MYSTERY OF
THE FJORD TIDE

A Novel of Sea Adventure,
Romance and Philosophy

Book II
Sequel to Found At Sea

By Mike Breslin

PublishAmerica
Baltimore

First printing

ISBN: 1-4137-2983-5
PUBLISHED BY PUBLISHAMERICA, LLLP
www.publishamerica.com
Baltimore

Printed in the United States of America

To Judith, Edward, Helge and
Baby for their stories of old Norway.

ACKNOWLEDGMENTS

My deepest appreciation to Anne Holland for her fine editing and friendship, and to my friend John W. Hurley for his expertise in all things Irish. To our relatives and friends in Flekkefjord, I beg your forgiveness for mixing fact and fantasy about the true center of the universe, thank you.

"I must go down to the sea again for the call of the running tide. It is a wild call and a clear call that may not be denied ...What am I, Life? A thing of watery salt. Held in cohesion by unresting cells, Which work they know not why, which never halt, Myself unwitting where their master dwells. "
—John Masefield

— CHAPTER 1 —

Henry loved adventure. The past year had been filled with it, more at times than he wanted. Over the past few months, however, he had begun to have bouts of restlessness. Now, he was experiencing one, as he surveyed the interior of their bungalow. It certainly did not look like the other luxury units at the Maura's Mandavu Hotel. It had never been finished. The furniture consisted of leftovers and damaged goods not fit for guests. A block of coral substituted for the broken caster on their bed. The walls, ceilings and floors were raw concrete.

He and Serene had been living there since shortly after they met and had neither the time nor inclination to re-locate for the contractors. As her busy schedule permitted, Serene tried to soften the room, and had succeeded to a large degree with a sense of the casually elegant. She had installed hooks for hanging plants, and artfully placed colorful wall hangings around the room, mostly from local artists and crafts people who brought their work to the gift shop to sell to tourists. Because she knew how much the islanders needed the money, she was a soft touch, and their bungalow became the overflow warehouse for the gift shop. It was small, cozy and comfortable, but Henry secretly craved more–more for himself and more for Serene. What that 'more' was, he didn't know. Maybe he wanted a life of their own separate from her family's hotel.

Framed through the open door was a band of fast-moving white clouds scudding across a perfect blue sky. Below, the turquoise sea broke steadily with ribbons of white foam sliding up and down the white coral sand beach. He walked outside in his bare feet and slumped down in a beach chair. To his left he saw the startling green of the most fabulous golf course in the Fijian Islands. He mused that there are two types of people in the world–those who love golf, and those, like himself, who saw no point to the game. Where was the satisfaction in knocking a little, white ball around a perfectly manicured park? Looking down the beach he saw bright, red aluminum umbrellas staked in the sand and guests sunbathing, bodies gleaming with tanning oil. A man and a boy of about five were making a sand castle at the water's edge. A few people were actually splashing in the ocean, although most guests, by far, preferred the fresh water pool.

He was living in paradise by anyone's definition, living with a wonderful woman, a beautiful creature that he passionately adored. Yet something was missing. He had a stinging pang of guilt that these thoughts were even occurring. He felt blessed to have found Serene, to have survived the accident at sea and even luckier to have escaped death from the mob only by a freak accident. It was not enough.

It was time for Henry to take stock of himself. He reviewed the past year and a half. Everything from his old life had changed, even his name. Oddly, he felt like a different person, too. All the pain he had suffered from the death of his wife, Amy, had dissipated. Most of that, he reasoned, was due to intense activity, not having the time to indulge in the past. These precious months with Serene had been filled with passion and hard work. Now, for the first time he was gaining perspective on the monumental changes that had rocked his life. A reassessment was certainly due. It was natural for him to have this emotional stutter at this time for he had no idea what he wanted to do with the rest of his life.

In his former life, his name had been Kevin McCall, but how effortlessly he had come to prefer Henry Langston. It had a richer ring to it. A well established New Jersey filmmaker who made industrial programs; he had been on-track and stable until the unfortunate death of his wife. After her horrible auto accident, he lost interest in everything and his deep sorrow gradually deepened into a black depression that would not subside. In desperation, he felt he had to regain control of his life, do something, change his field of view.

Through a former client he had befriended, he finagled a berth as an ordinary seaman on the container ship, the *Pacific Star*. With sea air, hard work and a change of scenery, he slowly began to have a brighter outlook. Then, during a Pacific typhoon he was washed off deck and nearly drowned. But he kept his wits and stayed afloat through a stormy night. The next day he found a floating container, which had also been blown off his ship during the storm. Fortunately, there was a steel lashing rod dangling from the container, which he used to climb aboard and later used to break through the top. Inside was a shipment of Red Cross medical supplies and emergency rations which had been bound for the victims of a tidal wave disaster in New Guinea. While rummaging through the container he also found ten million dollars in cash. From his experience shooting videos on the waterfront, he suspected, and later found out for certain that the money was being smuggled by the Jersey mob. As the container slowly began to sink he built a raft from packing materials and loaded it with supplies and the money. After narrowly escaping being trapped inside the container as it went under, he swam to his raft, erected a sail and spent weeks going westward. Finally, he landed on a tiny deserted island, which he later learned was named Mindavu, an atoll in the Fijian group.

Meanwhile, Philly "Gumdrops" Costello, a mobster who ran a freight forwarding company, learned that the cash he was smuggling for his client was lost in a storm. Costello couldn't believe that the loss of a novice seaman at the same time as his money was a coincidence so he dispatched Dom Scardino, his most lethal enforcer, to find Kevin McCall and recover his money.

Kevin, knowing first-hand the ways of the mob, figured they would come looking for him, so he assumed the name of Henry Langston, the name of a disturbed acquaintance who had gone missing.

To further protect himself, he burned the raft, buried the money, destroyed his identification papers and made up a cover story that he was working for a yacht delivery company and had asked to be left on Mindavu so he could test his survival skills and write a book about the experience. He would later claim he lost his passport.

After several weeks on the island, a group of tourists on a day trip from a nearby island arrived. Their guide was Serene, a ravishing Polynesian-American whose family owned Mindavu as well as a larger island, Mandavu, where they had recently opened a luxury resort. Later, Henry and Serene agreed it was love at first sight.

Henry glanced at his watch. He should stop daydreaming and get ready for their anniversary dinner. Perhaps he would mention his restlessness to Serene, but certainly not tonight.

Serene had never looked better since the day they had met, and she was a knockout then. Tonight, she was wearing make-up, a first for Henry's eyes. Even the faint traces of acne scars on her cheekbones had disappeared. Now her otherwise flawless face was truly flawless. Had she gained a few pounds?

Her brown shoulders looked less angular than he remembered. Yes, her face had grown somewhat fuller. Before his eyes was beauty and contentment personified, although she seemed more pensive than usual.

She sat across the table and daintily stirred her espresso with a tiny spoon; a new item at Lee's, demanded by the new generation of tourists, primarily those coming from Silicon Valley. As Henry watched her dainty gold spoon flow in slow circles through the black coffee, he had a pleasant thought. Too few moments in life contained this perfect serenity. He dared not disturb this rare peacefulness.

"What's up with you tonight, Henry?"

"Just savoring the moment."

"It's been quite a year. Remember our first date here?"

"How could I forget? It was the most decisive night of my life. I was deeply worried how you would react to the truth, learning whom I really was and that the mob was after me. What I most clearly remember was instinctively knowing that you would not tolerate another lie. Somehow I knew that one more lie that evening and you might be lost to me forever."

"Yes, honesty is our strongest bond. If you hadn't 'fessed up that Scardino was chasing you, we both might not be sitting here tonight. We faced death together and survived. Now, we should be in that happily-ever-after phase, but I sense something's gone sour. What's bothering you lately? Getting bored with me?" She leaned back in her chair and braced herself.

"Never in life! Don't even think that. I love you more than anything. And always will."

Serene let out the breath she had been holding. "What is the problem, then? You've been brooding. It's unbecoming to you and unflattering to me. What's up?" She crossed her arms and waited.

Henry was acutely aware that a satisfactory explanation was expected. "I suppose I have too much time on my hands. The phones are in and the telecommunications system takes care of itself. We've stopped marketing because we're booked solid for the next two years. All the bungalows are finished except ours, and we'd have to move out to finish it. We're fully staffed. Everyone is well trained. Lani and Malcolm have the hotel running like a well-oiled machine. The fact is there's not much for me to do. So, I've been thinking about us ... about our future together."

Serene unfolded her arms, leaned forward, put her elbows on the table, and kissed Henry softly on the lips and whispered, "Us ... together in the future. A very pleasant thought, darling. Sounds to me like you're getting a bit *island happy."*

"There's probably some of that. I really don't know."

"Come now Henry, everybody *knows* what they want. They're just unwilling to confront themselves and less likely to admit it to another."

"My ideas are vague at this point," said Henry.

"In other words ... too vague to tell me."

"Yup, maybe ... let me gather my thoughts. Tonight's our anniversary. I don't want to cloud our evening."

"The cloud *has* descended. Out with it!" Serene said with a wry smile.

Henry toyed with his espresso spoon. "I'll try. I don't think I'm *island happy* so much. It's more a feeling of being becalmed, not moving. Earlier today I was thinking about an experience I had on the raft. The wind had been blowing steadily for days. I had this feeling of hope that I was getting somewhere. Then, one morning, the wind stopped. The sea went flat as glass, like the entire Pacific Ocean was in freeze-frame. It was an awesome scene that totally absorbed me. But after only a few minutes I began to feel uneasy. I told myself to relax, to enjoy a magnificent field of view, one that I might never see again. But I couldn't. I couldn't. I just couldn't! Something deep inside was prodding me to move forward. So rather than appreciating this spectacular phenomenon before my eyes, I just sat there like a bump on a log anxiously looking for any breath of wind to get me moving again. When I look back, it was one of the bleakest ... strangest moments of my life."

Serene weighed the tone of frustration in Henry's voice, and then she said in a cheerful voice, "Henry, you just made me think of something. Have you ever read Thomas Hobbes?"

"I've heard of him, some old English philosopher. Is this a Jeopardy question?"

"No, silly. Hobbes didn't believe that men are motivated simply to avoid the pain of life or just to experience its pleasures. He thought man's first priority was to seek security, that if a man had security he could endure any pain and sacrifice any pleasure."

"The point being ... ?"

"Well, Henry. By that remark that I am either boring you, or cutting too close to a truth you are reluctant to broach. I think the latter."

"Go on then," Henry said sheepishly.

"What you want – I think, and what Hobbes thought all men want – is to continually *increase* your power to *ensure* your security."

"But I am secure here with you!"

"No. No. It's not that. Hobbes thought it was quite natural for a man to seek power after power until the day he dies, because without gaining more power, it's like you being becalmed, you are stuck where you are … not moving forward toward accumulating even greater security. Security you think you need to live well and assure your future … which is also our future. I'm glad you're normal!" She roared with laughter drawing the attention of everybody in the restaurant.

Henry chuckled as well. "I suppose we all go through these bouts of self-examination. Yes, I have been thinking about our future. To be honest … I can't see myself working at the hotel for the rest of my life, living off your family. That's it."

"I understand, Henry. You must know if it were not for you the hotel wouldn't be the success it is. You made it happen with your web marketing; otherwise we might have faced bankruptcy. Beyond that, I also understand that you're a creative person. You crave new challenges. You wouldn't be happy without them. I know that. This island, beautiful as it is, doesn't have to be our whole world. The hotel was my mother and father's dream. It doesn't have to be ours. Remember, we both found ourselves here because we were lost. You, from falling off the ship. Me, recovering from the divorce."

"I'm glad you see it that way, Serene. It takes the pressure off. One thing that's been running through my mind over the past few days was how could I not be contented here. It's idyllic by any measure, and I'm with you. Those thoughts were making me feel guilty. There's so much here, yet I want more. Makes me wonder if I'll ever be satisfied?"

Serene reached across the table and laid her hands tenderly on his. "I think we can, but I'm an optimist. The least we can do is try for it, together. We'll find out where our life should be. So, where shall we look?"

"Let's leave that for another day. All this serious talk is making me dizzy. Tonight, let's celebrate." Serene nodded in agreement. After ordering big snifters of brandy, they sat in silence holding hands and shared one of those all too rare moments of bliss.

When the brandy arrived, Serene proposed a toast. "Here's to Manowee and his quest for harmony and to us in our search for ours."

"I'll drink to that old guy anytime and to us every time, hear, hear."

— CHAPTER 2 —

It was 7: 00 a.m. at 12 Carrington Drive in Short Hills, New Jersey. Philly "Gumdrops" Costello sat at his kitchen table while his housekeeper Juanita poured his second cup of coffee. Philly hardly noticed her as he scanned through the *Newark Star-Ledger* like a bloodhound on the scent. Every morning he read the paper and made notes in his spiral bound notebook. He wanted to know who died, who got married and particularly any news on politics and criminal justice in Essex County. Even Philly, corrupt as he was, became an outraged taxpayer when he read about the rapacious corruption in his county, which experts rated as one of the most corrupt political entities in the country.

Later in the day Philly would review his notes and have his people dispatch flowers, cards, and candy (always his privately labeled 'Philly's Gumdrops') and blank white envelopes stuffed with cash to the needy, indicted, incarcerated and the bribable. Everything was delivered by hand. Nothing was ever recorded or signed. Yet, Philly's elephantine memory knew the disposition of every gumdrop.

As he scanned the paper a small article arrested his attention:

Missing Nutley Man Returns Home
Nutley–After being missing for nearly two years, Henry Langston of 378 Chestnut Street, yesterday reported to the Nutley Police Department that he should be no longer listed as a missing person. Mr. Langston stated he had suffered a nervous breakdown and had been recovering at an out of state location. He apologized to the police for not having advised his family of his whereabouts and claimed to be fully recovered.

"Henry Langston? I know that name," Philly said under his breath. It was a matter of seconds before his vast memory recalled his last phone conversation with Dom Scardino. "That was the name of the guy Dom thought was Kevin McCall!" he said angrily.

"What's that, Mr. Costello?" asked Juanita.

"Nothing. Just another strange coincidence that needs looking into."

As Philly drove his black Cadillac down Interstate 280 he was steaming. He remembered the red-hot flush of embarrassment of losing a client's shipment. He had broken out in a clammy sweat that day over a year ago when he forked over the ten million to replace the loss. Raising the cash had nearly caused him a nervous breakdown. His net worth was much more, but he only had six million in ready cash. He had to wait on receivables. This forced him to go to a shark for a short-term loan for which he was still paying nosebleed vigorous.

By the time he reached his desk at Costello Fast Freight, he had quelled his anger and rearranged his priorities to getting his money back. Philly needed the right man for this job. Scardino was fairly bright and an efficient killer, but unfortunately dead. It would take pure intelligence to unravel this mystery, Philly concluded, as he flipped through one of his giant Rolodexes. He needed someone he could trust. Ten million in untraceable bills was too tempting for most of the people Philly knew.

Philly reached the R's and stopped cold at Boxer Ryan. "He'd be perfect, if he'd do it," Philly said to himself. He knew Boxer from grade school in Jersey City. They had remained good friends all through high school. Philly had stayed in touch with him ever since. Not closely, but he would call Boxer every couple of years and invite him to lunch at The Elbow Rest in the old neighborhood, sometimes with family members or old friends from school.

Boxer's given name was Francis Xavier Ryan. He wanted to be called Frank in grammar school, but the nuns at St. Catherine's would have none of it. In class, they called him by his God-given name, Francis, which often resulted in smirks and giggles from his classmates and later tauntings in the playground. By fifth grade, Philly vividly remembered, Frank could no longer tolerate the teasing. Frank devised a plan. He went to his Uncle Finn, who had been a professional boxer back in Ireland, and asked him to teach him the manly art. After several weeks of instruction and running exercises prescribed by Finn, he was ready to take on any provocateur.

After that, any boy in school, up to and including the eighth graders, who made fun of his name, was challenged to a fight after school at the vacant lot off Railroad Avenue. One of the boys called him 'Boxer' and the moniker stuck. From that time on everyone, including his family who were proud of him, called him Boxer.

In the first few fights with fifth graders, Boxer won easily. He was rather middle-sized for his age and thin, but he came equipped with a black Irish temper that generated enough adrenalin to punch through a brick wall. He was fearless as well and frightened his opponents with his ferocity and skill, that was until his reputation reached the boys in the higher grades.

Once again his name became his burden, but now the bigger boys made fun of his new nickname, and Boxer issued more challenges for fights after school, regardless of the opponent's size. Boxer was beaten severely many times, but not for lack of courage and none of his opponents escaped without Boxer's marks upon them. Eventually, all his schoolmates gave Boxer the respect he desired. Besides his tenacity, Boxer was a top student despite little effort or show. He sat attentively in class, spent minimal time on homework and he got straight A's all through St. Catherine's. He was offered a full scholarship to St. Peter's Prep, one of the best high schools in the state. Philly, on the other hand, scraped through public high school and dropped out in his junior year to work in the family trucking business.

For his senior year science project Boxer came up with the idea to use lasers to slice silicon billets for use in solar panels. They were being cut with diamond tipped circular saws at the time and each pass through the saw ground more than one-sixteenth of an inch of valuable silicon into dust. Boxer was unsure if lasers were capable of doing what he proposed at the time. If they could, he prepared a cost analysis that showed the saving would be substantial. His project caught the attention of Stevens Institute of Technology in nearby Hoboken, which offered him a full scholarship to one of the world's finest engineering programs. Boxer bloomed at Stevens and became fascinated with electrical engineering. After he earned an undergraduate degree, he was invited to stay on as an instructor. For three years he taught while he earned a master's degree. When Boxer went off to Stevens, Philly saw less and less of him. The few times they did get together, Philly noticed he had not changed like other college guys he had known. Boxer was always Boxer, and always behaved like the tough little, good humored street kid that he was at heart. Philly dialed Boxer's number.

"Ryan Investigations."

"That you Boxer?"

"Yea, Philly. How-ya-doin?"

"Fine Boxer. Where's the gal?"

"She's history. More trouble than she was worth. Always asking embarrassing questions like when are you going to pay the bills. So I let her go and paid a few bills. She was a fine person. Got her another job the next day. So no guilt."

"Business bad, eh?"

"Be better if I put more time in the business, but you know me. Anyhow, what's up?"

"I may have some business for you."

"Philly, how many times you tried to send me business and I've turned you down?"

"And you hurt my sensitive feelings every time."

"Philly, I love you as a friend. You know I can't get involved. Melissa would have a fit."

"This is different, Boxer. It's for me, personally. I need a professional investigator. Besides, you are the smartest guy I know. I really don't know where to go. And, it's totally legal. I swear to God."

"Okay, only because it's for you. I'll listen, but I won't make a commitment until I hear the whole story and discuss it with Melissa."

"Fair enough. How about lunch tomorrow at the Elbow?"

"About noon, okay?"

"Noon it is. See ya."

— Chapter 3 —

That night, Serene paced the patio in front of their bungalow while Henry slept. The anniversary dinner had shaken her. Yesterday, she was firmly rooted in her life with Henry and their work at the hotel. She had felt secure, content and as happy as she had ever been. Now her world was in turmoil.

Henry's restlessness was contagious. She began a major reassessment of her own, the first since the breakup of her marriage, she realized. After signing the divorce papers she was adrift for several weeks, confused as to how she would redirect her life. She had thought of retreating into the arms of her family and dismissed it as a step backwards, a negative flight from her inner pain. She decided to stay in San Francisco and work things out on her own. She was well educated, bright and had come into her own as a highly desirable young woman. She had everything going for her except a vision of a future. She decided that whatever that future would be it would not be dependent on a man. While thrashing about in the aftermath of the wrecked marriage, fate rang up one morning with a phone call from her mother.

Maru said that she and her father needed help to finish the hotel. From the sound of her voice she was serious. Cost overruns and unexpected construction delays were driving them towards bankruptcy; however her mother also secretly hoped that Mandavu would be good for Serene.

Serene joined her family and worked tirelessly to market the property, train the native staff and get the hotel open for business. Their family also owned the tiny island of Mindavu about 15 miles away. Her father thought this would be a good day-trip for guests and Serene was elected as the tour guide. Her first outing there with a group of travel agents was memorable. Shortly after landing her boat in the lagoon, Henry, looking like wild man, walked out of the jungle and introduced himself.

He told his well-rehearsed story about practicing survival skills and writing a book. He claimed he had left his bag on the beach with his passport and it had been washed away by the tide. Serene suspected he was lying because the tidal movement there was only a few feet. If his bag had been washed out it would still be visible in the shallow lagoon. She played along with Henry's story. First, because she liked him immediately. Secondly, she was curious to uncover the truth because oddly enough, Henry did not know the name of the island he was on, or even what island group.

Serene, with the help of her friend Bill Wilson at the American Consulate in Suva, helped Henry get a temporary passport. While Henry was in Suva, waiting at a bar for Serene, he had a coincidental encounter with Dom Scardino, the gangster sent by Philly "Gumdrops" Costello to investigate the loss of his money. Fortunately, Scardino had a poor photo and Henry's appearance had radically changed since the photo had been taken. In that encounter Henry successfully eluded Scardino and returned to Mandavu with Serene. On the way there he offered to work at the hotel for room and board. Working together, Henry and Serene fell in love.

Now that Henry knew that Scardino was on his trail, he began to fear for Serene's safety as well as his own. Finally, he confessed that his real name was Kevin McCall and that he was being hunted by the mob for inadvertently taking possession of $10 million dollars in laundered funds, which had been washed overboard in the same storm that left Henry stranded in the middle of the Pacific Ocean. Knowing the mob would never believe his wildly improbably story despite its truth, Kevin McCall changed his name to Henry Langston, a former acquaintance.

Serene became gravely concerned about Henry's safety and insisted Henry return to Mindavu to hide. A few days later, Scardino showed up in Mandavu, kidnapped Serene and forced her to take him to Mindavu to look for Henry.

"Thank God," Serene thought, "if it hadn't been for an act of God, the lightning strike that killed Scardino, we could both be dead now. So why worry if Henry is having second thoughts now."

She decided, then and there, that she would be totally open-minded toward Henry's plans, whatever they may be. He was, after all, the first man she truly loved. Whatever he wanted, she wanted for him … and for her.

The sun had edged up over the sea and she felt the cool morning breeze on her face when she heard footsteps behind her.

"Looks like another perfect day in paradise. What's got you up before the birds?" yawned Henry.

"Couldn't sleep. Too much on my mind. How are you this morning?"

"Great! Best night's sleep in weeks. Our talk last night relieved a lot of pressure on my tortured little brain."

"The pressure was transferred to me. That's why I couldn't sleep. We've got to sit down and resolve this. If you're not happy then I'm not. It's that simple."

"Please don't misunderstand, I am gloriously happy with you. It's just that I feel I have to 'do something' or go nuts."

"I have an idea. Let's play hooky from work today, grab the SCUBA gear and see if we can find Manowee's pearls."

"Really! What brought this on?"

"Well, if we are going to 'do something' we're going to need money. I haven't got much cash. My money is invested in the hotel, and you dare not withdraw yours."

"I don't know about that. It might be safe. It's been over a year, and maybe the mob isn't even watching my account."

"Henry, you may as well kiss that money goodbye. If you try to get it there's a chance your 'pals' will find out. As long they think you're dead, you are safe."

"You're right. Dead people don't need money. I always come to that conclusion, too. But I wish, it's my life savings, almost $800,000.00 with interest by now."

"Maybe you should have thought twice when you sent the entire ten million to the Red Cross."

"Actually," Henry laughed, "I shorted them two thousand, but I don't think they minded. I have almost two hundred left."

"Well, then, let's hope we can find Manowee's pearls! Otherwise, you are stuck here with me whether you like it or not."

They decided to overnight at Mindavu. They got the SCUBA gear from the hotel's dive shop and had the kitchen pack up some food. By the time they got everything together and had the Zodiac gassed up it was almost noon before they left the dock.

The weather was clear, the sea calmer than usual, and they made the fifteen miles to Mindavu's tiny lagoon in less than an hour. They dragged the Zodiac up the beach and unloaded the gear.

"Good thing we decided to stay the night," said Henry. "We'll have to make two trips up to the cliff house, and I guarantee we won't be up for much after that."

"I hope you'll have a little energy left," Serene said with a playful wink. "That's where we first made love. An encore perhaps?"

High on the steep slope of the extinct volcano, nestled on a small plateau and hidden from sight was Manowee's cliff house. Henry had discovered the ruin while he was marooned on the island and had rebuilt it. That night, sheltered by its stone walls, they lay in the dark on a blanket. Their lovemaking had been torrid, perhaps inspired by memories of their first night there together, perhaps as a validation of their love, perhaps stimulated by the dangers of their now uncertain future. In the quiet blackness, tightly entwined in each other's limbs there was hesitancy on both their parts to break the spell, but in due course the long silence became awkward.

"Henry, have you ever heard of the threefold fire that burns within us all?"

"More Hobbes, I take it?"

"No. Can't remember where I heard it. Just came to mind. The three fires that beset human nature and which we have to learn to control are desire, hostility and delusion. Any one, or any combination of the three can disturb our well-being and if intense enough can destroy us. Our problem is that we forget, or ignore, or are unaware that they always burn. If one or a combination suddenly flares up, it causes great damage. We only catch brief glimpses of these three states of being and have little understanding of how they affect our lives."

"What on earth made you think of this now?" muttered Henry.

"I suppose our present situation and the fact we'll be searching for Manowee's pearls tomorrow. Manowee discarded his most valuable possession to cleanse his spirit of greed, the strongest form of desire. Now we're trying to recover his pearls in order to satisfy your desire to find something beyond these islands."

"The point being?"

"Now that I think about it, Manowee relieved his spirit from material greed to quell yet another desire, his love, or lust for Ona. Yet, because he disposed of the pearls by throwing them in the pool where he knew he could get them again, rather than in the sea where they would be lost, he never completely conquered his greed. I wonder if he fully realized that?"

"If he didn't know, he would have been deluding himself. Is that what you're getting at?"

"I don't know if I'm getting at anything, just trying to work through my feelings. Tomorrow we will try to dredge up Manowee's pearls, his symbols of greed to fulfill our desire to leave these islands. I wonder if greed can ever find absolute rest?" said Serene with a hint of anger in her voice.

"I think I just caught a glimpse of your hostility, Serene."

"Yes, I suppose I have been repressing some anger, my hostility if you like. Trying to deal rationally with all of this. I was perfectly happy until I began to see that you were discontented. I guess I thought that that happiness, or contentment would continue indefinitely."

"Now, that was a genuine delusion. Happiness is transitory. So is contentment."

"Realistically, I agree with you. However, my dream imagines as much of both as possible. That's my desire and I pray I'm not deluding myself, or then you might see some real hostility," she added with good-humored laugh.

"Then we have no choice. We have to find that right 'something' for *both* of us, which gives us the happiness and harmony we *both* desire. And, we may as well be as happy and content as possible during our journey as we look."

"Yup, good idea. Life is, after all, to be lived one moment at a time. My only other option is to let you go off alone. Then I think we'd both be miserable. My desire for you is too great." She playfully nuzzled into his throat and feigned biting his neck.

"Enough! Enough! Stop. I'll tell you my preliminary plan, that is, if we find the pearls tomorrow, and if we can get enough money for them."

"An extremely conditional plan, then?"

"Yes, my preliminary, conditional, delusional plan. Now, you will be the first person who I have ever told this. Secretly, I have always wanted to sail around the world. When I was a kid I read an amazing book, *Sailing Alone Around the World* by Joshua Slocum…"

"I read that too!" said Serene as she suddenly sat up in surprise. "That's always been a fantasy of mine." She jumped to her feet. "Is it possible our most secret desires are in-tune … synchronized?" She was standing naked in the dark, flushed with joy.

"Well I'll be … and I was afraid to tell you because you'd think I was crazy. You're just as crazy as I am, you nut," said Henry as he grasped her ankle. "Come back down here, you wonderful woman."

— CHAPTER 4 —

Boxer always felt nostalgic with a twinge of sadness when he went to the Elbow Rest. As a boy he remembered being taken there by his father to buy him a draft birch beer. The real reason, his father needed a drink.

In those days he remembered it as a dark, damp place filled with smoke and noisy workmen. The floors were covered in sawdust, and sawdust was also sprinkled on the long, wooden shuffleboard that paralleled the bar. After a few birch beers, Boxer would get fidgety. His father would try to pacify him with a hard-boiled egg, or offered to buy him pickled pigs feet, which he always declined, and which always bought a laugh or two from his bar mates.

The men he saw at the Elbow Rest became his boyish measure by which he judged men. They were big, broad shouldered Irishmen and a few Norwegians. The Irish called the Norwegians 'square heads' and the Norwegians called the Irishmen 'micks.' These men were large by natural selection dictated by the demands of their vocation. They wore plaid wool shirts, even in summer, and dark whipcord pants with broad, black belts and suspenders, and hi-top work boots. They usually had red or blue bandanas tied around the neck and wore tan caps with pull-down earflaps. They were longshoremen who worked the Jersey City docks. Standing shoulder to shoulder at the bar they drank the only medicine that relieved their aching muscles, strained backs and the tedium of the endless stream of crates and sacks they hauled in and out of the holds of freighters. In those days before containerized freight and heavy machinery, there were cranes that lifted the pallets and cargo nets in and out of the ships and trucks to carry the freight, but all the in between moves were humped by these human donkeys.

Most vivid of all, Boxer recalled the Miss Rheingold ballot box on the bar with color photos of the contestants pasted on the box. He always voted for the Irish beauty and would sit there voting ballot after ballot, making up different names for himself as he scribbled away. He wondered what those

Miss Rheingolds of yesteryear now looked like and what they would make of the Elbow Rest today.

They might recognize the bar itself, but the old shuffleboard table was long gone, replaced instead by dainty wrought iron tables and wire, ice cream parlor chairs. Who knew that under all that sawdust were fine oak floors which had been sanded down and thickly coated with glossy plastic finish. No longer dark and damp, now it was trendy, light and airy with greenery softening every sharp edge and plants hanging as if it were a rainforest. Its patrons today were the new breed of urban pioneers and the white-collar back office workers from the financial industry. No more shots and beers. Now they sipped flavored ice teas, espressos and cappuccinos, or even the occasional imported beer or the black and tan on tap. The food was the only thing Boxer felt had improved.

His lunch with Philly had been much more than he expected. As he drove back to his office, he mulled over their conversation and began to have second thoughts. He parked his battered Chevy behind his office in Hoboken.

His office had once been a flower shop, a very small one, only ten-feet wide by fifty-feet long. It had the benefit of high ceilings and a big bay window on Jersey Avenue, but its most valuable asset was a parking space in back. It was cheap, too. Boxer had signed a ten-year lease soon after he obtained his private investigator's license. The lease was up in a year.

He had made virtually no improvements. He adopted an old wooden desk and some rusty file cabinets that had been left behind. He splurged for phone, fax and copier and had 'Ryan Investigations' lettered in gold leaf on the front door. Rather than an ad in the yellow pages, he sprang for genuine engraved business cards with copperplate lettering which he passed out among his many friends and acquaintances. From this base of support, he began his new career. Everyone knew Boxer was smart, but they puzzled at why he scrapped a lucrative career as a highly paid electrical engineer with several patents to his name to become a private eye. Of all things! For Boxer it had been an easy choice. Engineering, he discovered, kept his mind cluttered from morning to night with technical details of which he had limited interest. After work he found his brain too confused by his various projects to pursue any serious study.

When Melissa inherited her grandmother's estate and he saw a small, yet steady income from his patents, Boxer seized the opportunity for a second career. The timing was perfect, since Melissa had resumed her profession as a family lawyer after their son, Michael, entered high school.

What Boxer secretly wanted was to devote himself to research and writing. He determined he might be well suited to investigative work and obtained his New Jersey private investigator's license. He was, after all, an expert at acquiring information. Since childhood, Boxer had never stopped asking questions. It drove his parents and relatives to distraction. He was always looking for something, and he had a gift in recruiting people to assist him. People liked him. Strangers would go far out of their way to help. His friendly enthusiasm for a subject and his somewhat eccentric bearing were magnets. This was particularly true of the many librarians he befriended over the years with his natural charm and by challenging their science, which kept them in top form.

Over the years, his office filled up with books. His main objective in choosing detective work was to do as little work as possible and concentrate on what he liked doing best – reading. As books began to accumulate he thought about getting bookshelves. Armed with the wisdom that most problems in life take care of themselves eventually, he now found himself surrounded by books stacked from floor to ceiling and covering every wall. Volumes had been laid flat on the side with spines facing outward for reference. A rather efficient system he thought, except for the occasional avalanche caused a rumbling truck.

Pedestrians looking through his bay window naturally assumed it was a used bookstore. The 'Ryan Investigations' on the door led to the further assumption that the proprietor tracked down hard to find books.

People walked in off the street and browsed. At first Boxer politely explained it was not a bookstore and often got involved in long conversations about books, which he enjoyed to a point. Some people came in, browsed, and left without a word. Boxer ignored them. Occasionally, someone would ask him for a particular volume. He would answer, "If you can find it, it's yours for the taking."

If they found the book they wanted and asked the price, he would simply hand them a business card and say, "The book is free. Call me if you ever need a private investigator."

Upon returning to his book-strewn desk, he began to have second thoughts about the assignment he had accepted. He had always liked Philly personally and considered him a friend, but his father had warned him as a child to stay away from Philly and his family and to avoid involvement in any business dealings with them. Boxer had heeded that advice until today.

Boxer empathized with Philly's predicament, and his will melted as he had listened to the tale of woe, his life savings lost and in debt to replace the lost ten million. Philly actually admitted the shipment was illegal and vowed he would never do it again because of the problems it had caused him. Philly also swore that Boxer would not have to do anything illegal. All Philly wanted was for him to track down this mysterious Kevin McCall, a.k.a. Henry Langston, and let him know where he could be found. Moreover, Philly promised there would be 'no rough stuff' with McCall if he were found. He just wanted to recover his money. Philly offered to pay Boxer two thousand per week plus expenses, and as a bonus pay him 10% of whatever was recovered.

Under other circumstances, Boxer would have turned him down flat. Unfortunately, Boxer desperately needed money for the first time in his life. Over the past few years while his reading had increased, his attention to investigations had decreased. During this time, his son Michael had graduated from high school, applied to Harvard, and was accepted. The cost for the first semester alone nearly wiped out their savings account. Now he and Melissa were on a payment plan with the school and struggling to keep up. Two thousand per week would solve his immediate crisis. Earning a million dollar bonus would allow him to continue his philosophical studies in peace and comfort, perhaps forever. His need and his greed overpowered his common sense.

Again, he read the newspaper clipping Philly had provided. It crossed his mind to get Langston's telephone number from information and make a call. Then he thought better of it. "Tomorrow I'll go to Nutley and look-see," he muttered to himself.

— CHAPTER 5 —

Henry and Serene stood on the high rim of the crater. In the soft, dawn light, Paradise Pool looked more inviting than ever. They sat down to rest before making the final trek to the tiny, round oasis located in what had once been the center of the volcano. Henry remembered the first time he saw it and how he had deduced that the lush, green center was a result of gravity, how the scant rainfall on the west side of the island all drained to the center of the lopsided crater to create the pool and its surrounding greenery.

"Really think they're still there?" asked Serene.

"I've been wondering about that, too. It's pretty deep. About forty feet, I'd say. I dove down and touched bottom once. It was sandy. I fear the pearls may have dissolved in fresh water after all these years."

"You're kidding!"

"Don't know much about pearls, but common sense tells me that anything that grew in salt water must be largely composed of salts. And if they've been in fresh water all this time ... well, I just don't know ... and if we do find them, we don't even know if they're worth anything."

"Could you please try to be a little more negative," said Serene with heavy sarcasm.

"Sorry. Didn't mean to sound that way. I suppose I'm trying to temper our high expectations in case we are ... disappointed."

"For now, let's be totally neutral, okay. You should know that this spot gives me the creeps anyway. Over there is where Scardino was killed." She pointed to the grassy summit not fifty yards away from where they sat.

"Well, he was trying to kill you at the time. That lightning was God's way of saying he shouldn't."

"I know. I know. I've gone over it a thousand times in my head, yet I still feel guilty."

"I know what you mean, Serene. The image of him holding my steel spear

26

in the air is forever seared in my mind. The expression on his face was frightening. Hate and triumph personified."

"It's not so much him getting split down the middle by lightening that bothers me. It's what we did with the body. That was illegal and dishonest."

"We had no choice, Serene. How could we have explained what really happened. If we had told the truth the mob would have sent someone worse … if that's possible. The new thug would have killed both of us. In effect, all we did was move the body from here to the hill on the golf course so the body would be found the next morning."

"That night was, without question, the most disgusting of my life. The smell of his roasted flesh in the boat. Landing on the beach in the black of night. The two of us like ghouls dragging him to the green in the boat cover. What gives me nightmares was you over the fire heating the putter. The expression on your face was barbaric. And, when you pressed the red-hot shaft into what was left of his poor hand it turned my stomach. I still wonder how you could do something like that."

"Life is simple, when you don't have any choice, Serene. Scardino had to look like he was playing in a thunderstorm. It worked. The mob bought the story."

"We won't find out anything here," said Serene as she abruptly shouldered her pack. There were tears in her eyes.

For two hours Henry's methodology had proved ineffective. Now he connected the last air tank to the regulator. The pool was round and about twenty feet in diameter. On his first dive he found that the skimming net they appropriated from the hotel's swimming pool worked effectively. It was two feet wide, had a steel rim and a short handle that in its intended use connected to a long aluminum pole. He had already covered the bottom once in a circular pattern. He had begun on the outer wall of the crater and pushed the net through the fine white sand. Every few feet he examined the contents of the net. Except for some small rocks, he found nothing.

"Well, princess, this will be the last dive. I won't have enough air to cover the entire bottom again. I'll concentrate on the center and try to dig deeper into the sand. If the pearls were there, that would be the most likely area. The turbulence has probably settled down by now."

Serene had changed into her black bikini and sat on the bank dangling her long, slender legs in the water. "I may try the extra mask and visit you at work."

"Be careful, it's very deep."

"Hey, I may not know how to SCUBA dive, but I'm half Polynesian remember … which means I'm half fish. How much air do you have left?"

"About twenty minutes."

Serene looked at her watch. "Okay, in exactly eighteen minutes, I'll come down to check up on you. I don't want to pay the overtime."

"Nag. Nag. Nag. See you later." Henry smiled, inserted his mouthpiece, adjusted his mask, held it tight to his face and jumped into the pool.

For some time he had been scooping through the sand in the center of the pool. He stopped and checked his air gauge. The indicator was almost touching red. Then Serene came into view from above. He saw her straining to swim downward. He waved and motioned his head from side to side and pointed up. She shook her head in agreement, and Henry began his assent. Henry broke the surface and swam to the bank. He pulled off his mask and turned to speak to Serene. She was nowhere in sight.

Henry became concerned. He put on his mask and swam downward. As he did, Serene flashed past him. He turned and followed her up. Henry was greeted with a gleeful smile. Panting heavily, she lifted her hand out of the water and held up a small, red pot.

Boxer sat in his car across the street from 378 Chestnut Street. He had been there since 7:00 a.m. No one had come in or out of the small house. It was now 8:20. What was left of his coffee was cold. From his briefcase he pulled out his notebook and the newspaper clipping. He made notes as he reviewed what Philly had told him at lunch.

Kevin McCall had been washed off the *Pacific Star* in a typhoon over a year ago along with several forty-foot cargo containers. In Philly's container was ten million in small denominations, all untraceable. Philly said he was helping a client launder the cash in the Far East.

He made notes: *Research McCall, interview his friends and family, order a credit report, check his bank account. Get a copy of the container's manifest.*

Philly had also briefed him on Dom Scardino's ill-fated search for McCall. Scardino had been on the trail of a man named Henry Langston whom he suspected of being McCall. Philly did not know if it was true, but he remembered the name, Henry Langston. "Philly always had a fantastic memory. I wonder if it's photographic," Boxer chuckled to himself. The last time Philly had spoken to Scardino, Scardino was about to travel by boat to the island of Mandavu to follow up on Langston. A week later Philly got a call from the American Consulate in Fiji telling him Scardino was killed in a freak accident, hit by lightning while playing golf in a thunderstorm he was told. Philly flew to Fiji and identified Scardino's body and was convinced it was lightning. Philly's gruesome description of his burnt corpse convinced Boxer as well. Boxer added *Research hotel on Mandavu* to his list.

Boxer heard the lawnmower start and saw a middle aged man on the front lawn. If first impressions are important, Boxer's engaging personality began with his appearance, which sparked curiosity. He dressed like a workman usually jeans, with a bright red, pocketed tee shirt, white socks and a pair of beat-up brown Sperry Top-siders. He was of medium height and well built, but his most striking feature was his disproportionately large head supported by a thick neck. His dark brown hair was usually in need of a trim and was rarely combed. With not a gray hair on his head, few people guessed he was in his late fifties. He sported a natural, broad smile and moved quickly in fluid motions. Since childhood he had often been told he had animal magnetism, that animals and people seemed naturally drawn to him. He knew he had a gregarious personality. The last time someone mentioned animal magnetism, Boxer did some research. He found that it was apparently true. Many great leaders throughout history had it, a special ability to relate to animals and humans, or behavioral mannerisms that attracted interest and gave them extraordinary powers to affect the behavior of others. Alexander the Great, Julius Caesar, Napoleon Bonaparte and Adolph Hitler were just a few that were said to have this power. His favorite example was Ulysses S. Grant, who as a young boy was able to calm and handle the most willful teams of mules and horses that even the experienced drovers avoided. The more modern and fashionable description of this rare quality, he found, was 'charisma.'

Boxer exited his vehicle, crossed the street, walked up to the man and smiled. The man immediately smiled back, released the safety bar and the mower sputtered to a stop. "What can I do for you?" Langston asked.

According to inquiries Serene made among her relatives and friends, Wu Chow was the man to see about pearls. His family had lived in Fiji for generations, and their jewelry business went back almost a century. Although he traded in gold and silver, dealt in precious and semi-precious stones, he was a world-renowned expert in pearls. Wu Chow was reputed to be shrewd and honest.

The little red pot Serene had resurrected from Paradise Pool had been a lucky find indeed. Just as Henry had waved her off to discontinue the search, she saw a red, crescent shape in the sand where he had been working. With her last ounce of breath, she forced herself to the bottom and scooped up the tiny vessel.

The top of the jar had been sealed with resin and had remained watertight for about two hundred years. Manowee had hedged his bet. While he had disposed of his last earthly treasure in his spiritual battle against greed, he had left his options open. Even though he had married Ona and never retrieved his treasure, Serene wondered if Manowee truly believed his spiritual purification was complete.

Inside the pot, nested in dried grass were thirteen exquisite grayish-white pearls, one of which was exceptionally large and perfectly spherical.

At Wu Chow's shop in downtown Suva they were politely greeted by a clerk who escorted them upstairs to Wu Chow's office. Wu Chow was seated at a large desk. Behind him a large bay window overlooked the harbor. A small, frail man in his sixties, he was dressed in a black suit, starched white shirt and a bright blue bow tie. He stood, bowed from the waist and greeted his guests in perfect English.

"Pleased to meet you. I am Wu Chow. Welcome to my humble place of business." He extended his hand in friendship.

"Pleased to meet you. I am Serene Bronte, and this is my friend Henry Langston."

"Please be seated. Your message said you wanted me to appraise pearls."

"That's right," said Serene as she opened her pocketbook and one by one placed the pearls in a row on the desk. As she did this, Henry watched Wu Chow's face for any sign of expression. There was none.

"May I examine?" asked Wu Chow.

"Certainly," Serene replied.

Delicately, he picked up the large one, swiveled his chair toward the window and held the pearl to the sunlight. He slowly moved it around in his bony fingers looking at it from every angle. He swiveled back. "I must perform a small test if agreeable to you. It may seem somewhat unusual. I assure you it will not harm the pearl."

"By all means," said Serene.

Wu Chow smiled, took the large pearl and brought it to his mouth. For a second both Henry and Serene thought he was going to eat it. Instead he rubbed it gently across his teeth. His smile grew wider. "A *real* pearl!" He sat back in his chair and gazed at the big pearl unaware of Henry and Serene's existence.

After a several seconds, Serene asked, "What do you mean by a *real* pearl?"

"There are many artificial ones and excellent cultured pearls these days. An artificial feels smooth and slippery across the teeth, but this one is gritty. I would say it is from the silver-lipped oyster. At first, I didn't believe it was real. I must measure it." Now the formerly reserved little man became highly animated as he ferreted through his desk drawer and extracted a micrometer and a jeweler's loop. He placed the pearl on a blue jewelers' cloth, put the loop in his eye, and adjusted the micrometer with a thumb wheel until he had its exact diameter between the calipers. "Twenty-eight millimeters," he whispered to himself followed by a long exhale. Then Wu Chow relaxed back in his chair.

"What's it worth?" asked Henry.

Wu Chow leaned forward and placed his arms on the desk. "Most difficult to say, Mr. Langston, because this pearl is virtually priceless. The only way to determine its actual value would be at auction after proper advance notice to the gemological community."

"Are you serious Mr. Chow?" asked Serene.

"Quite so. It is a perfectly spherical natural sea pearl with hardly a blemish. It is twenty-eight millimeters in diameter, which is ... to the best of my knowledge ... the largest perfectly formed pearl ever found."

Henry and Serene looked at each other, speechless.

"May I ask how you acquired this pearl?"

"You might say I inherited it from my great, great grandfather who died in 1840. His name was Manowee. He was the head man at Mandavu."

"Ah! I have read of him. He was with Cook. Very famous in our local history. I wonder if? Excuse me for a moment please." Wu Chow rose and walked to a bookcase that covered a wall of his office. As he scanned the volumes he muttered, "There was a pearl ... a Dutch captain's journal I recall ... he saw it here in Suva ... yes, here it is." Wu Chow brought an accordion folder to the table and withdrew several sheets of paper. "I made these copies from the journal of Captain Jan Von Hartog at the library. I have always enjoyed history, especially when it refers to pearls. Let's see. Yes! He landed on Suva in December 1789 in the brig *Voss*. This is a translation of what he wrote. 'I go to visit trader. He have large collection to show. There was a very big and lustrous one. I made him offer, but he say no. The pearl called Daughter of the Moon and sacred to his people; he would not sell for 500 Guilders.'"

"Manowee was the largest trader in Suva at that time. And he had learned English with Cook. The Dutchman must have known some English, too, otherwise he could not have dealt with him. So it must have been Manowee. But what is this Daughter of the Moon about?" asked Serene.

"I'd wager this is it," and Wu Chow pointed to the big pearl on the desk. "I have heard other references to the Daughter of the Moon from Fijian folk tales, but the Von Hartog reference is the only historic evidence I have found. In the mythology the ancients called it that because of its size … just look at its shimmering pearlescent luster and color. It looks like a miniature full moon. They believed it had magic powers to calm storms and tides. Believe it or not, it will look much better with a light polishing."

"No wonder Manowee had a problem throwing it away," quipped Henry.

"And I'd have a problem selling it, Henry. I'd like to keep the Daughter of the Moon and enjoy her for a while," said Serene.

"I can easily understand that, Miss Bronte. I would be honored if you would let me polish it for you, at no charge of course. But are you interested in selling the other twelve?"

— CHAPTER 6 —

Boxer was carefully reviewing his findings for his report to Philly "Gumdrops". He had spent over an hour chatting with Henry Langston and was even invited for ice tea on his porch. Boxer posed as a freelance writer who was researching a book on missing persons and told Langston that he had read the newspaper article about him. Langston had been most cooperative and related the tale of what he called his "nervous breakdown."

By nature, Langston had always been a quiet person. One day on a whim he decided to stop speaking and after the first day became intrigued that no one noticed his silence. He was amazed. *It was like he didn't exist,* he thought. So he continued in silence slowly withdrawing and avoiding his coworkers, friends, mother, wife and two children. For a few days no one seem to notice until his odd behavior caught the attention of his boss when, during a tour of the office, his boss introduced a new customer. Henry stood and nodded politely. When the customer asked Henry a question, he simply nodded again and sat down. When the boss pressed him for a reply, Henry shrugged his shoulders in defiance.

After he was fired, he still did not feel like talking. Henry pretended to go to work but instead he spent the days walking and sitting in the park. He realized that this was first time in his life he had ever given any serious thought about his life. Every day he read the classifieds. The more he read, the less he felt like working.

At the end of the month his wife discovered the secret when she received his direct deposit statement and noted a sum annotated as severance pay. When she asked about it, he spoke for the first time in weeks and said, "It must be a clerical error." Then he said he was going to the convenience store.

He never returned. Rather, he hopped a local bus to the Port Authority Bus terminal in New York City. For no particular reason he bought a one-way ticket to Birmingham. This left him with about a hundred dollars in his pocket. He found a seat at the back of the bus and slept most of the trip. "When I woke up in Birmingham, I felt like I was really awake for the first time in my life. The city's slogan is 'Magic City,' you know, and it worked its magic on me. I started talking again. Got a job as a bookkeeper and rented a room," he told Boxer.

Boxer asked Langston if he knew why Birmingham was called the Magic City. Langston said he did not know. Boxer said, "It got that name in the '60's because they made freedom riders disappear." It blew right by Langston. He was, after all, an accountant.

After their talk, Boxer's psychiatric evaluation of Langston was not that of a nervous breakdown, but rather an abrupt, necessary escape from an overbearing mother, an unappreciative and hateful wife and a dull, mind-numbing job. He was now living with his mother temporarily, and his wife and two kids had moved to Ohio to live with her parents. Langston planned on getting a job and saving to pay for a divorce and child support.

"While you were missing, did anyone try to contact you or your family?" Boxer inquired.

"Yes. My mother mentioned something odd. All the time I was missing she got just one call from a cop out west looking for information. He wanted my social security number and passport number of all things. Mom didn't know my passport number and gave him my wife's number in Ohio."

"Have you ever heard of the name Kevin McCall?" Boxer asked.

"Yes." replied Langston, "He was married to one of my wife's friends, Amy McCall. Poor thing was killed in an auto accident. They had a house over on Elm Street. I didn't know him very well. He made TV commercials or something like that. Why do you ask?"

"He is also missing." Boxer knew his next step would be to go to Fiji.

Thanks to the sale of the twelve pearls to Wu Chow, they had enough cash to buy a boat and travel for some time. Henry knew his limitations as a sailor, but felt confident that he could upgrade his skill with instruction and by getting a boat that was not too demanding. Serene was a more experienced sailor. She had grown up learning to sail on the San Francisco Bay, a challenging body of water.

Before they started shopping for a boat, they discussed what they wanted in their ideal craft. They wanted it large enough to live on comfortably for an extended period. They also wanted quarters for a crew of two or three, or

34

guests. Most of all they agreed that they wanted seaworthiness and stability in heavy weather, a sail rig that could easily be handled by the two of them and a strong, reliable motor. They agreed that a fairly new, broad beamed, low maintenance fiberglass motor sailor of about seventy feet with state of the art electronics would fit their requirements perfectly. Henry searched the Internet for such a craft. The search yielded yacht brokers as well as sites that listed private sales. Being thrifty by nature, Henry first scrolled through the private sales, which were divided into two categories, power and sail, and listed according to length. He soon realized that a seventy-foot late model boat was actually a 'yacht' and the prices were far beyond what they wanted to spend.

Soon he was looking at boats that were smaller and older. One listing intrigued him. It read: *37' Loki, the doer of good and the doer of evil. Click for photo and details.* He opened the photo and chuckled. Serene walked over to the monitor to see the object of amusement. It was a wooden boat with two masts. It looked rather odd, but graceful in a peculiar way. The photo showed the craft at full sail against a background of lush foliage. The dark background and the deep blue water perfectly showed the contours of a white hull. An emerald stripe ran the length of the boat just under the rub rails, which were painted gold. It had a small, square cabin set far aft. The smaller mast toward the rear had a gaff rig, as did the main mast. The jib led out to a wooden bowsprit.

"What's that triangular sail between the jib and the main mast?"

"That's called a Genoa, Henry."

Henry read the description below the photo. *37-foot double ender, built in Norway, 1939, double planked white cedar on ash frames. Restored and upgraded by Nate Nevins. New Volvo 180 HP engine, 150 gal. fuel tanks, 200 gal. Stainless water tanks. Two sets of sails, one heavy weather handmade by Nate Nevins. Ideal for long range cruising. On cradle. Wellfleet, MA. You must love it to own it. Best offer.*

"Just for fun, let's email and ask the price," said Henry.

"Go ahead. It's not at all what we talked about, although it's kind of cute. Just remember, darling, old wood boats are *work.*"

"Not buying, just inquiring … more curiosity than anything else."

"Email away, my dear!"

The next day Henry received a reply, which read:

Dear Henry,
*   I wish I could give you a price. Fortunately I've learned not to concern myself with such matters. I had great joy in restoring her and cannot put a value on that either. I figure the right person will come by one day and make me a fair offer and Loki will sail off to her destiny. If you want to meet her, it's up to you.*

Nate
P.S. About the doer of good and evil ... consult Norse mythology.

Henry printed out the message and showed it to Serene. She read it carefully and pondered it for a moment and said, "I understand how Nate feels. You can't place a value on love. It's sweet." She took another look at the printout of the photo. "Obviously, this is our boat. So, our adventure starts with an adventure!"

A week later their rental car was speeding across the Sagamore Bridge spanning the Cape Cod Canal. It had been a long flight from Suva. They had flown to Sydney and then boarded a non-stop to San Francisco. They had a six-hour layover there before boarding another non-stop to Boston's Logan International. They were both so tired they slept most of the way to Boston. After renting a car at Logan, they stopped for breakfast and now were sipping from containers of coffee as they entered the Cape.

"So far Nate's directions are perfect. We should be there in an hour. Serene, you really look like a tourist with your guide book."

"Hey! It's my first visit to Cape Cod. I like to know where I'm going, unlike some people I know who float around the Pacific Ocean on a raft and then land on an island and have no idea where they are," said Serene in a sarcastic tone as she lowered he sunglasses and flashed Henry one of her phony smiles. "Want to hear about where we're going?"

"Certainly, my dear, I cannot think of anything more pleasant than your reading to me."

"I'll skip over the boring stuff. Wellfleet is located some seventy-five miles out into the Atlantic Ocean on the outer elbow of Cape Cod. Even before the first settlers arrived, Wellfleet Harbor was well known for its abundance of fish and oysters. By 1707 whaling had become a thriving industry. 3,500 year-round residents ... swells to 17,000 in summer ... beaches ... wildlife, blah, blah, blah. Here's something! It has the only church in the United States with bells that chime in nautical time. Cool. Henry, get this ... it's well known as a vacation haven for psychiatrists. Maybe we should have our heads examined before we look at this boat."

"Definitely," laughed Henry.

Past the welcome sign to Wellfleet, their first landmark was the Wellfleet Drive-In Theater. One mile past that, they made the next left at the house with pink flamingos on the lawn. This took them down a narrow, sandy road through a forest of stunted, weather beaten pines. Occasionally they would see a modest summer cottage, but they could not get lost according to Nate's directions because his was the last house on the road. *You can't miss it* he had written, *the little gray house with the big boat next to it. If you go past it, you are in the marsh.*

They both knew it was Nate the instant he walked into view with a paint can in one hand and a brush in the other. Henry's first impression was that of a cement block. A short man with short legs. His torso was square from his shoulders to his hips. His head looked like a smaller block stacked upon the larger one. His face was friendly with a lantern jaw and big brown eyes, which were opened wide in expectation. Tufts of white hair flared up from a darkly tanned scalp. He put down the paint and wobbled up to the car.

Nate maintained a genuine look of surprise even though Henry had called from the airport and gave Nate a fairly accurate estimate of the time of arrival in Wellfleet. A big warm smile bloomed on his face as a resonant voice called out, "God protect ya. Ya made it from Boston against the onslaughts of our Massachusetts crashers." With that pronouncement he ensnared Serene in a bear hug. "Ah! Serene you are as beautiful as your name." A second later, Henry found himself in a similar hug, though Nate's head was buried under his jaw. "And you Henry, welcome. You're not as beautiful as Serene. I have seen uglier men, however."

Henry and Serene were flabbergasted as Nate stood back and removed his wallet. "Let me make my formal introductions," he said as he presented each with a business card, which read:

Land – Whiskey Nails – Used Cars
Manure – Fly Swatters Bongos – Racing Forms
NATE NEVINS
Expert
Wars Fought – Revolutions Started
Assassinations Plotted – Governments Run
Uprisings Quelled – Tigers Tamed – Bars Emptied
Virgins Converted – Mexican Gold – Orgies Organized
Also Preach and Lead Singing for Revival Meetings
Religious Conversions

By the time Henry and Serene had finished reading the card they had silly grins and were momentarily speechless.

"Come on, let's get out of the sun. Our bodies are seventy percent water, ya know … we might dry up and blow away. I've made up my special veranda ice tea … got the recipe from a nice young fancy boy in P-Town … he serves it on a veranda. So do I."

Nate led them down a footpath towards back of his house which was covered with dark weathered shingles and adorned with deer antlers, plastic lobsters, old buoys, horseshoes and other assorted *objets d'art* according to Nate's tastes. They arrived at his rear deck, which was cleverly fashioned from wooden shipping pallets arranged on the ground in a checkerboard pattern and deeply shaded by old pine trees. The view was breathtaking. Nate's house was situated on a sandy knoll and overlooked the vast expanse of marshland that edged Cape Cod Bay.

"I see you're admiring my free deck. It's astounding what people throw away these days. Sturdy hardwood pallets, already built, for the taking. All I had to do was arrange the squares on the ground and fill in the gaps with boards from other free pallets. Then I swabbed it down with a homemade stain made from kerosene and old paint. Orange paint, as ya see. Ya know, several people actually asked me to build them one like this. Who's got the time? Any thing you can't buy at Home Depot is considered artsy these days. But ya know, ya got to have time on your hands to conjure up the crazy side of yourself. Have a seat. I'll get the tea."

Henry and Serene sat on plastic chairs at a big round table, the base of which was an old wooden cable spool which had been covered with odd sized driftwood planks which were perfectly fitted together. They both stared across the yard. At the back of his barn was the demasted boat sitting on a cradle and covered with bright blue tarpaulins. Nate returned with a large pitcher of dark liquid spilling over with ice cubes and he filled the three large glass tumblers until they were overflowing.

"Wow! Fantastic ice tea!" said Serene.

"Truly," agreed Henry. "So, Nate, how long have you lived here?"

"Over twenty years off and on. Born right up Route 6 'bout twenty minutes in P-Town ... Provincetown. Lived on the Cape most of my life off and on ... when I wasn't at sea or some such. Ya folks from Fiji. Never been near it. What ya folks do there?"

Henry gave a sketchy account of his life before meeting Serene, told Nate about the islands and the hotel. Finally, he asked about the boat.

"Plenty of time to talk about boats. Tomorrow the boat. Today we get to know each other. I'll make ya some crabs for dinner. Spruced up the spare room for ya shipshape and Bristol Fashion."

"We have reservations at the Wellfleet Inn," said Serene.

"Jack Nickerson's place! Why he's got all these loony college kids working there. Most of 'em hung-over from partying all night. He even lets them cook food! Jack's a good man and all, but that's for tourists. You're my guests. That's that. I'll call Jack and tell 'em what's up."

"Thank you," said Henry. Serene nodded in agreement.

"Come on, I'll show ya the room. Freshen up. Take a nap. Ya must be exhausted."

Nate had read their minds. No sooner had they unpacked than they both flopped into the big, white feather bed. They slept till dusk and when they emerged on the deck, Nate was nowhere in sight. Out back heavy smoke billowed from a fieldstone grill. The air blew cool with the fragrance of salt and pitch pine on the evening breeze. The sky, a hue of pastels in pink and blue cast a unique quality of softly filtered light, which was new to their eyes. They strolled up the driveway. Nate's pickup truck was gone.

To the side of the barn sat the *Loki* all covered with tarps. As they walked around it, Serene remarked, "I know his ad said thirty-seven feet, but it looks much, much larger."

"It's because it's out of the water and up on a cradle. Besides, it's very broad beamed ... wide."

"Sweetie, I know what broad beamed is. Remember, I sailed for years on the bay ... more sailing than you I bet," Serene said with a wink.

"So glad you're not broad beamed," said Henry as he patted her behind.

"Hang around for a few years. You may get more than you bargained for."

Nate's barn was old but the metal roof looked new. The old double doors were open. They took a peek inside. Big windows revealed a tidy workshop with a huge table in the middle of the room. A row of power tools lined the rear wall and a staircase led up to a loft. The walls were mostly covered with white pegboard and were hung with all sorts of hand tools and nautical hardware. Set up on sawhorses was the freshly painted hull of a dinghy flanked by varnished oars and spars.

"You can tell the quality of the work by looking at the workshop," said Henry.

"In that case, Nate must be good. It's rare to see such thorough organization. I can't wait to see the *Loki*."

"Me too. However, let's not push it. Nate sounded adamant about not discussing it tonight. By the way, did you look at his library ... or living room ... the big room off the kitchen?"

"Just through the doorway. Looked cozy."

"I looked over his books while you were drying your hair."

"Snoop!"

"Guilty. He told us to make ourselves at home. Quite an eclectic collection ... philosophy, psychology, psychiatry, mythology, history, biology, religion. From what I saw, I was impressed. No, more surprised."

"I haven't seen a TV..."

At that moment Nate's pickup rattled up the driveway. He had a boyish grin on his face as he got out of the cab and pulled a burlap sack out of the bed. The sack was dripping and wiggling. "Sorry, no crabs today. We'll have to settle for lobster ... again," he said with a smack of his lips.

"You didn't have to go to all this trouble. We could have taken you out to dinner," said Serene.

"Trouble? No trouble. These restaurants charge you forty bucks for a two dollar lobster which I get for free from a pal 'o mine. Asides they don't cook 'em right. Let's eat!"

Nate's idea of a good dinner was lots of lobster, fresh Portuguese bread, enough butter to clog a garden hose and iced tea. During dinner, Henry asked Nate about his background, and he gladly provided it.

He was born in Provincetown. Henry and Serene had guessed he was in his late 40's, but Nate was actually in his late 50's. His father had been a tailor and his mother a seamstress. His family had moved to the Cape from Providence, Rhode Island, a few years before Nate was born. As an only child, he played on the floor of the shop and later found himself to be the only Jewish boy in his school. That was never a problem, however. The townspeople, with a long seafaring history, were extremely tolerant because of the many nationalities represented on the crews of the fishing boats. Nate mentioned that his parents were hard workers and that his father was particularly well educated, having studied to be a rabbi before losing interest in the vocation.

Nate spoke fondly of a childhood when the town was more of a working community than a summer resort. He helped in the shop after school and learned to cut and to sew. He talked of fishing, crabbing and clamming with his pals and cooking seafood on the beach at night. During summers he worked sport fishing boats and occasionally helped out a sail maker where he made good money because of his skill with a sewing machine. The sail maker taught him how to splice rope and do 'fancy work', the intricate braiding and weaving of rope at which he became expert.

After high school Nate did what most of the boys in town did, he went fishing. "For ten years, I fished for everything that swam, crawled, or burrowed. I worked commercial boats for cod, lobster, crabs, even went for whales one time. Hauled oysters and clams, too. Love the sea in tolerable weather. We fished from early April right to winter … as long the weather held. When it got cold, it was brutal, I'll tell ya. Ya was always damp or wet. Could never get dry and warm. That did it for me. Must be my Mideastern genes." Nate chuckled.

"So up to Boston with a pal I go, and we sign on with the old American Line. Freighters running to the Med and back. Wasn't long before I wangled a job as a machinist mate. Nice, warm, inside work. I learned an honest trade. After a time, there was nothing on them ships I couldn't fix. I studied for the Merchant Marine tests and rose to be a chief machinist. Can't get higher in that work. Stayed at sea for near twenty-five years, 'til my accident. Banged up my knees moving some machinery. So, I was beached. Gave me a chunk of cash 'cause of the accident, and I got my pension. Had some operations, and now I walk as ya see. These days do fairly much as I please. Make a sail. Fix up old boats. But, ya know, my specialty is hanging out with the rich folks.

"Ya see, after they make a lot of money, they buy themselves these big, expensive yachts. Most of 'em can't tie a knot! Not that they need or even want to, mind ya. But, they wants things just so and nautical-like. I got pals in Wellfleet, P. Town, Hyannis, even out on Nantucket and the Vineyard who know me as the best fancy splicer in these parts. So I get calls for my craft. I always fib to the owner and tell 'em it's best I'm aboard when she's workin', so I can understand her needs, ya see. It's a white lie, if there be such a thing. After they get to know me, I eventually tell 'em my scheme, and they laugh. No harm done.

"So, I cruise summers with the rich folks. Teach 'em a few little rope tricks, do what needs being done, mooring splices an' such. I had a man who wanted a thirty-foot rope gangway mat with the boat's name wove in gold letters! They want to look 'salty', and I can whip up the genuine stuff. Best thing is most of these men are smart, some real smart with a sense of humor, too. Guess they had to be to make the money for them yachts. I've had some humdinger talks, I tell ya … . some all night. Been some prize jerks, too, but I make a fast wake of 'em. The ones I like seem to get along with me. Made a lot of pals that way. Now I get invitations to cruise as a guest. Great food. Good company. What's not to like? Speaking of food … let's eat!"

— CHAPTER 7 —

It took a dozen phone calls before Boxer connected with Peter Sieffert the Executive Director of the Red Cross in Papua, New Guinea. Boxer introduced himself as the insurance broker from Costello Freight Forwarding, which was not far from the truth. He inquired about the lost shipment. Sieffert confirmed what Boxer already knew: the claim on the goods had been paid. Boxer thanked Sieffert for the confirmation and prolonged the conversation by asking about the status of the victims of the tidal wave. Sieffert was proud to report the progress and mentioned that their work had been expedited by a large, unexpected donation. Boxer asked who made the donation, and Sieffert said it had been made anonymously.

"How much was the donation, if I may ask?" asked Boxer.

"Sorry. Can't disclose that information. That's our policy with anonymous contributions."

"I completely understand," said Boxer. "Did you know I have psychic powers?" he added.

"Really!" Sieffert replied.

"I believe the donation was ten millions dollars ... all in cash."

"Well that *is* amazing, Mr. Ryan. But I suspect you already know the donor."

"Yes, in fact, I do. When I see him, I'll tell him how well things are going for you."

"Please ... thank Mr. Costello for us. We guessed it was him."

"I'm sure he'll be *very* interested to hear that."

Boxer's next call was to Philly.

"Hi, Philly. Got some information. Went to Nutley. Had a long talk with Mr. Langston. He's not your man. This guy had a nervous breakdown and has been in Alabama for over a year. Confirmed it with his employer down there. There's a connection to McCall, however. Langston was acquainted with McCall. Odd thing. After Langston went missing, both his mother and wife received only one inquiry about his disappearance from a guy out west who claimed he was a sheriff. Wanted to know Langston's social security and passport numbers. I think McCall assumed Langston's identity and is traveling under his passport."

"So McCall is alive!"

"Yup. Think he is. The other news is bad. I found your money." There was a long silence on the phone. "Philly, you there?"

"Yeah, go on," Philly said in a dead monotone voice.

"I talked to the head man at the Red Cross in Papua. A few months after the typhoon, they received an anonymous donation of ten million in cash. They think you sent it because of their lost container."

"Hold on a minute, Boxer."

If Boxer could have seen Philly's face, he would have been stunned. Philly's skin went ash white. His eyes bulged. He was breathing heavily. The arteries in his neck were throbbing. His fat face was oozing perspiration, and his teeth were locked like a vice, struggling to control his rage. With his hand over the phone, Philly took three deep breaths, as he learned from his anger management therapist, and slowly exhaled through his nose.

"Sorry, Boxer, another call. Where do we go from here?"

"I wish our deal had been for finding the money, not recovering it," jibed Boxer.

"Forget about the money. I'll have my lawyers look into it. If they think I sent it, maybe there's a way of getting it back. A long shot, but our deal stands. I'll pay you a million if you find McCall. It would be worth it to get that dirt bag. Same day rate and expenses. Go first class. Just find him."

"Philly, remember our deal. I don't want to be an accessory…"

"Just locate McCall. Then you're completely out of it."

"Okay, Philly. What was the name of that island Scardino was killed on? I have it in my notes somewhere."

"Mandavu. There's also a guy at the American Consulate in Suva who I met when I identified Scardino's body. Bill … something … Bill Wilson. Scardino mentioned he saw a photo in Wilson's office that may have been McCall. That's why he went to Mandavu … to check it out. That's where he was struck by lightning."

"I'll get right on it, Philly."

"Keep me informed. The faster you find him, the faster you get the million."

"Bye, Philly."

After Boxer hung up the phone, he realized how first his greed and now his curiosity overruled his judgment in taking the case. A million would solve his financial dilemma, but now he was intrigued by the case itself. Did McCall find the money and give it away? Why? What kind of guy would do that? Boxer knew, however, what would happen to McCall after he located him. He had an unnatural feeling in the pit of his stomach.

Nate's cottage was cold that night. Henry and Serene had slept soundly and were reluctant to crawl out of the cozy feather bed. The big, fluffy, goose down comforter had been a godsend. A low angled sun was beaming through the pines and cast razor sharp shadows of needles, cones and branches on the white walls. The images, Henry thought, looked like engravings. The friendly sounds of pots and pans, and the aroma of coffee triggered a race between them to the kitchen.

"Good morning," they said in sync, as they greeted Nate working busily at the stove.

"Another fine day. Ya folks bring lucky weather, I'd say. Belly up to the bar, buckwheat flapjacks with homemade cranberry syrup and scrambled eggs. Help yourselves to coffee."

"Can we ask about the boat today?" said Serene with a wink to Henry.

"Sure. Nothing better or more useless than boat talk. Problem is, I can't talk about boats with people I don't care for. Too serious a business. But I like you folks."

"Thank you," said Henry. "The feeling is mutual."

"I'll tell ya about her. Five years ago I was helping a pal with a charter. So, I'm bright and early at the town docks. While I'm unloading my truck, I see this odd looking boat tied up at a slip that belongs to a guy I know. You should have seen the *Loki* then. Looked like a derelict. Dirty. Paint peeling. Sails in tatters. Frayed lines everywhere. The messiest thing afloat. I see smoke piping out this crooked stack just fo'ward of the cabin. So, I walks over and give 'em an 'Ahoy there', and this lively blonde gal pokes her head up. At first, thought she was a boy. Short hair. She was this Norwegian, name of Randi. They speak perfect English, them people. Next thing her boyfriend Harold pops out. I say nothing about them being in my friend's slip, and we get to chattering. Seems they sailed down from Norway over the summer. They had put in at the Orkneys, Iceland, Greenland, St. Johns in Newfoundland, Halifax and Boston. Just like the old time Vikings they were. This boy Harold inherited the boat from his grandpa. They was either crackerjack sailors or just plain lucky to get that wreck here to Wellfleet. They were students, ya see, on their summer vacation! They wanted to sell the *Loki* in Boston and fly back to Norway. After two weeks there, they didn't get a decent offer. A broker suggested they sail down to Mystic Seaport and show her to a man who deals in old wood boats and would give them a fair price. That's where they were headed when their engine blew. So they sailed in here and tied up. Ya see, they were headed down the bay to go through the Cape Cod Canal. Big time-saver going that way, but you need a motor to get through the canal. They could have sailed back out around the Cape, but they would have had a hell of a time sailing into Mystic Harbor, narrow entrance and heavy traffic. They were in a pickle, all right. Had to get back to university. The engine was an antique. A big ol' cast iron one-lunger…"

"One-lunger?" asked Serene.

"Sorry, a single cylinder, diesel engine, maybe twenty horsepower when it was new back in 1939 when she was built. Well, my party was late. They usually are. I'm always early. So I start poking around the boat. Take a look at the engine myself. Sure enough cracked like a nut, and there's nothing to do about it. I suggested my pal, Shep, might have a used engine that might do.

"Then my fishermen come, and I got to go. Told Randi and Harold I'd stop by to see how they made out when I returned.

"Had a fine day on the water. Nothing like fish to make happy fishermen. After I filleted the fish and hosed down the boat, I dropped by the *Loki*. Randi and Harold had been to Shep. He looked at the job and gave them a fair price for a used engine and installation. Turns out that the Norwegians only had a few hundred bucks, and the estimate was several thousand.

"Well, to be honest, I'd been thinking about her while we were fishing. She had clean lines and was built like a bull. So, I asked them how much they wanted. It seemed like a fair price what with the blown engine and all. So, I offered them a deal. I would pay for haulout to inspect the hull. If she were in reasonable shape below the water line, I'd give them their price.

"Next morning Shep heaved her up, and everything looked great considering her age. I walked over to my bank, got cash and bought her. There wasn't any title or anything, just some registration papers in Norwegian. I had them write the facts of the sale in the logbook which is perfect maritime legal."

"What happened to the Norwegians?" asked Serene.

"They stayed here a couple of days. Sat where you two are right now. Nice young people. Both studying to be mathematicians they was. Happy as spring ducks with the sale. Harold told me all about his grandpa and the *Loki*. Enough chatter. Let's go disrobe the ol' lady."

Nate climbed the ladder like a squirrel, untied the lines that held the blue tarps and scurried back down. As he pulled off the tarps, he said, "Here's my masterpiece!"

Serene and Henry were awestruck. The bottom was painted a rich, dark copper. At the waterline, a thin, glossy, black stripe separated the brilliant white of the hull above. Dark green rub rails pinstriped in fine gold lines ran the length of the boat.

"It looks seamless. Did you fiberglass the hull?" asked Henry.

"No way! Only a moron would put fiberglass over wood. What I did was soak the wood with about a dozen coats of two-part epoxy to strengthen and waterproof her. That hull is over eight inches thick, double planked with white cedar over ash frames. About as good as it gets. Ya know, when I first looked at the engine, I noticed the framing. Massive I tell ya! Them Norwegians been carving boats out of wood for centuries. Know their business. Harold's grandpa hauled it out every fall. Had a big winch and steel train rails to ease her into his boathouse. Scraped and painted her during those dark winters. It was his pride and joy.

"When I first got her, I hired a couple of boys to scrape her down to bare wood. Must've been a hundred coats of oil paint on the hull. Near as many in the bilge. Used blowtorches to soften the paint. They scraped their hearts out for two months. After we soaked her with epoxy, I sprayed on six coats of paint. Come on. Let's go topside." Henry and Serene followed Nate up the ladder. The deck, wheelhouse and spars were of natural wood. The workmanship could only be described as museum quality.

"I had to rip out the old deck and a few beams to get that big old beast of an engine out. So, I replaced the old pine deck and trim with teak. Nothing better," said Nate as he led them aft. "She had a hand tiller originally, if you can believe it. I fixed up the old rudder and installed stainless steel, worm gear steering with two wheel stations. This here in the cockpit for fair sailing. The other in the deckhouse for foul weather. The aft mast steps into that socket there, just fo'ward the rudder post. Ya notice I put bronze safety rails all 'round. Stainless is cheaper and less maintenance, but the bronze hangs well on her. Them kids sailed here with a few old ropes strung around. Imagine that!

"Come fo'ward, and watch your footing," said Nate as he led them around the narrow deck alongside the wheelhouse. "Up here used to be a big hatch to the fish hold. She was built to fish mackerel in the North Sea, ya understand. That's why she's so rugged built."

"She was a trawler?" asked Henry.

"God no, Henry. With the engine she had she could barely push herself. No, they used to go out for weeks at a stretch and drift along on the current. Let out these long lines with baited hooks set about a yard apart. After a spell, they'd haul in with a hand winch, take the catch and throw 'em in the hold. Iced 'em down with what they cut out of the lakes in winter.

"Fact is, on a hot, humid day, she still puts out faint, fishy scent. It's soaked in the wood. Not so much to offend, mind you. I think of it as her perfume. Kind of like it myself," said Nate with a wink.

"Can't wait to see below," said Serene.

"Sure enough, but first see that new power winch on the fore deck. There's another like it on the aft deck. Whole boat's been totally rewired."

Nate walked them to the deckhouse hatch, stopped and said, "This whole deckhouse is new. The old one was a wreck 'cause it was mostly open to the weather. There was a windshield of sorts and some side curtains. They used to rig a tarp overhead when it got foul. I enclosed it. Installed these heavy weather hatches and ports. Doors and windows ya landsmen call 'em. Remember last night, when I said I didn't like the cold. Truth is I don't like hot either. That's why I closed her up. To put in the heat and air conditioning."

Nate opened the hatch which was on the located on the port side and motioned for Henry and Serene to enter the deckhouse. Everything they saw was new and handsomely crafted. Directly forward of the hatch were stairs that went below deck. To the starboard side were two plush, brown leather captain's chairs equipped with armrests and footrests. The chair toward the port side faced a bronze and wood wheel and state of the art controls. Directly behind the chairs was a built-in island. Since the chairs swiveled, Nate explained the island doubled for eating or was used as a chart table. On other side of the counter was a built-in, brown leather sofa set up on a platform to make it the same height as the captain's chairs. With the chairs faced toward the sofa it was like booth in a diner. The deck was covered with heavy-duty, gray rubber matting with a skid resistant surface. The electronics were all state of the art and rather extensive. Besides radios, GPS, radar and sonar, the boat had been wired for hi-fidelity audio, television and computers. Besides VHS and DVD playback to several monitors throughout the boat, there was satellite feed via dishes mounted on the deckhouse roof.

"Hope you like what I've done below!" Nate said.

— CHAPTER 8 —

Getting a reservation at the Maru Mandavu was not easy. It appeared to be the most popular resort in the Fijian group. Even with his considerable powers of persuasion and charm, Boxer could only get a bungalow for two days during the middle of the week. Thus, he arranged his flight schedule to give him two days at the Imperial Hotel in Suva before he traveled to Mandavu and then two days back at the Imperial after Mandavu. He thought this time would be more than sufficient. If not, he was prepared to stay as long as the job took. This part of the case was no chore for Boxer since he had always dreamed of visiting the South Pacific. Now he was an hour from landing at Suva.

Reluctantly, he closed Henri Bergson's *The Creative Mind* and felt a twinge of guilt because he had not even thought about the case during the long flight. Even though Bergson was infinitely more interesting, Philly was footing the bill for this first class seat. He pulled a notebook from his briefcase and reviewed the 'to do' list he made back at the office.

1. See Bill Wilson at the American Consulate.

2. Check at the Imperial to see if anyone remembered Scardino or Langston.

3. Inquire around Mandavu and at the hotel to discover if anyone remembers Scardino, or knows Langston.

4. Be discreet. Avoid direct questions and try to uncover information through extended conversations.

Boxer was an expert at extending conversations with his breezy style, eccentric manner, and storytelling. He had obtained a better photo of McCall from a video trade magazine, and Philly supplied a good photo of Scardino.

There really was nothing more he could do on the case for the moment, he concluded. His thoughts reverted to a theory he had just read. Bergson believed that the human brain evolved over millions of years as a direct

50

reaction to a hostile environment by learning and remembering all those immediate physical actions necessary for self-preservation. As a result of this long process, these survival instincts were brought to the forefront of consciousness. All other types of learning, the more subtle and associative kinds of knowledge acquired during a lifetime also reside somewhere in the intellect, perhaps in what many have called the subconscious or unconscious.

Boxer speculated that maybe this other wealth of knowledge, which is not readily available for use in moment-to-moment existence, exists nevertheless as an untapped reservoir. Then he had a personal intellectual breakthrough, which he always found was accompanied by a particularly clear state of mind and a mild tingling sensation on his scalp.

If he proceeded on the premise that all useful knowledge is retained as a necessity for survival, it *could* be that all other knowledge beyond which is necessary and is acquired during a lifetime, is also stored away as some kind of coalesced wisdom. Boxer recalled that H.G. Wells had thought that man, contrary to accepted beliefs, is not a *remembering animal*, but evolved and was designed by nature to be a *forgetting animal*. While many sensations and perceptions are interesting and compelling, those that are of little practical utility in daily survival must be pushed to the rear to make room for those that do sustain life. Boxer now wondered if there was more knowledge in our heads via genetic inheritance than we ever imagined.

Boxer questioned whether everything he had ever learned, and everything all of his ancestors had ever learned, was lodged someplace in his large head. Many times he had heard the unsupported claim that we use only a small fraction of our brainpower. He had never come across any substantial scientific support for this claim. Why would we have brainpower that we never use? How could unused power have even come into being if it had not been created by necessity? Nature, he pondered, is lean and stingy with little or no tolerance for the useless or superfluous. It was true, he knew, that the brain is an electro-biological organ composed of billions of synapse where nervous impulses pass from one neuron to another. How the brain actually *thought*, science believed would take hundreds of years to begin to unravel and may not ever be fully understood. Boxer had also learned that as far as the understanding of how memory actually worked, the world's greatest minds in science and philosophy had speculated and argued the subject endlessly with few, if any, conclusions. The more Boxer had read and studied over his lifetime, the more he appreciated how little science has comprehended about the physical world and even less about the mental realm. Perhaps, Boxer thought, he might find a way to use his own conscious mind to retrieve his legacy of forgotten wisdom, if it resided within him. Maybe there was a way for him to tap everything that had been forgotten and apply this wisdom to an immediate problem. His own IQ had always tested in the high 130's. He decided to use this yardstick to measure his progress. Like many people, he had discovered that he could remember obscure information, but it often took a long time to recall it, and in some cases his memory failed him. He resolved to work on his new theory. It could be as simple as devising a method for his conscious mind to connect to his subconscious to ask for the information. These thoughts led to slumber, which were soon broken by a jolt and screeching tires as he landed in Fiji.

After a busy morning of inspecting the *Loki*, Henry and Serene thanked Nate for the tour and excused themselves for a walk. Hand in hand, they ambled along the sandy road that led back to Highway 6. Both were silent as they welcomed the quiet of nature after the whirlwind of new and dizzying information.

They limited their sparse conversation to the landscape, the diffusion of the bright sun as it filtered through the canopy of pines, and the dappled light that fell upon the forest floor of reddish brown needles. Their tranquility was momentarily disturbed by the speeding traffic on Route 6. After they crossed the highway, they saw the entrance sign to Marconi Beach. Walking toward the sign, they noticed an inviting needle-covered pathway. As they wandered down the path, it became quiet again, and the light scent of pine was displaced with heavier, saltier air. The trees grew smaller, and wider spaces between the pines revealed patches of white drift sand edged with low stands of scrub oak. Faintly, they heard waves breaking. The forest gave way to an open area of tan and green dune grasses and ground hugging masses of dark green vines. With great expectancy, they climbed a high dune and saw spread out before them the Atlantic Ocean. They sat down on the ridge of the dune and marveled at the seascape. There was not a soul to be seen on the long expanse of beach. Just the two of them, facing a decision.

"Marconi Beach! It just hit me. This is where Marconi transmitted the first transatlantic radio signal. It was in the guide book," said Serene.

"Makes sense. Cape Cod sticks out far into the Atlantic. These high dunes would have been perfect spot for a transmitter." Henry paused for several seconds, and said softly, almost to himself, "I guess everything has to happen someplace."

"You're sounding very philosophical this afternoon. Don't try to attach any historical significance to buying a boat for God's sake."

"I won't," chuckled Henry. "I suppose looking at this vast expanse of water puts the little *Loki* in perspective."

"Even if the *Loki* were a thousand times its size, it would still be a speck compared to that."

"I know. It's just that my dream of sailing around the world has collided with the hard reality of actually doing it."

"Oh, I thought it was *our* dream, my dear?"

"It is. My dream reawakened yours. Now it's ours. My real concern now is for you ... your safety. I wonder if we have enough experience to tackle that," said Henry as he panned his arm across the horizon.

"Maybe our deal with Nate could include some *Loki* sailing lessons in the bay. After that we take it slow. Stick close to shore, watch the weather, take it mile by mile, and we'll soon be there ... wherever that is," said Serene as she broke into one of her bouts of uncontrollable laughter and lay back on the sand. Henry, who always found her sudden outbursts funny, smiled and waited until she had regained her composure. He lay back as well, resting his head on his crooked arm with his face close to hers.

"So I suppose we buy *Loki*?" Henry whispered.

"Of course," replied Serene. "It's *our* boat."

"Shall we seal the deal with a kiss?"

"Cheapskate. I won't settle for less than lot."

"Hi, Philly. It's Boxer. I'm in Suva. Can you hear me okay?"

"Sure. What's up?"

"McCall *is* posing as Langston. He showed up here a few months after he went off the *Pacific Star* and claimed he lost his passport. He got a temporary passport in the name of Henry Langston. He had all the information to get it, which, as we figured, he wangled out of Langston's mother and wife posing as a cop. Now he's hooked up with this babe, Serene Bronte. Her family owns the Maru Mandavu Hotel. That was where Scardino was hit by lightning ... on their golf course. And guess who reported the 'accident'?"

"Langston!"

"Right ... and Serene Bronte."

"So where's McCall now?"

"Here's where it gets complicated. I nosed around Mandavu and learned that they came into some money from the sale of some pearls that Serene inherited. About a week ago they left the islands together. No one knows where. When I got back here in Suva, I checked out some pearl dealers. This Chinese guy showed me one of the pearls they sold him. I asked how much he wanted for it and he quoted me $25,000.00. I don't know how much he paid. He bought twelve of them. But here's where it gets interesting. Serene still has this big pearl she wouldn't sell. It even has a name, The Daughter of the Moon. It's huge and old. The dealer said it's priceless."

"I believe that pearl rightly belongs to me," said Philly in an ominous tone.

"Whatever, Philly. I made a friend at the airport here for five hundred bucks. He checked the departing flights and found they were routed to Sydney, San Francisco and finally to Logan in Boston. They arrived there about a week ago."

"So, you're on your way to Boston?"

"Not quite. Back to Jersey first. I have to check with some friends in the car rental business. Just hope they rented a car. It takes me a couple of days to get that info. If they didn't rent and somebody picked them up at the airport, then it becomes harder. I can also check the hotels in Boston from Jersey. In any event, I'll drive up to Boston and track them from there."

"You know best about these things, Boxer. Just don't let the trail get cold. Good job so far."

"Thanks Philly. I'm working on this new theory. I'll be thinking about it on the plane."

Philly put down the phone, scratched his chin and wondered what Boxer's tease about his 'new theory' was about. He dismissed Boxer's eccentricities, because he had more pressing business, namely who should handle McCall after Boxer found him. Philly had great faith in Boxer. He had never known him to fail at anything he set his mind to. Now Philly had to choose the men to kill McCall and his girl and bring him that valuable pearl. The job called for cunning, intelligence, loyalty and ultimately ruthlessness. In the end he wanted McCall to suffer horribly for the trouble he had caused him. Philly had paid back the lost ten million. It nearly broke him. His cash reserve was gone. He had sold property, borrowed from the bank against his receivables, and borrowed nearly two million. Every spare dollar was now going to pay off the loan because the interest was killing him. Now for the first time in his life, he was strapped for cash. McCall had to pay the hard way.

— CHAPTER 9 —

They returned late afternoon to find Nate sitting on a lawn chair in front of his workshop, gazing blankly at the *Loki*. His reverie was broken by the crunch of footsteps on his gravel driveway.

"Admiring your work?" asked Henry.

"Yup! Thought you folks was here to buy a boat, not for a hiking trip," Nate jibed.

"We always go for a hike before buying a boat." Serene replied.

"So ... what have you good folks decided?"

Henry took a folded scrap of paper from his shirt pocket and handed it to Nate. Nate unfolded the paper, looked at the number Henry had written, closed his eyes and thought a moment. He stood up, spat on his hand, held it out and said, "It's a fair deal." Henry and Serene gleefully spat on their hands and in turn shook on the deal with Nate.

"We have another proposal Nate. We'd really appreciate your help in getting her into the water and rigged ... and since neither Serene or I have ever sailed anything like her ... perhaps give us a few sailing lessons. We'd be happy to pay you," offered Henry.

"God, no," Nate replied. "I already figured on getting her wet and rigged up nice and proper. That's part of the deal as far as I'm concerned. As for lessons, well I'd be pleased to show you the ropes. From what ya folks told me at dinner about your sailing experience, it shouldn't take more than a day. God! Serene, you told me you sailed for several summers on Frisco Bay and raced to boot."

"We even won a few," said Serene with a sly wink at Henry.

"Well that bay is about the meanest hunk of water on the planet. Ya folks shouldn't have any problems at all. The *Loki* is about the easiest sailing boat that ever was. Very forgiving. 'Bout as good a heavy weather hull ever built. Stable, too. Watertight top down and bottom up."

"And remember, Henry, we'll also have that new engine Nate installed," said Serene.

"To tell ya the truth, I didn't tell the whole truth on the Internet about the 'new' engine. Fact is, I understated it. The engine was a year old but never used when I got my hands on it. Shep, my pal who owns the boatyard, gave it to me for favors I done him over the years when he'd run into a problem. I am a master machinist, remember. Shep ordered the engine for a commercial fisherman for a sixty foot steel trawler but the poor guy's financing fell through. So Shep refunded his deposit and held on to it, knowing I'd need an engine for the *Loki* by and by. When I got my hands on it, I made a number of improvements before I dropped her in. Still a bit overpowered for the *Loki*, but ya never know. When I had her out last season for the shakedown she really clocked along. Ya see, the *Loki* ain't got no keel. Just hull resistance. Had her up to twenty knots and that was at two-thirds throttle. People in the harbor was amazed. Run her at ten knots with the 150 gallon tanks I installed, she'd take you about five hundred miles. Go slower and who knows how far. So even if ya never hoisted a sail, you'd be fine and dandy. Ya know, I never showed the dinghy that goes to her."

Nate arose and led Henry and Serene into his workshop.

"We saw that tiny boat when you went for the lobsters yesterday," said Serene.

"Yup. A little jewel she is. Just gotta slap a couple of coats of bottom paint on her. She'll mount on top the main cabin. In the barrel there's a seven horse outboard for her." Nate pointed to a fifty-five gallon drum of water with an ugly green motor clamped to it. It's an old Merc I picked up for next to nothing and fixed. Should fly! Made a cute little gaff sail for the dinghy, too."

"We can't accept the dinghy as part of our deal, but we'll buy it from you separately," said Henry.

"Nope. Sometimes a deal includes the unexpected," said Nate with a playful grin.

Boxer was hard at work on his new theory. To the other passengers in the first class cabin, he appeared to be sleeping. Upon careful observation, there was a faint smile on his face for he was experiencing the pleasure of a new intellectual discovery. In all his considerable study, he had never come across an idea quite like the one he was pondering. Now he was solidly determined to pursue his new idea but not mention a word to anyone, lest they would think him deluded.

If he postulated correctly, all sensory information and its distilled wisdom reside somewhere, somehow, in our cells, central nervous system and brain; there, genetically deposited from billions of experiences over millions of years of evolution, it is briefly supplemented by life experience of the living individual. Boxer decided to proceed on the basis that there must be a method of accessing it.

His thoughts flashed to the Kundalini system of yoga, which has been practiced by Indian aesthetics for hundreds of years. In this system, the yogi through meditation and verbal pronunciations works his way up from the bottom of his spine to the crown of the head through a series of six *chakras*, or psychological/spiritual centers that are distributed along this line. As the yogi travels upward through the *chakras* via this mystical channel up the spine, his spirituality is increased as he attains each stage. The ultimate hope is to attain a seventh state, which is beyond all categories, descriptions, thoughts and feelings called *Sahasrara,* the thousand petal lotus at the crown of the head.

The yogi's path is a purely spiritual one, a way of transcending reality as most of us know it. But, Boxer thought this practice might also be incorporated as one of the component ways to access our unconscious intellectual resources; to resurrect these powerful assets to the conscious mind and bring them to bear on reality.

For many years Boxer had practiced self-hypnosis, mostly as a technique to relax his body and his mind. It was useful when tired to renew his energy, or when his thoughts became confused to calm himself for improved concentration, or when he had difficulty falling asleep. He was an expert at it and could bring himself into a hypnotic state in a matter of minutes. He would take several deep breaths and slowly exhale each through his nose. Then, counting backwards from ten to zero while he visualized each number, he would let his mind's eye pass through the center of the zero. At that point he entered a hypnotic state, which was accompanied by a mild physical tingling sensation. He could remain in the state for hours or suggest to himself to pass into sleep after a given period of time.

Boxer thought he might be able to combine the Kundalini system of meditation with self-hypnosis, as a way of tapping that deeply forgotten knowledge he believed existed. He resolved to create and test a series of verbal prompts to use during meditation and self-hypnosis to help release the stored information. Self-hypnosis might be the first step. Then he might compose several incantations to address each of the seven *chakras*. He had work ahead, and he needed time with his books for research, he concluded. He almost wished that the McCall case would go away so he could concentrate on more important matters.

Henry and Serene had never worked harder in their entire lives. As they sat on pier in Wellfleet Harbor, totally exhausted and filthy from the day's work, they agreed that trying to keep up with Nate Nevins was impossible.

The day after they concluded the business details, Nate arranged for his friend Shep to lift the *Loki* from Nate's yard, carry her to the town docks and lower her into the water. All the while, Nate darted about like a hummingbird to make sure not a scratch marred his masterpiece.

Once afloat, Nate turned on the ignition, and the big engine started instantly with a low, powerful sounding grumble. He nudged the *Loki* away from the dock, put the motor in neutral, and went around the boat putting large rubber fenders over the side. Nate brought the *Loki* into the boatyard dock and tied her up under the crane. They drove back to Nate's barn in Shep's flatbed truck. They lugged and loaded what seemed to be tons of masts, spars, sails, rigging and dozens of cartons filled with assorted parts. By the time they returned to the dock, it was late afternoon. Everyone was bushed, so they left the loaded truck under the crane. Since it was only a mile to Nate's place, Nate, Henry and Serene decided to walk back and stop at Captain Higgen's for dinner.

As they were being seated in the restaurant, Henry said, "Nate, we insist that dinner is on us tonight."

"I'm too weak to argue!" replied Nate. "We put in quite a day."

"*You* put in quite a day, Nate. You should take it a lot easier, because you're killing us. We're not in a hurry, you know," said Serene.

"Sorry. Just my way. My pop used to say there's plenty of time to do everything ya want to do if only ya get to doing it."

"And when you finish up with us, how will you keep yourself busy?" asked Serene.

"There's always an old boat that needs fixin'..." Nate stopped in mid-sentence as a dark, slender man with a bushy black beard placed his hand on Nate's shoulder. Nate turned and a warm glow came to his face. "Doc Lieberman!"

"Hi Nate!" said Lieberman.

"Come, have a drink with us. I want you to meet my new friends." Dr. Lieberman sat down. Nate made the introductions and then said, "The Doc here is a famous psychiatrist, ya know, written about a million books, right Doc."

"Only several textbooks, Nate ... and whatever fame I enjoy exists mostly in your fruitful imagination, I must say."

"The Doc's being modest. He's a top New York City shrink and makes like a million bucks an hour knockin' dents outta heads, right Doc." Everyone burst out in laughter. Dr. Lieberman laughed loudest.

"How long have you known Nate?" Henry inquired.

"Forever it seems ... over ten years actually ... we fish together."

"Ya mean we fish and talk and talk more than we fish," said Nate with a wink and a chuckle.

"Some of the most enjoyable hours of my life have been spent with this man," said Lieberman as he nudged Nate with his elbow.

"I'm sort of a consultant, ya see. The Doc here always has these knotty cases, and I help unsplice 'em."

"So you're a psychiatrist along with all your other talents?" asked Serene. Nate sat back relaxed in his chair, folded his arms and a childlike smirk of self satisfaction appeared on his face.

"In many ways our friend Nate here is better than most psychiatrists I've known. He is certainly more widely read and has a clearer understanding of human nature. Some of his theories are a little far-fetched in my opinion, but he may be onto something ... It remains to be seen. One of his techniques, however, I've adopted for my own practice."

"The poor man's psychotherapy. Make 'em go fishin', right Doc," said Nate.

"No question. It's been a very effective treatment if I can I convince a patient to actually do it. That's the tough part. But with Nate's help, I worked out an incentive system. If a patient agrees to go fishing on a boat for one full day every month for three months and he's not satisfied with his progress, I refund a session fee. Even with the incentive, it's hard to convince some people to go. I've had lawyers, doctors, brokers, bankers, entertainers; all types of people who have never held a fishing pole in their life take up my offer. And, I've never made a refund."

"What's the magic in fishing?" asked Henry.

"Two basic ideas," piped in Nate. "Most of these fellows that the Doc deals with are strung too taut. They have demanding jobs, families, friends ...

belong to all kinds of clubs and associations. They are preoccupied with everything but themselves. So when they hit a strong gust in life, sometimes their rigging snaps, or when they do find a few minutes to think about themselves, they begin to churn up all kinds of doubts and problems in their noggins. I say, they're better off going fishin'. Gives 'em something to do that gets them out of their own heads for a few hours. They get their little selves out in a small boat under a big sky on the vast ocean, which in itself is beyond understanding. Instant perspective they get. As an alternative therapy, I also recommend periodic walks through a graveyard, but the Doc thinks that's a hard sell 'cause it's kind of morbid. Secondly, it's a proven fact ya can't hold two different thoughts in your mind simultaneously. Just try it! When you're fishin', ya mostly think fishin', 'cept, of course, when the Doc and I go out." Nate and Dr. Lieberman laughed together until tears came to their eyes.

When the waiter arrived, Dr. Lieberman excused himself and vowed to call Nate and arrange their next fishing trip.

After placing their dinner orders, Henry said, "The Doc certainly has a high opinion of you, Nate."

"He's one of the good guys. Some of the other shrinks I've talked to make my head hurt."

"Have you been in therapy long?" asked Serene.

Nate's eyes widened with theatrical surprise. "Never been! For some inexplicable reason, Wellfleet has become the summer roosting habitat for these odd critters. Ya can't walk about without bumpin' into them. 'Mental mechanics' I call 'em."

"I read that in the tour guide," said Serene. "Isn't it odd that a lot of psychiatrists and psychologists vacation here?"

"Not really. Birds of a feather always flock together. I suppose they feel more secure in greater numbers. Lots of artists in Wellfleet, too. Very similar to the shrinks in many ways."

"How so?" Henry asked.

"Both seem to be consumed in looking for that elusive 'something' in life. The artist searches for it by trying to create his ultimate satisfaction while the shrink looks for it by attempting to understand his own inner life by exploring the inner life of his patients and thereby find the same satisfaction. People seek the same answer in many occupations and ways. Of course, the majority of folks have just given up or have never begun to search. They may be better off," Nate said with a laugh.

"What are you searching for, Nate?" asked Serene.

"For answers, like everyone else. Problem is the more questions you ask, the more it begets more questions. Answers are as elusive as they are rare. Still, I keep poking through the debris hoping I can find a few pieces that fit together."

"By 'debris,' I take it you mean books," said Henry.

"Why yes, Henry! How astute of you to parse my meaning! You're a man after my own heart."

"I took a look at your library ... quite impressive," said Henry.

"I keep a few books about the place. Most of 'em wind up in the fireplace and at least provide a bit of warmth to this cold world for what they're worth. At sea I'd just throw 'em overboard not wanting to waste another fellow's time. Yep! I'm a book burner and a litterbug in service to mankind." Nate laughed. "At sea, that's the place to read, ya know. Probably the best benefit of the trade. You'd be surprised at how well read many seamen are. Ya got plenty of time off watch and there's not much else to do 'cept drink and gamble ... and there's a might of that, too. But I'm a Jew. That's not our tradition. We to like to read it seems ... at least I always have."

"We have a lot in common. Serene and I are both lifelong bibliophiles. That was one of the things we liked about the *Loki*, how many bookshelves you built into the cabins."

"Yes, with those cute little bars to keep them from falling out," Serene added.

"Them's called 'fids', Serene. Same fids on the edge of the table to keep your dishes from sliding off. But don't take no books you won't miss. Salt air chews 'em up terrible."

"Looked like you were planning on taking more than a few, Nate," ribbed Henry. "I got the impression you were planning on sailing the *Loki* yourself. Were you?"

"Yep. For a time I thought so. There are a few places I'd still like to see. Someday, maybe. But the *Loki* is yours now. Tomorrow we'll rig her, and soon ya folks will be off to follow your own dreams."

"Nate. Where were you thinking of going?" asked Serene.

"I'd rather not say if you don't mind, Serene. Dreams are very delicate things, ya know. Best to leave 'em in one's own imagination lest they escape. Here comes dinner. Let's eat."

— CHAPTER 10 —

Tracing Henry and Serene from Logan Airport was easier and faster than Boxer had thought. Twenty-four hours after he landed at Newark Airport, Boxer knew that Serene Bronte rented a mid sized car from Hertz and charged it to the Maru Mandavu corporate American Express card. She took the car on a weekly rate and left no local contact information. Boxer was still waiting to hear from his man who was checking hotel reservations in the Boston area.

He was glad to be home again. Melissa had welcomed him warmly, and he was eager to catch up on family news. He had already reported to Philly that he was waiting on the hotel information. This gave him a little time to work on his new theory.

All the way back on the flight, Boxer had reviewed what he knew on the subject of memory. Now, alone in his office he looked at the notes he made on the plane and laughed out loud when the list prompted him to recall his freshman basic electricity class at Stevens Institute. It was taught by Mr. Winslow, an elderly, world-wise professor who began the first class with the words, "In this course I will attempt to educate you on how electricity works and a few of the innumerable applications man has found for it. You will learn how electricity is generated, transmitted and controlled by numerous electronic devices to provide our world with light, sound, heat, cooling, pictures and instrumentation. I hope I can tell you a lot about electricity; however, if one student this semester asks me what electricity actually 'is', I will refer him to either a theoretical physicist for possible explanations, or to his god of choice for an absolute definition."

Boxer concluded that human memory is like Mr. Winslow's electricity. We can learn a lot about it, but it is highly doubtful we will ever know what it is. In the past Boxer had delved into the subject from psychological, philosophical, and scientific viewpoints. He had read quite a lot about memory and while endless and interesting theories had been put forward by

Aristotle, Hume, Locke, Freud, Jung and Russell, among countless others, even these great thinkers admitted it was mostly speculation. Yes, by general agreement, it is believed that humans have memories, however the content of our recall can be deceiving. We can remember things that did not actually happen or are untrue. The ultimate philosophical test for any belief must consist of facts, which the believer knows to be true with absolute certainty. How can we be certain about memory? How can we be sure that we have memories at all? It's a paradox! It certainly seems as if we get images, ideas and representations of the past, which come to exist in our present thoughts, but no one knows why or how they operate.

Boxer also firmly believed that there is no duality of mind and body, that they are one in the same. He had learned that entire portions of the brain are devoted to activities that our conscious mind is not monitoring, by performing numerous bodily functions automatically, like breathing, or by instructing the body to do something before the conscious mind is aware of it, like taking a hand from a hot stove.

Boxer had also learned that he could use his own brain to instruct itself to do things, such as memorize a passage of text, set what he called his 'inner clock' to awaken him at a specific time, or cue him to perform a task at a certain time. Some might call this ability willpower or concentration, however Boxer thought that these type of self-instructions might be used to unlock the knowledge which he thought resided in his genes and central nervous system and bring it to his conscious mind for practical application.

Boxer began to think of the human body as a long-term storage battery. The human body is, in fact, a kind of magnificent electrobiological battery composed of approximately 70% water and 30% solids, which generate minute electrical nerve impulses. Scientists estimate that these impulses switch one hundred trillion synaptic connections bridging one hundred billion neurons. Who knows what might be stored inside this massive complex? Moreover, he wanted to know how he could retrieve his stored information, not simply knowledge, facts and figures, but the resolved associations of perceptions and sensations that have been clarified into instinctive knowledge gleaned from his genetic ancestors as well as his own experiences.

To be scientific about it, he resolved to measure any progress made. He decided to take three separate intelligence tests before he began experimentation, each to be taken at a reputable organization under professional supervision. This benchmark would provide an accurate record of his average IQ before he began his experiments, and he would repeat the same three tests every three months to measure any progress.

Now he had to develop the actual method by writing the programmatic phraseology, the incantations he would use, as well as devise the sequences of the meditations and self-hypnotic exercises. Then he considered the conditions under which he would perform his experiments. Factors such as time of day, environmental conditions, and place should be noted and taken into consideration, as they might prove important to the result.

True to his word, Nate had the *Loki* fully rigged by the end of the second day. Henry and Serene worked alongside Nate as he "showed them the ropes," as he put it. Nate had shaken down the *Loki* the previous summer so all the rigging went together quickly and perfectly.

It was early afternoon on the second day of Nate's sailing lesson. The unseasonably warm May weather had held, and a light breeze was pushing them back to Wellfleet.

"I don't think there's much more else to tell ya. She's by and large a simple lady to handle. If ya get in a blow, just pull in her cloth and batten down the main sail like I showed ya, and crank up the engine."

"Nate, we appreciate everything you've done for us. We were a little nervous when we decided to buy her, but now we feel very comfortable," said Henry.

"Don't ever feel *too* comfortable with any boat," Nate warned. "Remember she's the *Loki*. You know what her name means?"

"Yes," said Serene, "One of the first things we looked up. Your ad was so mysterious, 'the doer of good and the doer of evil.' From what I read *Loki* seems to me to be one of the more interesting Norse gods, extremely multi-dimensional. Most of their myths have characters that are so stereotypical, either very good or very bad. He seemed to be the most human of them all."

"Ya know ... I think you're right Serene! Never thought about him that way. He was a trickster for sure, sly, cagey, but he did some noble deeds. Like when he fooled the giants into giving Thor back his mighty hammer. But in time his evil doings became worse. Know why?"

"No, I don't," said Serene.

"Boredom was his problem. He was too clever with too much time on his hands. A deadly, dangerous combination. In that respect, as you mentioned, he was the most human of all. Ya gotta avoid boredom. It's like quicksand ...

before you know it you're swallowed up."

"I don't think boredom will ever be a problem for you, Nate," said Henry.

"Ah! There's where you are wrong. It's a problem for most everyone. The breeding ground of unrest and unwise decisions. But it's also the fountain of all man's inspiration. When you're sitting around and bored, any number of crazy ideas come into your head, and ya can take up the most nutty ones just to relieve the boredom."

"Boredom ... 'the doer of good and the doer of evil'," said Serene with a giggle.

"Ya got it! Ya know when ya got it?"

"When?" answered Serene in a puzzled voice.

"When you got it ... and not before!" Nate laughed loudly, and Serene and Henry joined in.

With tears running down her cheeks, Serene said, "Nate, you and Henry make the most obscure statements I've ever heard. Sometimes I don't quite get it, but I always find them amusing. Please, don't stop, either of you."

By this time the *Loki* was nearing the harbor entrance, and the expression on Nate's face turned serious. "Well, folks this about does it with the sailing lessons. Everything is about as shipshape as I can make it. You're both better sailors than you think you are. So I figure you are on your own once we dock. Of course, you are more than welcome to stay at my place for as long as you like."

"We've already discussed that, Nate. Serene I plan to start living on the *Loki* starting tonight. You might have noticed that we loaded our luggage in the car this morning. We've imposed long enough, and you've been a generous host. We will always think of you as a friend."

"That's a deal, too!" said Nate, and he spat on his palm and shook hands with Henry and Serene. Serene finished by hugging Nate and kissing him on the cheek. Nate actually blushed.

"If ya don't mind me asking, where ya folks headed from Wellfleet?"

"We have a general plan," Henry said. "As we mentioned we want to sail around the world. We thought we'd spend a week or so doing day trips out of Wellfleet while we stock the boat for a transatlantic crossing. We'll be calling the car rental company to see if we can drop it off locally. When we're ready, we'll probably head east until we hit the Gulf Stream and follow it up to Ireland."

"Ah! That's a beautiful sail. You won't even have to use the engine in that current. You'll have all summer. And when it starts to get chilly, you can always head south and winter in the Med. You planning on … coasting along Norway?" Nate asked in a curious tone.

"That's a wonderful idea. I've always wanted to go there. I understand the scenery is breathtaking. Can we, Henry?" asked Serene.

"Of course, my dear. Norway has always been on my list of places I'd like to visit. Nate, what's the North Sea like?"

"To tell ya the truth, don't know it that well. Been to Copenhagen and around the Baltic a few times but never set foot in Norway. Seen it off in the distance a few times. Tell ya what though, I can lay my hands on all the charts you'll need for those waters. And I'd be honored if ya let me help out with the provisioning for the voyage. As ya may have gathered by now, I know how to buy things right."

"We'd love it, Nate," said Serene as Henry nodded in agreement.

For three days, they had neither seen nor heard from Nate. They cherished the time alone together in their first new home. Below deck was roomy and comfortable. The master stateroom located under the foredeck had its own head with a shower. Nate had built in lockers of exquisitely finished mahogany. Their bunk was actually a queen-sized bed set up on a high platform, far forward, with a short stepladder to climb up. Beneath the bunk and accessible from three sides were a series of drawers each secured by a brass latch.

Alongside the bunk, on both sides of the hull were built in sofas which could be used as extra bunks should the need arise. Above the sofas and running all around the cabin were bookshelves ready to be filled for a long voyage.

Exiting the hatch from the master berth was a short hallway around the main mast. On one side of the hall was a small mate's cabin, also comfortably appointed. On the other side was another head with a shower and in front of that a small storage cabin. The next hatch opened into the main cabin, the largest of all. The lantern skylight made this Henry and Serene's favorite room. The skylight was original to the boat and fashioned from odd panes of old, irregular, pastel colored glass, which was leaded into stout iron frames. Depending on the strength and color of the sun and the position of the boat, it lit the cabin with a variety of kaleidoscopic effects. Set to the starboard side of the main cabin was a well-upholstered dining booth with a table Nate had made from an antique hatch cover. It almost glowed from many costs of spar varnish. Along the port side was a long, comfortable seating area with storage lockers underneath and a high coffee table that was also made of an old hatch cover and as artfully finished as the table. Aft of the main cabin, on the starboard side was a small but modern galley and to port side the steps led up to the wheelhouse.

Although in a practical sense, Nate had done a masterful job on the interior appointments, the cool, gray, nonskid rubber decking and the gray leatherette upholstery gave Serene, as she said, "the feeling of being inside a meat locker." Her problem was soon remedied by a shopping spree in Provincetown, a scenic twenty-minute drive from Wellfleet. While most of the tourist shops were still closed, several of the year 'rounders were still open, including a few antique shops. Luckily for Serene and Henry, one antique shop had a nice selection of oriental rugs from a recent estate sale. They purchased several small, colorful ones that fit the *Loki*. At the local Kmart, Serene bought a dozen inexpensive throw pillows that she matched to colors in the rugs. She also picked up tableware, cookware, bedclothes, curtains, towels, food, beverages and all sorts of household supplies for the boat. At the checkout counter Serene spied a display of beach hats, and a blue denim one caught her eye. She picked it up and placed it on Henry's head.

"Somehow how this hat is *you*," said Serene. Henry walked to the mirror on the display rack and looked quizzically at himself.

"I can now impersonate McMagoo or a blue mushroom." Henry chuckled. "But if it pleases you that's all that counts.

"We'll take it!" Henry said to the cashier.

By the time they finished shopping, there was no room to spare in the car.

The next day Henry did the lugging and stowing while Serene decorated the boat. Serene's experience in her father's construction business and her good taste paid off. The rugs fit perfectly, and her sense of color was uncanny. The predominantly scarlet Oriental rug in the main cabin complemented the colors in the skylight, and the scarlet throw pillows in the seating areas brought the scheme together miraculously. In the master cabin she used several smaller rugs in blues and greens and accessorized with yellow pillows.

Even the small mate's cabin did not escape her attention. The light, cream-colored Oriental rug with delicate maroon designs made the room look more spacious, and goldenrod bedclothes and pillows sparked up the cabin considerably.

By dusk the interior had been magically transformed into a warm and cozy nest. Bathed in soft candlelight, Henry prepared their first hot meal aboard, vermicelli with garlic and oil with a fresh green salad. The scent of the garlic peaked Serene's appetite as she opened a bottle of a good Chianti Classico. As she slid in the dining booth, it occurred to her that she had never been as content and happy as she was at that very moment. Henry served the meal, and they ate in silence as the *Loki* gently bobbed on the outgoing tide.

The next morning it rained, and they cancelled their sailing plans. Instead Henry and Serene decided to return the rental car a few days earlier than they had arranged. In a sense, it was a statement of their confidence in themselves and the *Loki* as well as a commitment to soon depart land.

After dropping off the car in Harwich and paying a substantial penalty for the return of the car to Boston, they called for a taxi and returned to Wellfleet. There they stopped for coffee at a café and then browsed through several arts and crafts galleries before ambling down the road to the harbor. Along the way they came upon a small shop called Well-Read Used Books. Upon entering they found an older woman reading at a battered rolltop desk. She merely smiled to acknowledge their presence and returned to her book. For several minutes Serene and Henry scanned the tightly packed shelves.

"Henry, I expected to find a large collection of beach reading, but this is outstanding."

"Hey! I like beach reading. It's like cotton candy for the brain."

"I do too, sometimes. Good therapy."

"It is a rather high brow collection. I suppose these are the leavings of all the artists, writers and doctors who vacation here."

"Lucky for us," said Serene as she nudged her elbow into his ribs.

The clerk watched with growing interest over the next hour as Henry and Serene picked through the stacks until they had assembled a sizeable collection, which they piled on the counter.

"Serene, I just thought of something."

"What?"

"We no longer have the car."

"Yipes. Good point."

"We'll call for another taxi," said Henry.

Upon overhearing this, the clerk rose from her desk and walked to the cash register and asked, "How far do you have to go?"

"We live on our boat, the *Loki*, down at the town docks," said Henry.

"No problem. I'll have my son Bruce deliver them tomorrow. He has a truck. Looks like he'll need it."

Henry paid the bill, which seemed very reasonable considering the treasures that they had discovered. They left the shop and were strolling arm in arm down the winding harbor road when they heard the rumble of a vehicle and a horn honk behind them. It was Nate. He poked his head out the window and yelled "Ahoy, mates! Need a lift?"

From the minute Henry and Serene entered truck, Nate began talking more excitedly than they had ever heard before. "Ya know, I been kind of worried about ya folks making the Atlantic crossing. Not that I don't think ya can't handle her. Sure ya can. But you're short handed for the distance. Ya should have an extra hand, maybe two for the watches, ya know. Days are long at sea. And there's plenty of commercial traffic out there."

"Ya know, we were talking about just that last night over dinner," said Henry as he grinned and winked at Serene. "You wouldn't happen to know anyone who would be interested?"

"Ya know, fact is, I got a curious notion to get over to southern Norway myself. Be glad to work for the passage. I'm a fair hand ya know, and I like to cook."

"Nate, we couldn't dream of anyone better. We'd love to have you as our shipmate," said Serene without hesitation.

"Good it's deal. We don't even have to spit on it," said Nate with a broad smile. "By the way Henry, that blue hat suits you," he added.

— CHAPTER 11 —

Early the next morning, Nate backed up his truck as close as possible to the *Loki*. "I rummaged through my barn and got a few things you'll need ... I mean we'll need for the voyage." Nate pulled the tarp off the truck's bed. "I brought some fishing gear, poles, tackle, gaff, net and such. Here's good axe in case any rigging breaks away. And I had some extra foul weather gear. One's small size, never used, which should fit you Serene. Here's an inflatable life raft with built in emergency supplies, some water, food, flares, flashlight and compass. This charcoal grille mounts so it swings out over the transom, and here's a few bags of charcoal. I also rustled up this swim ladder if ya ever get to warm waters. Brought a few safety harnesses and a couple of extra life jackets." Nate picked up a round, black case. "In here ya got all the charts ya need for the voyage." Finally, he went to the truck's cab and returned with a battered black violin case and handed it to Henry. "Here's a special present for you."

"But I don't play," Henry said somewhat confused.

"Open it," Nate demanded.

Henry placed the case on the tailgate, unsnapped the latches and opened the case. Fitted inside the case was a tiny, sawed off shotgun with a stubby pistol grip and a box of shells. Henry and Serene both starred at the gun, speechless.

"It's an over 'an under .410 gauge shotgun. Cut her down myself. Should always have a gun aboard for sharks and the like."

Henry's thoughts flashed to his encounters with sharks on the raft and the stories he had heard aboard the *Pacific Star* about the extent of modern day piracy and the dangers posed from drug smugglers. "Why thank you, Nate, it may be useful for emergencies."

"Well, let's get this gear aboard," said Serene.

After several trips, the truck was unloaded, and the gear staged on the aft deck. Serene suggested a coffee break and they went below. As Nate entered the main cabin he froze in an overly dramatic pose. "Why you've made her into a regular Persian pleasure palace." While Serene put on the coffee pot, Nate quickly inspected the rest of the boat and returned with a satisfied look on his face. "Ya made her nice and cozy. I like it!"

"How do you like your cabin?" asked Serene.

"Wouldn't change a thing. Might bring a few books aboard, however."

"As many as you like. Serene and I were at the Well-Read yesterday, just before you picked us up. They'll be delivering our books today."

"You've probably got a few of my old ones mixed in," Nate chuckled.

Serene poured coffee into three Cape Cod souvenir mugs and placed a box of donuts on the table.

"When were ya folks planning to sail?"

"We have no schedule, Nate. When will you be able to leave?"

"Just need a few days to close up the house. Have you provisioned the boat yet?"

"Fairly much," said Serene, "but we were hoping you'd go over the supplies and make any suggestions."

"Be glad to. I may have a few more things in the barn that will come in handy. Ya folks have your passports?"

"Yes," answered Henry. "Why do you ask?"

"You're supposed to have a special visa to land a boat in Norway. It's that way with most of them countries. I checked it out a while back. Whole lot of crazy paperwork. But chances are good nobody will bother us as long as we have our passports. Easy going people, them Scandinavians."

"So you've been planning to go to Norway for some time?" asked Serene.

"Yes. There's something I've been wanting to check out there, even before I ran into Harold and Randi and bought the *Loki*. The *Loki* renewed my interest in the idea, and I started thinking about it again while I was restoring her. Did a little more research on making the voyage. Even toyed with the idea of sailing there myself, but I thought better of it, and that's when I decided to sell her. Wrote it off as another one of my pipe dreams."

"So … what do you want to see in Norway?" asked Henry.

"Nothing really. It's what doesn't happen there that sparked my curiosity many years ago. I'd better explain it to you now, 'cause if I told ya this after we was out to sea ya might think I was touched, which may yet be a possibility," Nate said with chuckle.

"About twenty years ago I was working on the old President Line and

71

shooting the breeze with shipmate named Alf. He came from a little town in southern Norway named Flekkefjord. Alf was about the most even-tempered, agreeable fellow I ever met. A gem of a human being, although he did like his whiskey. One day we were coming into Boston Harbor, and the ship had to anchor to wait for the tide. Alf and I were standing at the rail grumbling about having to wait, as we were both anxious to get ashore. Then Alf mentions that where he comes from they don't have to mess with tides because they don't have any! I tell him that's impossible. There are tides everywhere. But he swore up down that they don't have any tidal movement where he comes from. I have to believe him, 'cause Alf wasn't the kind to make up stories."

"So you want to go there just to confirm there are no tides?" asked Serene in disbelief.

"I already know there aren't any tides there. I checked that out years ago. Fact is, up until a few months ago I was corresponding with the leading expert on Norwegian tides, a professor of mathematics at the University of Oslo to find out exactly why. He says Flekkefjord is located at 'amphidromic point.' He says an amphidromic is caused by destructive interference of tidal waves with different phases, one with high water the other with low water. Sounded like mumbo jumbo to me. Besides scientists always have an explanation even when they don't have a clue as to what's really happening. Ever hear a scientist say he doesn't know? The fact is, no tide. I find that terrible curious. I want to know why. Ya folks know much about tides?"

"Only what I read in the tide tables," Henry jested.

"That's about what most people know. Those are useful schedules made up over the years by sheer observation and timekeeping. This Flekkefjord is up on the North Sea, mind you. A terrible hunk of water at times. Now at most seaside places like that the water reaches its highest level approximately two times a day, the average interval between two successive high waters being about twelve and a half hours. At the head of the Bay of Fundy up there in Nova Scotia the range of tides is nearly 50 feet. In Fiji I'd guess the tides are about two feet?"

"I believe that's about right," said Serene.

"It's around two feet for most of the Pacific islands, and the range is about the same in the Mediterranean. Here at Wellfleet it ranges about nine feet as you've seen and is why we've got those long spring lines to dock the boats and compensate for the change. Wellfleet is about 41 degrees north latitude. Flekkefjord is 58 degrees north latitude, way farther north and yet no tide at all. Now, I suppose ya both know what causes tidal movements?"

"It is caused by the spinning of the earth and gravitational pull as I recall," said Henry.

"And the pull of the moon," Serene added.

"You're both right, but there's a whole lot more to it. Just imagine how primitive people must have scratched their noggins about the tides. Strange thing the phenomenon of the oceans going out and then coming back in twice a day. The old Greek philosophers pondered on it. Ever since, scientists, mathematicians, and physicists have been trying to figure it out. It's like trying to explain why the world goes around or why there's a vast universe out there. Tides can get downright metaphysical when ya think about it. There's been every kind of speculation about the earth's hydrospheric tidal flows. Now, of course there are multi dimensional effects that cause the tides. Mostly the gravity of the moon, but also the gravity of the sun is involved. And innumerable spheres of our own galaxy, not to mention the gravitation effects of the universe at large play some role. But since the moon revolves around the earth and is pretty close to us, considering, the largest impact that the moon has on the earth is through tidal forces. The moon's gravitational pull does indeed pull on bodies of water creating the high and low tides. Land, of course, doesn't move as easy as water, yet in some places land itself rises and falls a couple of inches due to the moon's gravitational pull."

"Nate, I'm impressed. You've really studied the subject," said Serene.

"Yep, but it's like anything else ya look into. The closer you look the more there is to see, and the longer you look the more confused the so-called experts make ya. I even delved into the nonastronomical crap ... excuse my French ... nonastronomical anomalies such as variations of the sea level caused by changes in ocean basins and the total quantity of water they contain, meteorological effects due to atmospheric pressure on the sea surface and tangential stresses on the sea surface exerted by the wind, and the heating and cooling the sea surface."

"Wow! And what conclusions have you reached?" Henry asked.

"Aside from learning that it's a very complicated subject and that there are endless theories and mathematical formulas attempting to explain tides, I found that I still don't know why there is no tide in Flekkefjord."

"I don't quite get it, Nate. If you already know that there's no tide, why the fascination?" asked Henry in puzzled confusion.

"Don't know myself. What I do know is I have some kind of personal affinity, or sensitivity to the tides. From when I was a kid, I've noticed subtle physical and mental changes in myself during the ebbs and flows. Whenever

I go down by the marshes on an incoming tide I feel good … a rush of energy and optimism. When the tide goes out I feel sad, somehow weakened and deprived. May sound nuts to you, but to me it's the most intimate feeling I've ever had as actually being a part of nature. Ya got to remember that the human body is 70% water and 30% solids, roughly the same proportions as there is water and land on the surface of the earth. The key thing is that the water in our bodies has roughly the same amount of salt as in seawater. Now, if the gravitational pull of the moon has such great affect the tides, why shouldn't it have a great affect on me? That's my question. To my mind, and to many others, the moon is a mysterious, powerful creature. Just look at western literature. All kinds of tales about unusual behavior caused by the phases of the moon. The myths about wolf men alone should tell ya something. Not that I believe in wolf men, mind ya, but everybody knows that folks get even crazier during the full moon. Ask a cop, doctor or anyone who works in a mental hospital. They'll tell ya. There's also a lot of hard science out there that connects human, animal, and plant behavior to the phases of the moon. One study I read said that more animals are born during the full moon than any other day of the month. Years ago I worked with an English sailor. He told me it's a fact among his people who live along the east coast of England that most deaths happen at ebb tide. He was as sure of that as his own name."

"So, Nate … you believe there's a link between tidal movement and human behavior?" Serene asked timidly.

"Absolutely! I'm convinced of it. But what really peaks my curiosity is what is the effect on people who experience no tide at all."

"Now you've got me thinking about it, and, frankly, I can't argue with your logic," said Serene. "Henry, why don't we go to this place in Norway and then visit Ireland later?"

"Sounds like an adventure to me. Let's do it!"

— CHAPTER 12 —

Boxer sat in the lotus position on the floor of his office in dark shadows. The blinds were closed, and he had unplugged the phone. He had completed his breathing exercises and brought himself into a light state of hypnosis. He had memorized the script he had spent so many days composing. Now he was prepared to say the words that he hoped would unlock the wealth of knowledge within him. Slowly he said the words, "I call upon my conscious mind to work with my unconscious mind and ask my unconscious powers to harmonize with my entire physical body to bring to my conscious mind all the useful knowledge and wisdom that has been accumulated by me since my birth. Further, I call upon every cell in my body to release all embedded learning and its resulting wisdom of my genetic ancestors into my conscious being so that I may have full use of it. Now, I will count backwards from ten to zero and upon reaching zero will go to a deeper state of hypnosis and wait for this request to commence."

Boxer kept himself under for about twenty minutes and then slowly brought himself back. He stood up, feeling relaxed, alert and optimistic. He vowed to perform this ritual twice a day before having his IQ retested in three months.

He opened the blinds, turned on the lights and plugged in the phone. It rang a few seconds later. It was Philly.

"Any news?" Philly demanded.

"Yes, in fact, I was going to call you. My guy called this morning. No luck with the hotels. They must be paying in cash or staying with somebody. But he tracked down the car they rented at Logan. The day before yesterday they turned in the car in Harwich, Massachusetts. That's up on Cape Cod."

"So why are you still here?"

"Philly, I just stopped at the office to get some papers and the pictures of them. Was going to call you from the car."

"Isn't it faster to fly up?"

"Nah. Not really. It's about six hours by car. I'll be up there by mid afternoon. If I screwed around with planes and rental cars it would take longer."

"You know best, Boxer. From now on keep me informed the minute you find anything. Call day or night."

"Righto, Philly."

Nate did not want to waste any time getting underway. He often labored over decisions, but once his mind was made up, he was action personified. His enthusiasm was infectious, and Henry and Serene became just as eager to depart. Their discussion over coffee about the tides had carried over to lunch at Captain Higgins and a planning session for the voyage. Serene made lists in her notepad while the three of them went over the supplies that would be needed. Surprisingly, they found that they already had most of what was needed. The fuel and water tanks were full, and the boat was fairly well outfitted. Nate suggested the purchase of some additional food supplies and insisted on picking them up himself.

Later that afternoon, Bruce arrived with their books. He insisted on lugging them aboard and flatly refused the gratuity offered by Henry. "Could be the biggest single sale in the history of the Well-Read. Mom said you didn't even haggle with her. It's our pleasure."

Henry and Serene spent the rest of the day stowing away the books and the gear Nate had brought. As evening approached, they walked over to Mike's Seafood Shack, ordered scrod sandwiches from the window, and sat at a picnic table overlooking Wellfleet Harbor. A stiff breeze tried to blow away their meal. As they ate, holding down their napkins and paper plates, Henry said, "Serene, we've been so busy we've hardly had any time to talk about anything but boats and trips. How are *you* doing with all of this?"

"Oh. I'm fine with everything ... really. I feel guilty about not having called my father yet and letting him know what's up. In fact, right after we eat, I'm trotting to the pay phone over there and give him a call. Otherwise, you've been just wonderful. I'm so happy that Nate is coming, and I'm excited about the voyage."

"What do you think about Nate's tide theory?"

"I have an open mind. He's a smart man. Much smarter than he often lets on I suspect. Notice how he slips in an out of that down home New Englander accent?"

"Yes. He's somewhat of an actor. A genuine character, nevertheless. I have the feeling there's something he's not telling us."

"Strange, I got that feeling as well. Considering the way he rambles on, he's very reticent in some ways. For instance, I've never heard him utter a word about women. For a man that is very unusual."

"Do you think he's..."

"Not for a minute! I think he's still shopping around myself."

"At his age?"

"Certainly. I'm still looking myself, *ya know*," as Serene burst into one of her hysterical bouts of laughter that immediately infected Henry. A passer by would certainly wonder why this handsome couple was doubled over.

Later that night Nate arrived at the dock with literally a truck load of food, supplies, additional gear and his clothes packed in two large sea bags. He announced that he had made all the arrangements for his house and that Shep would keep his truck at the boatyard while he was away. He was, as he said, "ready to ship out whenever you folks are ready."

"We're about as ready as we're going to get," replied Henry.

Serene added, "How about we leave first thing tomorrow morning?"

"Good choice. I listened to the marine forecast on the way down and it looks clear for the next couple of days. Let's stow the rest of this stuff, and I'll be back at first light. I have a few errands, and there may be a few things back at the barn we'll need."

— CHAPTER 13 —

Boxer opened the car door. He was stiff and tired from the six-hour drive. He yawned as he raised his hands above his head and stretched. The tiny, weathered sign read East Harwich Auto and Truck Rentals. He entered the office set with his most disarming smile. A well-groomed middle-aged woman sat behind the counter.

"Good afternoon. I'm Frank Ryan from Ryan Investigations in New Jersey. Can you spare a minute?"

Of course the rental lady cooperated with Boxer. Most people did, especially so after Boxer spun a sad, soap opera-ish tale about father who abandoned his wife and four small children and ran away with a younger woman. It was critical he find this man. His youngest boy had been in a serious auto accident and was begging for his father. Boxer saw this fabrication more as entertainment than lying, giving the woman something to talk about for weeks. With tears in her eyes, she looked at the photos and recognized Henry and Serene. They had returned a car a few days ago. She did not know where they were staying but she remembered they called a taxi for a ride to Wellfleet. Boxer thanked the lady and inquired about motels and restaurants. He would drive to Wellfleet in the morning.

Somewhat disoriented from the long drive, Boxer slept later than usual and then stopped for a leisurely breakfast at a diner. By eleven o'clock, he arrived in Wellfleet. As it was early in the tourist season most of the shops were closed. He cruised slowly through the sleepy little town until he spotted the Well-Read bookstore and the 'Open' sign in the window. Boxer was not even thinking about Henry and Serene when he pulled into the gravel parking lot. He could never pass up an interesting looking bookshop. He smiled at the young man at the cash register and began looking through the titles. In the psychology section, he was surprised at the number of quality hard covers and selected several volumes. Only after he had paid the clerk, as an after thought, he pulled out the pictures of Henry and Serene. "Have you seen these two?" he asked bluntly.

Bruce was somewhat taken aback at the abrupt presentation and guilelessly answered, "That's Henry and Serene."

Boxer aware that he had startled the young man softened his approach with a warm smile. "Thank God! I knew they were staying in Wellfleet, but didn't know where. Hi, I'm Henry's cousin Frank. Know where I can find those two rascals?"

"Sure. They're docked at the town pier just down the road," he said as he pointed the way. "Can't miss it. Beautiful old double ender called the *Loki*, or something like that. Delivered a load of books to them yesterday. Nice people."

"They're the best. I'll tell them I ran into you. Thanks."

A few minutes later he was at the docks. Upon arriving he visited the Harbor Master's office and learned the slip number of the *Loki*. When he found the slip, it was empty. As he stood there, he distinctly heard eight bells chime. The sound seemed to be coming from the church tower on hill. He looked at his watch. It was exactly twelve noon. They had better take up another collection and fix that clock, he thought. Shaking his head in confusion, he walked back to his car, disappointed.

Upon hearing eight bells earlier that morning, the crew of the *Loki* cast off and departed Wellfleet Harbor. The bells which confounded Boxer later that day kept time according to ship's bells which mark off one half hour periods of watch duty, disregards A.M. and P.M. and makes little sense to the landsman because eight bells occurs three times over a twenty four hour period. Time at sea is different than on land in many subtle ways.

Under diesel power, they had moved slowly down the harbor channel in the early light. As soon as they passed the last buoy, Nate cut the engine, and they hoisted sail. A few hours later they were nearing Race Point, the northeastern tip of Cape Cod. Nate suggested they lower sail and restart the engine. "Currents get tricky up here. Let's get well offshore and see how the breeze sets."

They were blessed with yet another brilliant spring day. Henry, Serene and Nate had settled comfortably into the open sunny cockpit. Nate adjusted the throttle to one-third speed, which pushed the *Loki* smoothly through the mounting rollers. "I'd say we're out of Cape Cod Bay about now and in the great Atlantic Ocean," announced Nate.

"Great!" said Serene. "Now I feel the voyage has begun."

"Once out of sight of land has always been my benchmark," said Nate.

"Time. When things actually begin or end has always been a matter of conjecture," added Henry.

"I swear, Henry. Between you and Nate my little brain is going 'huh?' all the time. What is it with you two and your mysterious, pregnant pronouncements?" she complained good-naturedly. They all laughed.

"Henry and I are infected with the philosophical disease; a serious malfunction of the *what's* and *why's*—we question everything. Try to forgive our boyish pastime. It's our own particular waste of time, but it's fairly all we got to work with. Everybody's a philosopher, ya know. Some have the good sense use their fleeting time on earth wisely and be closed mouth about all the nonsense. But Henry and I aren't as bad as others I know. Think of all those folks who fritter away their lifetimes in fearful measurement of time itself.

"My God! Counting has become the god of everything these days. How long will it take? How many miles I walk today? How many calories? How many pounds? Not to mention the universal preoccupation with money counting. What seems to count is the accounting instead of the living. And, the counting that goes on about health matters is the most destructive of all. What's my cholesterol today? How much is my bad? My good? My blood pressure? My blood sugar? People are counting death a hundred ways each day and are not even consciously aware of it. Better to live than count. That's healthy."

"I agree," said Serene. "Nate, I've read a little on philosophy. I'm curious to know which school is most agreeable to you."

"Better watch out, Nate. She knows more than she's letting on," jested Henry.

"Oh, I agree with most all of 'em. To my way of thinking they all offer wisdom of one sort or another. I think I've learned more from the knuckleheads than the perceptive thinkers. At least the knuckleheads help you recognize bad thinking and help bump you along the right path. Ever since man learned to write, the most intelligent men have been looking for a cure for the human dilemma, for answers that satisfy and reconcile man's basic, restless thoughts.

"All genuine philosophers are writing to themselves, ya know. They jot down only those truths that they accepted as being true in their own minds. After a while of reading philosophy, you realize that the long line of philosophers throughout history is but the single, same voice of man repeatedly asking the same questions over and over again and attempting to answer them. It's the voice of humanity crying out for a reasonable explanation to this fix we're in named living. Of course, some theories are more substantial than others," said Nate as his attention drifted to an interesting cloud formation overhead.

"I know it's difficult to classify thought, Nate, but if someone were to put you on the spot, like now, which school would you most closely align yourself with?" asked Serene.

"Ya see them clouds yonder? Ya could say I belong to that school, the Cloud of Unknowing, ever hear of it?"

"In fact, I have. Some anonymous monk in England wrote it in the 5th century. Never read it though. Mysticism, right?" questioned Serene.

"Suppose you could call it that. More religious inquiry, I'd say. Just another guy trying to figure things out within the context of his own life. Just like us, or anybody who takes to pondering. At least that monk came to a conclusion, which is more than ya can say for most. He realized there's a barrier beyond human understanding that we'll never penetrate, even with the most advanced intellect, the highest powers of perception and the most sophisticated scientific instruments. He called that barrier the cloud of unknowing. I think that cloud is there for a good reason. It's as much a part of our life as those clouds up there. Not being able to know everything is what drives us to learn what we are capable of knowing. In a manner of speaking, it's the unattainable carrot of the universe. The fact we chase it is prime motive force of life. It's what Kant was meaning with his 'category beyond reason'."

"So you're of a school which disregards the metaphysical, I gather," said Serene.

Nate laughed. "I'm not laughing at you, Serene, rather the thought of even trying to ignore the metaphysical. It's the only game in town, so to speak, us trying to understand the prime movement. Without that challenge why would we even bother to investigate this vast layer cake of biological mass in which we find ourselves and of which we are ourselves are but a dominant manifestation." Nate pointed his hand down to the water and then up to the sky. "Or, instead, we can speculate, try to tinker with and explain away the material world as the scientist does, as most folks do, and confine the metaphysical to a part time activity through periodic, more easily experienced religious practices. That's fine in my book, but for some reason people like me, and perhaps you two, tend to philosophize by our natures and continue to seek knowledge of the unknowable."

"So, in essence you are saying philosophy is mostly a waste of time," said Serene.

"Yep! For the most part. What we glean from the effort is meager. Philosophy is the work of making simple things into the absurdly complex. What's there to be learned is barely sufficient to sustain our interest. Except for fools like me. I am egged on by the humorous grand design. The elusive carrot."

"And in the end, what do we get out of it?" asked Henry.

"It can lead to a better understanding of ourselves and perhaps a wiser use of our brief time here. Perhaps harmony in our thoughts and inner peace in our hearts in view of all the mysterious paradoxes we confront. And, maybe, just maybe, a little of us rubs off on someone else."

"Let's hope this voyage leads to something good for all of us," said Serene.

"It already has," Henry added.

Lying about important things was not in Boxer's character. In investigative work, it is a necessary part of the business in order to obtain information and placate clients. After the *Loki* sailed, he spent the rest of the day trying to find out where they were headed. In a small town like Wellfleet, especially off-season, it was rather easy. A few questions around the docks led him to the boatyard and a friendly chat with Shep. Shep told how his friend, Nate Nevins, sold the *Loki* to Henry and Serene, that they sailed off to cross the Atlantic, and most importantly, that they were headed to a town in southern Norway where there are no tides. Shep did not know the name of the town.

That evening Boxer checked into the Wellfleet Inn. Now he had to give Philly the bad news. He decided to say the *Loki* had departed the previous morning. The guilt from his Catholic upbringing nagged him that he should have driven to Wellfleet directly from the rental agency instead of overnighting in Harwich. Boxer dialed Philly's home number.

"Philly, I almost found them."

"What?"

"McCall, Serene Bronte and a local guy named Nate Nevins left Wellfleet in a 37 foot sailboat early yesterday morning…"

"So wait for them to come back. I'll send some people up, and when you spot them you can take off."

"The problem is they won't be back for a long time. They're going to Norway I am told."

"Norway! What the … Where in Norway?"

"That's the other problem. Nobody knows. All I know is that it's someplace that has no tides."

"No tides!"

"It's a clue at least. I'll have to work it."

"Don't they have to file some kind of flight plan or something?"

"I think that's only for airplanes, but I will check with the Coast Guard and the Norwegian embassy. Maybe they have a radio channel or need some kind of visa. And of course, I'll research this tide angle. I've never heard of such a thing. No tide! I think that's impossible."

"Yeah, sounds nuts to me. This whole thing is nuts. Anything about the pearl?"

"No. She probably has it with her. I'm driving back to Jersey in the morning, and I'll start investigations on several fronts. It'll probably take them about three weeks to get to Norway. By that time we should know something."

"Boxer, I'm counting on you. I can't tell you how crazy this whole McCall thing is making me," said Philly in exasperation.

"We'll find 'em, Philly."

"You better," and Philly slammed down the phone.

The tone of Philly's voice and memories from high school when Philly got 'crazy' again gave Boxer serious doubts about having accepted the assignment.

— Chapter 14 —

Life aboard the *Loki* was more pleasant than Henry and Serene could have imagined. Nate was appreciating the fine sailing qualities of the boat. Her wide beam and rugged Scandinavian construction kept her moving smoothly and quietly through the Atlantic swells. In two days they reached the edge Gulf Stream. Now with the aid of the steady current they sailed northeast at a steady ten knots. Nate trolled the blue green wake and caught a tuna that he broiled on the charcoal grill. Serene made a big salad with the last of the fresh vegetables, and Henry opened a bottle of Chianti and made iced tea for Nate. After dinner, they lounged in the open cockpit and drank black coffee under a starry but moonless sky. Serene emptied her coffee dregs over the stern and then she exclaimed, "There's light in the water!"

Startled, Henry and Nate looked in their wake. Nate chuckled. "Not to worry, dear. It's only bioluminescent *Noctiluca*, a phytoplankton."

"A what?" asked Serene mesmerized by the phenomenon.

"It's a luminous form of plankton. Sometimes you also see it in waves breaking on the beach. You know about plankton?"

"Only from high school biology. The smallest animals in the sea, right? I don't remember anything about them lighting up."

"I saw them while on the raft in the Pacific and had heard about them," said Henry. "But I didn't know their name."

"Well, it's common *Noctiluca*, a dioflagellate which is one of the two major forms of phytoplankton. The other form is the diatoms."

"So why do they light up?" asked Serene.

"Well, they're not exactly 'small animals' as you said, rather free floating photosynthetic organisms that trap the sun's energy and create chlorophyll. Noctiluca's chlorophyll happens to be highly bioluminescent so they give off light when the water they're in is disturbed, like our boat plowing through their home water. The other major group of phytoplankton, the diatoms, are even more unbelievable. Imagine this – diatoms are enclosed within a unique glass 'pillbox'. Each round pillbox is composed of two valves with one valve fitting over the top of the other, just like a top and bottom of two pieces of Tupperware. The living cells of the diatom are within this box, and the box is made of silicon dioxide, the same material in glass and silicon computer chips. And you can't beat this! Each diatom is decorated with highly ornamented, geometric designs! That's one for the books, I tell ya. When they reproduce, each diatom divides into two halves. One takes the top half of the original box, and the other takes the bottom half. Then each secretes a valve to create their own pillboxes. How they do it, I don't know. They must have some very basic cellular memory."

"Nate, you really believe these tiny creatures have memory?" asked Henry skeptically.

"Tend to think so. After all, they always remember to reproduce!" said Nate as he alone smiled as his own quip before continuing. "Basic memory even if called instinct, habit or nature exists in all living cells for both animal and vegetable. We humans undervalue the intelligence, capability and genetic richness of our smaller friends as well as the larger organisms such as ourselves."

"How big are these little diatoms?" asked Serene.

"Tiny. Need a microscope to see 'em. There's even smaller phytoplankton. That ocean out there is a rich saltwater soup. The larger zooplankton eat the phytoplankton, and fish eat the zooplankton, and we eat the fish, like tonight, and once in while, a shark gets lucky and eats one of us. We're not that far removed from the diatom, kinfolk in fact."

"You sound like a marine biologist, Nate," said Henry.

"Made a good living on the ocean. Thought I should read about what I was floating on."

"Is that when you became interested in tides?" asked Henry.

"I suppose it triggered my childhood curiosity about them. Remember, out on the Cape, we've an eight to ten-foot tidal flow. As a small boy I was intrigued by this mysterious phenomenon. I used to sit on a bridge that had a large steel culvert under it. When the tide went out, water from the salt marsh squirted through that pipe like a fire hose. Just amazing! Same thing coming in. Exhilarating! Seeing that raw power of nature twice a day like clockwork had to make ya wonder. So, I figure if tides are driven by the gravitational pull of the moon and our bodies are mostly water and there's plenty of evidence that the moon affects our thoughts and behavior, then I also figure there must be some kind of effect on folks who live in a place where there's no tidal movement at all. That's what I want to look into."

"What do you expect to find, Nate?" asked Henry.

"Don't know, but I have an inkling it's some type of counter effect. Ya see, I'm very sensitive to tidal movements. My many years at sea told me a lot about them. First started to notice it in the Mediterranean. The intertidal movement there swings about two feet. Not much compared to farther north or south. Noticed that I always felt better, more relaxed in the Med, better able to read, study, think. Folks who live about there are more relaxed and friendlier than a lot of other places I'd been. Found the same to be true in many Pacific island ports where the littoral zone is about the same as the Med."

"Littoral zone?"

"Sorry, Serene. It's the measurement between mean low tide and mean high tide also called intertidal. Many ports in the Pacific have about the same intertidal as the Med, two to three feet.

"But back to your question, Henry. I expect to hang around Flekkefjord for a while and simply see how I feel. I'll observe the people, too. If I feel and think better there, then I'll know there's a connection to the tide."

"But you said that Norwegian professor explained some special currents that cause the no tide effect," said Henry.

Nate grinned. His eyes sparkled. "Henry, scientists can always find an explanation for anything. When they can't find one, they're likely to conjure one up. I've seen all kinds of currents bumping together everywhere in the oceans and seas. What's that got to do with the price of peanuts? Ya can't escape one basic fact. No tides in Flekkefjord! I believe it means something."

"It won't be long before we find out," said Serene.

"About two weeks, I figure. Plotted a course this morning. We just stay in the Gulf Stream and follow it into the North Atlantic Drift up to the top of Scotland and make for the Faeroe Shetland Island passage. That will bring us into the North Sea, a few hundred miles north of Flekkefjord. When we turn south the Norwegian Current will be against us. We'll have to tack south or use the engine along the coast. Whadya think?"

"I wouldn't mind a slow chug down the coast taking in the scenery. We've hardly burned any fuel so far," said Henry.

"Should have bought a guide book on Norway before we left. I'd like to learn more about the country, especially Flekkefjord," said Serene.

"You're in luck! I have one in my cabin," said Nate.

It was early June when they entered the North Sea. They were welcomed by the first foul weather of the voyage. For three days it rained. Visibility was poor, and a damp, brisk wind whipped up whitecaps on waves reaching nearly four feet. They had retreated from the sunny days of the aft cockpit to the warmth of the wheelhouse. Long hours were slowly measured out by the clop, clop of the windshield wipers. They were in the heavy traffic lanes now, and long, careful watches had put them all on edge.

At the helm, Henry watched the radar and compass and periodically adjusted their course to compensate for the strong currents. Nate was working at the chart table when Serene climbed up from the galley carrying a tray with steaming mugs of hot chocolate and a book tucked under her arm. She served the mugs with a forced smile and a theatrical curtsy of a French maid. Immediately the tension brought about by the gloomy weather was broken. She sat next to Henry in the other captain's chair, stretched out her long legs so her feet rested on the instrument panel, and opened her book.

"You boys ready to play Norwegian trivia? For starters, how many islands does Norway have?" she teased.

"Do we get points for this? Win a prize?" Henry asked.

"Only my admiration of your knowledge. That should be prize enough," replied Serene with a wink.

"From the maps I've seen ... lots of islands. I'd guess 10,000."

"Way more," said Nate, "maybe 100,000. I have the map right in front of me."

"Both wrong! According to the Norwegian government, there are over three million islands!"

"They must be counting every rock that sticks out of the water. That's what they call 'skerries' those little islands we've been seeing all along the coast. Didn't think there was that many though," said Nate.

"Next question. According to the United Nations, where does Norway rank among countries that are the best to live in?"

"Fairly high on the list, I'd guess ... about six or seven," said Nate.

"Higher. Maybe fourth or fifth," said Henry.

"Both wrong again. It's actually ranked number one for the past few years by the UN. The data compared income, standard of living, quality of life, crime, unemployment, literacy and health."

"When I think of Norway only fish and Vikings come to mind," said

Henry with a smirk.

"They got fish all right and plenty of forests, too, but since the 60's they've had that North Sea oil. That's where the money comes from, I'd wager," said Nate.

"It's a highly socialized country, I understand. Cradle to the grave government services and high taxes," said Henry.

"Maybe," added Nate. "But maybe you get something for your money."

Serene continued reading, "The town of Flekkefjord is located in the most southwestern part of the country, the earliest settled area of the country."

"Interesting," said Nate.

"It has a population of 6,000, a historic downtown district ... some summer tourism ... ship building ... salmon farms, a big jigsaw puzzle factory ... and, oh yeah, get this: the word 'Flekke' in Norwegian means 'spot.' It literally means a spot on the fjord," said Serene.

"Like a bump in the road. That's the spot we're headed for," said Henry.

"A very curious spot to me," chuckled Nate. "And, if all goes right tonight, I figure we'll enter the fjord tomorrow morning. We'll be entering the Hidra Sound shortly, and it's extremely narrow. In fact, the chart has a chunk of it marked as a canal. I suggest we anchor before dark. Looks like there's some good holding ground a few miles ahead off Hidra Island. And the good news ... I just checked the weather fax. Forecast says clearing overnight."

"Ah! Scenic Norway. All I've seen so far is rain and fog," said Serene.

— CHAPTER 15 —

"That must be it!" said Serene excitedly, as she pointed to a large expanse of exposed rock on the mountain. "That must be the spot!"

The *Loki* had just entered the fjord on a clear, crisp spring morning, and in the middle of the light tan rock face she indicated a small area of darker discoloration.

Henry looked through his binoculars. "You're nuts. I think it's just a shadow. Maybe the angle of the sun. Hard to tell at this distance."

The fjord was a magnificent sight that morning. High mountains covered with bright evergreens and raw stretches of bare rock shot up on both sides of the of the purest blue water. A chain of small, rocky islands sprinkled with pine trees dotted the entrance of the fjord. Many islands had small, colorful bungalows perched on them. Some of the little houses and their boathouses nearly covered the islands. They were surprised to see kids diving off a dock into water that they knew to be icy cold.

Past the islands, the fjord opened wide to its full width of over a mile. As they cruised past pristine forests rising on the flanking mountains, Serene asked, "Where's the town?"

"Ahead about 10 miles at the end of the fjord. Not really the end. Looks like there's a narrow channel that runs through the town into another body of water, maybe a continuation of the fjord or a large lake."

"I don't know about you guys but I'm looking forward to eating a big breakfast on a table that doesn't move," declared Henry.

"Nate, have you seen any tides?" asked Serene.

"No. I've been watching the watermarks on the rocks, however. There's just a single, thin black line. No other tidal marks," he said with a nod of satisfaction.

Soon the town of Flekkefjord came into view. Tall, narrow, brightly painted buildings with garage-like boathouses lined the shore. Nate shifted the engine to neutral, came out of the wheelhouse, and scanned the waterfront with his binoculars. "Just to the starboard of that park with the statue is the channel that goes through town. Let's go up the channel and look for a berth, hopefully near a restaurant."

When they entered the channel, the traffic increased, mostly families in pleasure boats who looked like they were off for an outing. Everyone they passed waved, smiled or tipped a hat at the *Loki,* which was flying a small American flag. Happily they returned the salutes and felt welcomed. Across the channel from the modern looking Maritime Hotel, they saw an expanse of vacant bulkhead in front of a building with a sign that read *The Pizza Inn.* Nate brought the *Loki* about while Henry and Serene scrambled to hang the bumpers over the side. With a line in hand, Henry jumped to the dock and tied it to a bollard.

Nate left the engine running and leaned out of the wheelhouse. "Henry, could you ask if it's okay to tie up here?"

"Sure! And by the way, welcome to Norway!" Henry shouted gleefully as he disappeared around the corner of the restaurant. He saw a young man cleaning a table on a patio. The young man smiled as he approached. "Excuse me," said Henry. "Do you speak English?"

"Yah, but not so good," replied the young man.

"Is it okay to leave our boat at your dock for a little while?"

"Yah, it's good, it's good."

"How long can we leave it there?"

"As long as you like. It's okay."

"Are you the owner of this place?" asked Henry.

"No," he answered quizzically.

"Perhaps I should speak to the owner?"

"No. It's okay with Mr. Rom as well. That's why he have dock … for boats."

"Thank you. I just wanted to make sure. Do you serve breakfast here?"

"Sorry, only lunch and dinner. Across the street is good for breakfast. The white building," he said as he pointed.

"Thanks again." Henry returned to the boat.

By this time Nate had the boat securely tethered to the dock. Before Henry could utter a word, Nate said, "I kinda thought we'd be okay here for a while."

"They say we can stay here as long as we like. That's what I was told by the young guy at the restaurant."

"That would be wonderful. It's a nice protected berth, and there's water and electric hook ups. I'd like to hose the salt off her," Nate replied.

"Me, I just want food!" yelled Serene.

"Let's go then. I found a breakfast place." They walked through the parking lot, past the patio, to a narrow but busy, one-way street.

"This is cute. I just love it. So tidy looking and clean!" Serene exclaimed.

"Sure is. Immaculate. And look at that beautiful, old wooden church up the street," said Henry.

A well-dressed man passed by, tipped his hat and smiled. Two middle-aged women carrying packages nodded and smiled.

"Very friendly and so healthy looking," Nate remarked.

The instant Serene placed her foot on the roadway, the traffic stopped abruptly. A man in a blue Volvo with a pleasant grin waved for them to cross. As they neared the café, the aroma of bacon greeted their noses. Nate stopped and read a bronze plaque at the doorway.

"Can you read Norwegian?" asked Serene.

"No. But I know enough German to parse it out somewhat. Says this building was Gestapo headquarters during the war. Many brave citizens and resistance fighters were questioned and tortured here. It gives thanks to God for the bravery of the men and women who helped rid the country of the Nazis. Interesting. Let's eat!"

Without a word and a winning smile, a young blonde girl guided them to a cozy dining room decorated with black and white historical photos of the town, and they were seated at a round table by a window overlooking the street. The waitress, who spoke excellent English, served coffee and took their breakfast orders. Serene said, "I'd almost forgotten that the Nazis invaded Norway, and frankly, I know little or nothing about it."

"I really don't know that much, either," said Nate.

"I used to be a World War II history buff," declared Henry. "Norway had an ambitious ex-minister of defense named Vidkun Quisling. This clown went to Germany and conspired with the Nazis to invade his own country. He thought he could get rid of the royal family and run the country under German occupation. He even worked with the Nazis to plan the invasion. Quisling betrayed his own country. That's why 'quisling' is now in the dictionary as a word for traitor.

"With Quisling's help, Germany invaded in 1940 and took over the country. The royal family fled to England, and the people here were outraged. Their tiny army went into the mountains, and resistance groups popped up all over. A lot of men went over to England, some even rowed over. There, they were trained as spies and radio operators or joined a Norwegian brigade. The resistance movement here drove the Germans crazy. By the end of the war, the Nazis had 350,000 troops tied up here trying to control the country; troops Hitler sorely needed elsewhere. Just like the old time Vikings, these people were tough. Germans stationed here were terrified of them. Many said they'd rather be at the Russian front.

"After the invasion, Quisling asked all the Norwegian merchant ships at sea to go to Norwegian, German or neutral harbors and wait for instructions. Back then, Norway had the world's fourth largest merchant fleet ... modern, fast ships and a lot of oil tankers that Hitler wanted. Not a single captain heeded the request. They all went over to the allies. Quisling was named prime minister, but he never had any power, merely a Nazi puppet to the end of the war."

"What happened to Quisling?" asked Nate.

"He was tried, convicted and shot by a firing squad," replied Henry.

The cashier happily accepted American dollars and gave change in Norwegian krone. After the big breakfast, they wanted to stretch their legs after the long voyage. They walked through the narrow streets of the shopping district. Most of the buildings were simple, white, wooden structures, old but well maintained. Here and there they saw ornate Victorian buildings and wandered past a number of small parks and plazas. At a particularly inviting park they sat down at a bench and watched people passing by.

"Extremely well-groomed and dressed," remarked Serene.

"Notice they walk at a brisk pace, yet they don't seem to be in a rush," said Henry. "What have you observed, Nate?"

"By and large, a very handsome and healthy looking race. Even the older women look energetic, thinner and more athletic looking than American women."

"Whoa! Nate is eyeing the ladies. We better get out of town by sunset," jested Serene. Nate and Henry chuckled.

"I confess. Guilty as charged," said Nate. "There's something else I've noticed, their expressions. Not a frown or a hostile look among 'em."

"I agree," declared Serene. "Looks like a nice place to live, although like any small town, I suppose it has its limitations. By the way, guys, whenever I visit a new place I like to check out the real estate values. Just curiosity I assure you, Henry, but I have yet to see a real estate office."

"They're probably outside town. Looks like this area was sold out a few thousand years ago. Maybe tomorrow we rent a car and take a look around. Let's stop at that market we passed. Get some fresh milk, fruit, ice cream and vegetables. I'm looking forward to a peaceful night's sleep without watches," said Henry.

Henry was surprised that it was almost noon. He was barely awake and heard rain falling on the deck. He rolled over and cuddled up with Serene.

"Henry, do you know what time it is?"

"I know. Best night's sleep I've had in weeks. It's raining. Go back to sleep," he yawned.

"That's Nate washing the boat, silly. I was up earlier and made coffee. It's a gorgeous day."

"I better get up and help," said Henry groggily. "That man is a workhorse. It's embarrassing." Henry dressed, went to the galley, poured a mug of black coffee, climbed to the wheelhouse, and went outside.

"Morning, sailor," yelled Nate from the dock where he was coiling up a hose.

"And a beautiful day it is!" replied Henry. "You should have waited for me to clean the decks."

"Ah, no problem. Was up early, had nothing better to do. So what's the plan for the day?" asked Nate.

"No plan really. I want to go and talk to Mr. Rom, first. He owns the Inn. Just want to thank him for the dock here and to pay for the water and power we've used."

"Whenever you're ready, Henry. I'd like to meet him as well."

Henry drained the last of his coffee, put the mug in the wheelhouse, and yelled down to Serene that he and Nate would be back in a few minutes. Nate and Henry walked around the corner and entered the Pizza Inn. A large man with a bushy red beard was writing the luncheon specials on a blackboard behind the cash register.

"Hello. Are you Mr. Rom?" asked Henry.

"*Jah*, Rom," he answered in a soft, singsong voice.

"I'm Henry Langston, and this is Nate Nevins. We have our boat, the *Loki* tied-up at your dock."

Rom extended a large paw of a hand, "Ah my American neighbors! Happy to meet you both! Please sit with me for coffee and cake." Rom led them to a red leatherette booth and asked one of his waiters to bring coffee and cake.

"How you like Flekkefjord?" asked Rom.

"We're delighted to be here. It is a beautiful town, Mr. Rom," said Henry.

"You come from USA in your boat?" asked Rom.

"Yes, from Cape Cod in Massachusetts. You know it?" answered Nate.

"Is it near Brooklyn? I have aunts and uncles there," said Rom.

"Actually, not that far. About a six hour drive, I believe."

"How long you staying in Flekkefjord?" inquired Rom.

"A week or two, not sure really. Can you suggest another place for us to dock so we don't inconvenience you," said Henry.

"You are okay where you are. Please stay as long as you like," Rom said emphatically.

"We'd love to stay where we are, but insist on paying for the dock, the electricity and water," said Henry.

"No. Please be my guest. Use all the water and power you want. It costs next to nothing here. We have much hydroelectric, you know, and the water runs down free from a mountain lake. We are happy to have you here," Rom insisted.

"You are very kind and hospitable," said Henry. "You have yet to meet Serene. She is back at the boat. I'll introduce her to you later."

"You can't miss her, Mr. Rom. A slim young woman with short, black hair. Very beautiful," said Nate.

"Yes, Mr. Rom. By the way, she wants to visit real estate agent in Flekkefjord. Can you suggest one?" said Henry.

"Unfortunately, we do not have one. The nearest would be in Stavanger, about a two hour drive from here," said Rom.

"Interesting!" said Henry. "How do people buy and sell property here ... with ads in the newspapers?" asked Henry.

"Ours is a very small town, and as you see most houses are passed to children or sold to relatives. It's not like the USA."

"So, if you wanted to find out how much houses cost here, what would you do?" asked Henry.

"You should talk to Helge Austad, our mayor. If anyone would know about houses, he would. He is our local hero. There is a statue of him in front of the church," said Rom.

"A war hero?" asked Nate.

"Yes. He was in the resistance. Arrested when 15 years old as a spy and condemned to death," said Rom.

"Obviously, he escaped," said Nate.

"Not really. It is a long and interesting story. It is in our history books. You can find Helge at the town hall, the last building up Kirkegt, by the museum. But I must excuse myself now. I see we are starting to get busy for lunch. Again, welcome to Flekkefjord. Stay as long as you like," said Rom as he scurried to the cash register to assist a customer.

"They have a museum, too. We must stop by there," said Nate.

"I don't think we have to bother the mayor about real estate. Would be nice to meet him though. Can't recall ever having met a genuine hero," said Henry.

— CHAPTER 16 —

Upon returning to the *Loki*, Henry told Serene about his conversation with Rom. She was pleased they were staying put and suggested they buy him a gift to thank him for his hospitality. Serene, however, became more intrigued about real estate and was doubly interested to meet a war hero. Nate also thought it would be wise to see the mayor, not about real estate, but to announce their arrival. They had not seen a harbormaster's office or been visited by a customs official.

As they walked up Kirkget, Nate suggested they look for the mayor's statue in the churchyard. On the side of the church, they came upon a bronze statue of a thin, young boy, his chin held high. He was dressed in knee breeches and wearing a vest trimmed with folk embroidery. "Can you read the plaque, Nate?" asked Serene.

Nate peered at the writing for a few seconds and said, "Near as I can make out, it says that Helge Austad, a son of Flekkefjord, went into the night and something else in May, 1942 and returned from the night and something else … could be darkness, or fog in October 1945 and never gave up the light of Norwegian freedom."

A few blocks up the street they found the town hall, a simple, yet stately Dutch style masonry building. The front door was open, and there was no receptionist. They walked down the hallway and heard a voice call out from an open office door in Norwegian. A tall, slender man with gray hair and bright blue eyes rose from his desk.

"Sorry, we don't speak Norwegian," said Henry.

"It's okay. Most all speak English here. You are the Americans docked by Pizza Inn, I take it. I am Helge Austad. Please come into my office," he said. Henry introduced his party, and they sat in chairs in front of his desk.

"I welcome you all to Flekkefjord. How may I be of service?" he said with a warm, genuine smile.

"Thank you for seeing us. Mr. Rom at the Pizza Inn thought you might be able to answer a few questions for us, but first we have to let you know that we did not see any customs or immigration officials when we came into your port. We docked and thought someone would come to the boat, but no one came," said Henry.

"We are not so formal here. If you want a bureaucrat, you will have to go to Stavanger or Kristiansand to find one. You have American passports?" Helge asked.

"Yes," said Henry as he reached for the inside pocket of his jacket.

"I don't need to see them," Helge laughed. "Besides, I have no stamp. So that is that. What else?"

"I have a few questions about real estate," Serene announced. "I understand there are no real estate agents and that most sales are done privately, but I'm curious to know what's the average cost of a house here?"

"Are you in the real estate business, Serene?"

"No. But my family was in housing development and construction in the San Francisco area, and I always like to check the local listings. Habit and curiosity mostly."

"As you know, values vary according to location and quality. I would say on average a medium sized house would cost in US dollars about three hundred thousand."

"Thank you," said Serene. "Do you know of anything for sale? I would certainly like to see the inside of a few Norwegian houses."

"Not that I'm aware of, but if I hear of anything I'll let you know. If you want to see the inside of a typical house, you are most welcome to visit my farm. Our house is over 250 years old," Helge said proudly.

"That would be a treat, but I would not want to impose," said Serene.

"It will be my great pleasure. You will be here for some time?" Helge asked.

"A few weeks, I believe," Serene replied.

"Good. Then I will invite you. Is Saturday about 11 a.m. good for you?"

"Yes. Thank you. I will look forward to it."

"I will pick you up at your boat then. I only live five minutes away. By the way, can I ask you a question, Henry?"

"Certainly," Henry replied.

"What brings you to Flekkefjord?"

"It may sound strange, but our friend Nate here has wanted to visit here for some time because you have no tides."

Helge's expression froze for an instant. They he laughed. "Ah, that is nothing. We have much to offer here ... a scenic countryside, good fishing, and many islands in the fjord for picnics. One island is a town park. It has a dock, a small beach, and rest rooms. Ask anyone at the docks for directions. You will like it."

"Thanks for the tip," said Henry as he rose from his chair. "We're just on our way to visit your museum."

"It is very humble but we are proud of it," said Helge as he rose. "I will see you Saturday at 11:00 then."

They thanked the mayor, and they left the building. Once on the street, Nate said excitedly, "Did you see his face when you mentioned the tides, Henry?"

"Yes, quite unusual," agreed Henry. "I was surprised at how quickly he dismissed the subject. I thought he would tell us something more."

"Exactly. A phenomenon as extraordinary at that. You'd think there would be some town pride. It has to be a boon to folks with boats, not having to deal with tide tables and not having to re-adjust their mooring lines. If I were him, I would be bragging about it," said Nate.

"Nate, as long as we're on the subject," said Serene. "How is your measuring instrument doing? How are you feeling about this place?"

"Never in life have I felt better! Was thinking about it this morning while washing the boat. I have an unusual sense of well being here. Can't quite put it into words, but there's something about this place..." said Nate as his words trailed off into thought.

"Did you notice that he knew exactly who we were and where we were docked?"

"Yes, Serene," said Henry. "But I suspect in a small town like this, everyone knows everything that happens. And, I bet Helge knows most of all."

"Shall we check out the museum?" asked Serene.

"I'm game," said Nate. Henry nodded in agreement.

Across the street stood the museum, a rambling white clapboard structure that could have once been a commercial building. Since it backed onto the 'river', the name given to the channel that bisected the town, they supposed it probably was at one time. The sign at the entrance was in Norwegian, German, English and French. There was no admission charge, but donations were welcome. Henry placed a twenty-dollar bill in the receptacle. This was noticed by a woman standing behind the counter. She smiled and welcomed the group in perfect English. "Welcome to our little museum. My name is Lilly. If you have any questions, I would be pleased to try to answer them for you." She was a trim, sprite, woman in her mid-fifties with round, rimless eyeglasses and beautiful white teeth. She continued, "I am a volunteer here one day a week. My family has the bookshop on lower Kirkegt which I hope you will visit as well."

Henry thanked Lilly on behalf of the group, and they began to tour the exhibits. While modest, the exhibits were nonetheless interesting and the multilingual cards were helpful. They again learned that the town had been one of the earliest settlements in the country and home to many Vikings. Since the 1500's, it had been an export harbor for timber and in the 1600's for granite that was shipped to Holland to build dikes. Around 1750, herring fishing became important, and up until the early 1800's, the town was the largest exporter of herring on the southern coast. They browsed through exhibits of household items, furniture, glassware and folk art.

One exhibit arrested Nate's attention. He stood in front of a large, flat stone with runic symbols carved in it. A perplexed expression was on his face.

"What's this, Nate?" Henry inquired.

"It's called the Berrefjord Stone ... comes from Berrefjord and it contains a fragment of the Berrefjord Saga, about a Princess Ingvild and the legend of the moon. That's all the card says, but what *really* caught my attention is this." Nate pointed to a dark, black line running parallel to the runic letters across the stone as if the inscription was underlined. "That line is a tidal discoloration. Same as the ones I saw on the rocks when we came up the fjord."

Nate immediately returned to the Lilly's desk. "Can you tell me more about the Berrefjord Stone?"

"Oh that," she grinned. "Don't take it too seriously. It really hasn't been authenticated. My cousin Ingvild found it last summer in Berrefjord. She insisted we keep it here for her. That's what she thinks the runes say."

"Is she related to the Ingvild in the saga?" asked Nate.

"Yes, her name is Ingvild Berrefjord, and the Berrefjord was the home of her family going back forever. Ingvild has been a popular name for girls in her family for many generations. That I know to be a fact. Going back as far as she claims, I could not say."

"How can I contact this Ingvild?" Nate asked.

"I can give you her phone number if you like." Lilly began to search her purse and continued, "She lives in Oslo but also has a house outside town, and she comes home for vacation and holiday. Here it is." Lilly wrote the phone number on a slip of paper and handed to Nate. "Ingvild is a very special person. Everyone loves her, but she is, how you say, 'eccentric.' No, that's not quite right, 'different' is better. Perhaps you Americans might say a bit of a 'hippy.' Yes, that's better. But she has a good heart and a big job in Oslo. She is Director of our National Theater School."

"And you said you are cousins?" asked Nate.

"Yes," chuckled Lilly, "but that is no large distinction here. Almost everyone is a cousin of everyone else in one way or another. However Ingvild is a second cousin. Just tell her that Lilly gave you her number. She'll be happy to hear of your interest in her stone. She was very excited about finding it."

"Thank you so ever much," said Nate as he shook hands with Lilly.

"Tell her I said *Hai Hai!*" said Lilly as Nate, Henry and Serene left the museum.

— CHAPTER 17 —

"Hello. Is this Ingvild Berrefjord?" Nate asked as he stood at the pay phone in the Pizza Inn's parking lot.

"Yes, this is she. Who may I ask is calling," answered a pleasant voice in crisp English.

"My name is Nate Nevins. I'm an American, but I'm calling from Flekkefjord. Your cousin Lilly at the museum was kind enough to give me your telephone number."

"And how is Lilly?" she responded.

"She was fine when I saw her today. She said to say 'Hai Hai' to you."

"If you should see her tell her I said 'Hai Hai' as well. What can I do for you, Mr. Nevins?"

"Please call me Nate, I insist."

"Then you must call me Ingvild. I also insist," she said in a very professional tone.

"The reason I'm calling is because of the Berrefjord Stone I saw in the museum today…"

"Terrific! You noticed it!" and the demeanor of her voice became lively.

"Yes. I'm very interested in it. You see, I came to Flekkefjord to investigate why there are no tides here. Then, I noticed the water line discoloration across the stone and your reference to the legend of the moon. That's why I'm calling."

"You are a scientist, then?" she asked.

"No. Only a curious old seaman with an interest in tides, purely an amateur."

"You are an astute observer, however, and correct. That piece broke off from a rock face that was once by the waterline. I found it last summer while diving in Berrefjord. I think there are more rune stones underwater."

"That's astounding!"

"I believe it is an important find. I have been excavating at the fjord for several summers. This is a most important discovery I think. I will be resuming work next week when my holidays begin. How long will you be staying in Flekkefjord?"

"I'll be here for a while. I can't speak for my shipmates. Let me explain my situation. I owned a boat which I sold to my friends Henry and Serene, and we sailed here together from Cape Cod. If they decide to sail on, I will check into the Maritime Hotel, which is just across the river from where we are docked."

"Oh, you are by Rom."

"Yes."

"Say *'Hai Hai'* to him for me. He is my cousin."

"I certainly will. By the way, Ingvild, do you know anything about the tides here?" There was a pause before Ingvild answered.

"Nate, don't mention the tides to people in town. They don't like to talk about it. It's very silly. I'll explain when I see you. I have to run off for a meeting now. I will see you when I get to Flekkefjord."

"I look forward to meeting you."

"Same here. Bye-bye," and she hung up.

Nate hung up the phone and walked across the lot to the Pizza Inn. It was late afternoon. Rom was sitting on the patio reading a newspaper.

"Good afternoon!" Nate said.

"Ah! Nate. How are you this fine day?" Rom said as he put down his paper. "Please join me."

"I was just speaking with your cousin Ingvild Berrefjord on the phone. She sends her regards."

"Oh great! How is she?"

"She sounded fine. She will be here next week for vacation."

"Yes, it is already that time again. How fast it goes. How do you know Ingvild?"

Nate told of his visit to the museum, his conversation with Lilly, and the resulting phone number, and asked, "What's Ingvild like?"

Rom laughed. "Ah yes, Ingvild. I love her. She is a one-of-a-kind for sure." Rom continued to laugh. "I am sorry, Nate, the very thought of her gives me such joy. I was just reminded of her car being condemned by the police. It's so funny. Let me explain. You see, Ingvild is wealthy. She inherited both from her father and her uncle who was childless. She owns houses, apartments, farms … who knows what else. Plus she has a good job in Oslo. Yet, she is extremely conservative. What you Americans call *cheap*," said Rom as he rolled with laughter. "But she is only conservative when it comes to herself. She is very generous otherwise.

"So from her uncle, she inherited this old Toyota. It must be 25 years old. A real junk! It had been sitting in her uncle's farmyard for many years, all covered with chicken droppings and rust. Mice ate up the seats. Well, Ingvild is quite handy. She got the old car started and found the motor was good. She cleaned it up, started driving it, and was soon stopped by the police. You see, Nate, in Norway you cannot have a car on the road if it has any dents, or rust, or even missing paint, or anything wrong with the body. It's a law. So Ingvild began patching it up. She painted it with spray cans with whatever color struck her fancy that day. Even so, the car was very ugly. She was always being stopped. It was like those old black and white American movies where the crazy cops are always chasing around..."

"The Keystone Cops?" interrupted Nate.

"Yes. Those ones, ha ha. That was how it was with Ingvild. Finally, the police in Oslo got an order from a judge and got her car condemned. Just like an old building ... to tear it down. Ingvild would have none of that. She took the car in the courtyard of her building and spent a weekend patching and painting it before she went to court to fight it. She defended herself and made the judge come outside the court to inspect her car. The judge dismissed the order of condemnation, because all of the body was actually there and painted, although he did say it was the lumpiest and ugliest automobile he had ever seen. The story even made the newspaper with a picture Ingvild standing by the car with the judge. What's really funny, however, is that after that police continued to stop her. So she pasted the dismissal order from the judge and the newspaper picture on the back window. Now when she is stopped, she doesn't say a word but points to the window, and when the police finish reading it, she just smiles and drives off."

They both had a good laugh until their eyes were tearing.

"She sounds like a character," said Nate. "How old is she?"

"She is in her mid forties, but she looks younger."

"Married? Children?" asked Nate.

"No, never married. She was engaged as a young girl. Don't know much about it. She went as an *au pair* for a rich Jewish family in Brooklyn, and she fell in love with the son. But it didn't work out, and she came home after a year. Are you married, Nate?"

"No, never was. Spent most of my life at sea. Little opportunity."

"Ah! Then you will like Ingvild. She's quite a catch, you know," Rom kidded.

Nate blushed and stuttered back, "No, no. Too late for me, too set in my ways."

"Ah. It is never too late, my friend. There's always time to do everything you want if only you set about it," said Rom.

"Funny, that's what my father used to say," replied Nate.

They were sitting in the main salon, when from above deck they heard Helge calling, "Yoo-hoo ... Yoo-hoo ... anyone home?" He waited on the dock dressed in khaki shorts, a bright red shirt, sporting a white baseball cap and wearing dark sunglasses. After exchanging pleasantries and giving him a quick tour of the boat, Helge escorted the party to his minivan and began driving.

"You must know our place has not been a working farm for many years. We used to have several cows and would sell the milk. It is a small place, very modest, but my father and mother raised ten children there. When they built this new highway about ten years ago, they took a some of our land from both sides of the road, so the small farm became even smaller."

A few minutes later, he turned off the highway onto a gravel road and stopped the car. On a hill rising up before them was a small, white house with red shutters, flower boxes and Victorian style trim. Next to the house was a large red barn. Immediately behind the buildings and shooting up nearly vertically was a high, rocky cliff framed by evergreens on the top and sides.

"The farm has been in our family since 1725. On the other side of the highway are hayfields and a smaller barn. That barn over there is where we hid 40 soldiers from the Nazis for several days. That was some job, I tell you."

Helge put the car in gear, drove up to the farmhouse, and parked between the house and barn on the only level ground to be seen. A small, spectacled woman with a gracious smile came from the porch to greet the visitors. "This is my wife, Viola, but everyone calls her 'Baby'," said Helge as he made the introductions. Baby welcomed everyone and said Helge had been crabbing the night before and that crabs would be served for lunch shortly. After adamantly refusing Serene's offer to help, Baby excused herself and returned to her cooking.

Helge took them on a tour of the old farmhouse. The tiny rooms were spotless and decorated with antique furniture, family photos and framed needlework, many of which had been crafted by his wife, he proudly noted.

He took them upstairs and showed the bedrooms, each barely large enough to hold a small bed and a chair. "In Norway," he explained, "bedrooms are used only for sleeping. In the farming days we got up at 4:00 a.m. and worked until dark. We only came back to the house for lunch."

Helge guided them out the back door across the yard to the barn. He showed them through the ground floor which now contained his workshop as well the remnants of the dairy operation. The barn was built into the side of the hill, so when they exited the first floor, Helge led them up the hill and around to the back of the barn to reach the hayloft. They walked up a ramp, which led to large barn doors.

As he opened the doors, he explained, "This was once used only for storing hay. We had a trapdoor in the floor so we could pitch the hay down to the cows. Now it is our modest clubhouse, used as meeting place for civic groups from town and occasionally for reunions of the resistance fighters."

The loft looked immense due to its full ceiling height and old-fashioned post and beam construction made from hand hewn lumber. All around the large room and suspended from the ceiling was a collection of antique farm implements. Helge chuckled as he said, "As you see, my family never threw anything away. At least now, we've put them to use as decorations."

There were several folding tables and chairs set up meeting style with a large blackboard in front. A long bar with several stools lined one wall. On another wall hung a number flags including the national flag and several military banners. In the center, the largest and most predominant flag had a white field with head of a black wolf with teeth bared and drops of blood dripping from its mouth.

"That's a striking flag. What is it?" Serene asked.

"Oh. That's the flag we made up for our little resistance group. Come, sit down. Can I offer you a drink? Soda, beer, a glass of wine perhaps?"

Henry, Serene and Nate sat at the bar down and placed their drink requests. Helge went to an old, white refrigerator and returned with bottles of soda and beer.

"Can you tell us about your activities during the war?" Henry asked.

"That is a tough subject for me to talk about. Several history men have interviewed me. It's in some books. Each time I was interviewed, I would have bad dreams for weeks. I hope you don't mind," Helge said apologetically.

"Not at all," Henry said. "We understand. But it's great you still get together with your old war buddies."

A big smile came to Helge's face. "Yes, we have had some good times in this room. We have a few beers and tell the same old stories over and over again, and we laugh louder each time it seems. They are great fellows."

"And I really like your flag. Nice design," said Serene.

"We never had a flag during the war. One of the guys made it up several years ago. He did a good job," Helge said as he turned to look at the flag. Then in a soft voice, almost a whisper, he continued, "We called our little group the Black Wolves."

"Was that because you did your work at night?" Nate asked.

"Yes, that was part of it, but not the real reason. I'll explain. Have you heard of the word *berserk*," asked Helge with a sly grin.

"That means someone who's crazy, doesn't it?" said Serene.

" That's the meaning we understand today ... someone who is crazed or frenzied. But the word *berserker* comes from the Old Norse language. It literally means *bear shirt*. The skin, and often the head, of the black bear were worn by an ancient cult of fierce warriors called berserkers. In our old myths, berserkers were the bodyguards of Odin, the god of war. These were wild men who fought with inspired frenzy with no thought for their safety or lives. They howled like beasts in the madness of battle and trusted in the power of Odin to deliver them from wounds."

"But that's all mythology, isn't it?" interrupted Henry.

"No, not at all. They became part of our myths, but the berserkers actually existed. They were the bodyguards of the pagan kings of Norway. Berserkers were also the shock troops throughout the period of the Viking raids. They were sent first into battle to terrify the enemy with their ferociousness and break the enemy's will to resist. What is less known, however, about berserkers is that they fell into two classes. There were men who wore bearskins, but others who wore wolf skins.

"The bear-men, it is said, came from the mountains. They were bigger, stronger men than the wolves and extremely ferocious, but by nature did not seek war. They were content to build their houses of rocks, tend goats and chop the great trees in the highlands. They would only fight if provoked, or called upon by a chieftain or king. They would rather remain in their mountain homes like bears in a den. When they did go into battle, however, they were murderous and unrelenting.

"The wolf berserkers were different. They lived along the seacoast. They were ... how would you say ... more cosmopolitan. They were the sea traders, explorers and warriors. As they had more exposure to foreigners, they were more suspicious of strangers and crafty in their dealings with them. Some say the wolves were more intelligent since they wound up possessing the more desirable lands by the sea for fishing and farming. The wolves were aggressive and sly and preferred to attack by surprise, often at the full moon. It was after this old tradition of the berserkers that we named our little band the Black Wolves."

"Attacking at the full moon, Helge," said Nate. "Do you think berserkers had greater strength or more courage at that time?"

"Perhaps there is something to that. My friend Olav said that his grandfather told him that the ancient wolf berserkers actually worshiped the moon. They painted their round, wooden shields with silver to symbolize the belief that the moon gave them power to be stronger and braver. I personally believe the moon affects people. In the camps during the war the guards became more aggressive during the full moon. Many of the prisoners acted a bit crazy, too, including me," he said with a grin.

"Did you have any berserkers in your group?" asked Serene.

Helge laughed, "Well, you had to be a little crazy to fight the Nazis. If you were caught, you were put to death. They would also put your entire family to death and burn down your house to boot. Enough talk of those days. The hardest part is to forget it. Come now. I believe Baby has our lunch ready."

— Chapter 18 —

Boxer arrived early and sat in a booth at the Elbow Rest waiting for Philly 'Gumdrops'. It had been nearly three weeks since the *Loki* sailed from Wellfleet. Boxer had used some of that time investigating Norwegian tides trying to determine where the *Loki* might land. More time had been spent working on his new theory and practicing 'surfacing', the name he had coined for his hypnotic meditations. He had been doing these sessions three times a day.

He had calculated it would take at least three weeks for the *Loki* to reach Norway, and he had already booked a flight to Stavanger and packed his bag.

As he waited he thought to himself, "Either I am getting smarter through my surfacing technique, or I have auto-suggested that I am smarter. Either way, my self-confidence has increased, and I feel I'm getting smarter. Maybe it's wishful thinking. I can't wait for the next IQ test to see if there's been any increase. If there is, and if progress continues, what then should I do? Naturally, I would want to continue to practice the technique just to see what happens. I could write a paper and try to publish in a scientific journal. Maybe writing a book for the general reader would make more sense? Or perhaps I should test the theory on larger scale with multiple subjects? There's another possibility! I could teach the technique! Imagine that! Boxer Ryan from Jersey City, a self-appointed guru teaching my own 12 step system to higher intelligence … ."

"What's that stupid look on your face Boxer?" asked Philly as he sat in the booth opposite Boxer.

Boxer, caught unaware, quickly recovered and said, "Sorry, daydreaming again, Philly. How's things?"

"You always was a daydreamer, Boxer. Sometimes I wish I could escape from reality like you."

"It's an acquired art, Philly. I suppose you have to be predisposed to daydreaming by nature. After that, it requires hard work and persistence to efficiently waste time. It's tough overcoming the Judeo-Christian work ethic. Everybody worships fast action these days with as little thought as possible required. And look at the mess we created. Pure thought for its own sake is becoming a rarity, hardly ever considered as real work unless you work at a think-tank. Even then, people thinks it's a scam. Me, I consider daydreaming a leisure activity, although it's often the seedbed of useful ideas. I have also perfected lying in bed and doing absolutely nothing. A very difficult accomplishment."

"You are a card, Boxer. One of the reasons I always liked you. You are definitely different."

"Thanks, Philly. But each of us is unique, you included."

"That's what they used to teach us at Catholic school, but I've found that most people are pretty much the same."

"Philly, that's because you don't take the time know a person well enough. If you did, you'd see all the little eccentricities and foibles that make people a veritable sideshow."

"You're probably right, Boxer. As much as I enjoy our weird conversations, let's get down to the business of McCall. What's the next move?"

"Like I said on the phone, the only concrete lead is they were going someplace in Norway that has no tides. I made lot of calls to marine biologists, hydrologists and scientists. I've narrowed the area down to a small area of coastline in southwestern Norway, a stretch about ten miles long." Boxer put a map on the table and drew a circle on it. "This area, around the Lista Lighthouse. There are a several small towns, the largest being Farsund and Flekkefjord. My flight leaves tomorrow morning for Copenhagen. From there I get plane to Stavanger in Norway. I rent a car and start looking. I have their photos. If they're in that area, I should be able to track them down. That's the plan."

"Okay. Nothing else to do. If you find them, call me. I'll have people standing by to take over."

Nate had been polishing bronze fittings since dawn. His thoughts turned to the intriguing little town in which he found himself. They had been there a week. Henry and Serene showed no inclination towards leaving. He felt the same. It was as though he had arrived at a place he had always sought, like living on the flowing edge of a contented 'now.' He thought perhaps it was the novelty of being in a new and pleasant place. He wished this state of mind would continue.

Since their arrival he noticed something else. He arose before the others and sat alone with his coffee and tried to piece together the fragments of dreams. When he dreamt in the past, his dreams often left him with disturbed, uneasy feelings, darkly veiled and confused. Many times he had tried to analyze his dreams but had never gained much insight. He had been only able to classify his dreams in the broadest categories, such as being fearful, sexual, hostile or omnipotent. Since his arrival at Flekkefjord, he noticed his dreams had become much less emotionally charged and easier to reconstruct in the morning. Now the morning memories of his dreams were detailed, vivid and came to him in complete scenarios, which unfolded fluidly.

Nate's reverie was broken by the sound of a loud muffler coming from the parking lot. One glance told him it could be none other than Ingvild's car. Rom's description had not been exaggerated. The multi-colored sedan reminded Nate somewhat of a Jackson Pollack painting. The picture was further topped off by an exhaust pipe assembly tied to her roof rack. As she shut off the engine, there was a punctuating backfire. Nate laughed.

Ingvild got out of her car and look at it disapprovingly. Then, she shrugged her shoulders, and a pleasant smile came to her face. As she walked towards the *Loki*, the first thing Nate noticed was that she was well built even though she was wearing baggy denim overalls over a neatly starched white blouse. Her large, bright blue eyes were noticeable at a distance. Her short blonde hair bounced as she walked despite a bright blue sweatband that matched her eye color. If Nate had not already known her age, he would have guessed she was no more than thirty. As she neared, Nate felt excitement at the force of her personal energy. She called out, "*Hai! Hai!* You are Nate! I am Ingvild! Pleased to meet you face to face." She shook Nate's hand vigorously with a tight grasp. "This is a wonderful boat! May I take a look?"

Before Nate could answer she sprang to the deck and began inspecting the boat like a detective looking for a clue. She darted about so quickly Nate could hardly catch up. The image of a hummingbird came to Nate's mind. "This is an old fishing boat, built in Norway or Sweden. Definitely was a fisher boat. A beautiful restoration. Did you do it?"

"Yes," Nate answered.

"Fine job! I will show you my boat. Restored it myself. Twenty-two coats of varnish. A double-ender too. Inherited from Uncle Johann. It was a mess.

One of the last *snekkes* built in the fjord, double-ended, lapstreak. Company went out of business in 1965. Six meters, about 20 feet with an old Saab one cylinder. Sounds like this … dunk … dunk … dunk … dunk … dunk…"

Nate was bewildered and delighted by this fast-talking, whirling dervish of a woman. She went into the wheelhouse and took a quick look. Before Nate could utter a word she disappeared down the steps. By the time Nate caught up, she was introducing herself to Henry and Serene. As Nate joined the group, Ingvild asked Serene to show her the rest of the boat. The women scampered down the hall chattering like long lost sisters.

"She's the first big storm the *Loki* has run into," said Henry with a grin. "Who is she again?"

"She found the rune stone in the museum, Ingvild Berrefjord. I told you she might be coming," said Nate.

"Oh, yes. What a ball of energy! Let's invite her to breakfast, that is, if she can sit still that long," Henry kidded.

Ingvild did want breakfast, however she insisted on making it for them at her home, which she said was a few minutes away by car. When Henry and Serene saw her car, they stopped in their tracks, blankly looked at each other, and said nothing. As Ingvild started the engine, she apologized, "Excuse the noise. I just picked up the new exhaust pipe. I will put on this afternoon."

"Ya know, I'm a bit of a mechanic myself. Be glad to give ya a hand," said Nate.

"That's an understatement," said Henry. "Ingvild, Nate is a master mechanic."

"I can do it myself, but you are welcome to keep me company. There is an auto-pit near my home," said Ingvild.

"What's an auto-pit?" asked Serene. "I've never heard that expression."

"We have many in Norway. You'll find one in every town. Many people repair their own cars. You have two tracks built out over a hillside. You drive out on the tracks to work under the car. That's how they did it before mechanical lifts. This one is very old and made from stones. Fixed wagons on it long ago," Ingvild said with a laugh.

She drove up a steep hill leading out of town. At the top she made a left onto a narrow, winding road, which had been blasted out of the mountainside and ran along the upper fjord. This vast expanse of water narrowed to the river channel, which ran through town and into the lower fjord. Ingvild turned off the paved road, shifted into low gear and gunned the engine to climb a rough gravel driveway up a steep hill. At the top she parked in front of a tall, white frame house set in a grove of maple trees.

"What a fantastic view!" exclaimed Serene as she got out of the car.

"Marvelous," Henry agreed. Nate was speechless at the vista of blue water and green mountains.

"We like it a lot. On a clear day, you can almost see the end of the fjord twenty miles away. The only problem is snow and ice. Often we have to park at the bottom and walk up. It is not hard for me. I am mostly in Oslo in winter. For my cousin Vigdis and her husband Mike it is harder. They lease the bottom of the house. I have the top. We must go around back to enter," said Ingvild almost apologetically.

After climbing a steep flight of stairs, they entered what Ingvild called her little apartment. She gave them a quick tour. It was actually quite spacious and what Norwegians call *koslig,* a cozy, comfortable home decorated with family photos, mementos, figurines and lots of polished silver, pewter and copper. The walls were freshly painted in white and provided a museum-like backdrop for finely carved pieces of antique furniture and an impressive grandfather clock. The floors were of a highly polished, dark wood that was accented by colorful area rugs in abstract designs.

Ingvild was particularly proud of her new kitchen and bath which had been recently been completed. The bath was done in pink Italian marble. The kitchen was of a modern Scandinavian design with meticulously crafted oak cabinets and stainless steel appliances. The crowning moment of the tour was in the living room. She drew back heavy curtains to reveal French doors. They opened to a large balcony that offered an even more spectacular view than from the driveway.

Since it was a sparkling, clear day, they sat at the round table on the balcony. Ingvild brewed coffee and served a giant western omelet, which they all shared. It was accompanied by fresh bread and butter, an assortment of homemade jams and jellies, and assorted cheeses. The small talk during breakfast led to a probing question by Nate.

"Ingvild, please tell us about the translation of the Berrefjord stone, and what you know about Princess Ingvild?"

"Yes, of course. My favorite topic. I have bored my friends to death about it. What I know about my namesake, Princess Ingvild, has mostly come down through my family. There is a written account of the story by one of my relatives, a schoolmaster from the early 1800's. Of course, I am hoping to find more rune stones to flesh out the story. You have heard of Eric the Red?"

"He was the one who discovered Iceland," Serene replied.

"That's the one. His family lived south of here in a village near Stavanger. Okay then. Princess Ingvild was the only child of Edred. He was a small, but powerful chieftain in these parts. These were the most anciently settled lands of Norway because they were the most desirable. That's why it has been fought over for centuries. This land is fertile, abundant in timber, fresh water, and fish. Most importantly, it is blessed by a warm sea current, which flows up from the south and moderates the climate. I think one of the curlicue ends of the Gulf Stream hits this part of the coast. Anyway, this keeps the fjord free of ice well into the winter, and it melts here earlier in the spring, and that extends the fishing season.

"Also, as Nate discovered there are no tides here which has advantages. You don't have re-moor your boat with the rise and fall, and you can have covered boathouses right at the water's edge. Another major asset is our extreme southwestern location. Back in those days, it was an ideal departure point for Viking raids on England, Ireland, or wherever. The big island of Hidra is an asset, too. It protects the entrances of Flekkefjord and the Berrefjord from storms in the North Sea.

"Edred's clan, I understand, were more raiders and pirates than fisherman and farmers. They settled in Berrefjord for good reasons. It's a tiny fjord compared to Flekkefjord. The entrance is narrow and well hidden by a number of small, rocky islands that are difficult to navigate through. Even today with the channel marked with buoys, it's tricky.

"Anyway, to get back to Princess Ingvild and Eric. Many people think he was called 'the Red' because of his hair color, but in our family tradition it has been understood that he was a bloodthirsty, ambitious and vain dolt. Eric had heard tales of Ingvild's beauty, so one day he came to see for himself with a dragon ship rowed by twenty warriors.

"Edred was surprised by this unexpected visitor and rallied his men, about the same in number, and was ready to do battle. Eric, however, raised the hand of peace and indicated that he wanted to come ashore alone to parley. Eric's men put him ashore and rowed to the middle of the fjord to wait. When Eric saw Ingvild, he was smitten and began to bargain with Edred for her hand in marriage with a proffered alliance and the promise of gold. Edred, a good judge of men, had no use for Eric at all. He had heard many stories about him. He was brash, unpleasant and full of himself, an ill match for his only daughter, Edred concluded. Besides, Eric spoke of taking her away. Edred would have none of that. She was his only heir. There was also a need for diplomacy. Eric was feared as a powerful warlord with many ships.

"After a few hours of talking with Eric, Edred finally agreed to the marriage, but with the provision it would only take place when Eric returned with the agreed weight of gold for the dowry. Edred, of course, had no intention of losing his only daughter. He figured that Eric would be dead in battle or lost in exploration within a few years, as he was a reckless adventurer. After Eric sailed away, Edred conceived a plan to send Ingvild away to stay with relatives in Denmark, not far away. He put Ingvild, two of her handmaidens, and six of his best men in his *knorr*, a broad beamed cargo vessel, and they sailed away.

"Edred swore his people to secrecy with a blood oath and made up a story to tell Eric when he returned. The problem was, Eric never came back. The other problem was Ingvild never reached Denmark. She was in her early teens when she sailed, and she did not return for five years. By that time Edred had died. Why Eric the Red never returned for Ingvild is unknown. Later he made several voyages of exploration, and he is credited in the sagas as having discovered Iceland. His son, Leif Erickson, discovered Greenland and set foot on North America three hundred years before Columbus."

"So, what happened to Ingvild during those five years?" Nate asked.

"That's the answer I've been searching for. All we know from family oral tradition is they encountered a terrible storm, were driven south and after a long voyage landed far to the south, perhaps Spain, or even Africa. They called it the Land of the Sun. Two of the men and one of the handmaidens died, either on the voyage or during the years they lived there. Eventually, they found their way back to Berrefjord. That's about all I know, except she married one of her shipmates, ruled the clan for many years, and was well remembered because of her unusual adventure."

"And what have you learned from the stone?" asked Henry.

"A lot more over the winter. I took a rubbing from the stone at the end of my vacation last summer, and I left the stone at the museum because I didn't want to *schlep* it around..."

"What? *Schlep?* What's a nice Norwegian girl like you using a word like that?" Nate kidded. Everyone laughed.

"It's has just the perfect meaning. I learned some Yiddish words many years ago when I was an *au pair* for a Jewish family in Brooklyn. So don't interrupt me like a *schlemiel*, Nate," said Ingvild, and everyone laughed.

Ingvild regained her composure and said, "As I was saying, I made a friend of a professor at Oslo University, an expert in runic inscriptions, and I showed him the rubbing. He confirmed much of what I had translated.

Although I'm not that experienced with runes, I did recognize my name and the symbols for the moon. I also had a good textbook on the subject so I had a general idea of what it said. The professor thinks the style dates from the 10th century, perhaps carved during Ingvild's lifetime. The inscription you saw is only a fragment. And Nate, you are right; the black line is a watermark. I hadn't fully realized the significance of that until you pointed it out. It may help us find the rest of the stones.

"You see, I knew from the 18th century written record that there were runic carvings somewhere in the fjord, but I had not been able to find anything after looking for several summers. Then, I noticed the different color on the rock by the old village. It would have been the ideal place to carve a rune. Perhaps, I thought, some rocks had broken off and fallen in the water. So, I got diving gear from cousin Sven, and sure enough I found the rune stone. To get it out of the water, I got another cousin to bring in his trawler, and we pulled it up with his big winch."

"So what was the professor's translation?" asked Nate.

"Essentially, the runes read that Ingvild brought the moon from the land of the sun and that it was a curse on the people. That's about it."

"What do you suppose the moon is?" asked Henry.

"I have no idea. Something she brought back, I assume. What I want to know is where she went."

"Can we be of any help?" asked Serene. "That is, if it's okay with you guys," she added.

"Certainly. I could use help. Especially if there are stones to haul up."

"Sounds interesting, besides I like to see this Berrefjord," said Henry. "How about you, Nate?"

"Nothing I'd like better. And, Henry, didn't you mention you are a diver?"

"I've done some underwater film work in the Caribbean, and recently Serene and I did a little pearl diving."

"Quite successfully!" said Serene as she hugged Henry.

"My cousin Sven dives for the oil rigs. We can get all the gear we need from him. You know, we have to camp out in tents at Berrefjord. We can go in my *snekke*. She's only 22 feet. It will be a tight fit with the equipment, but we should be okay."

"Can we drive there?" asked Serene.

"Oh no!" laughed Ingvild. "There are no roads. You'd have to be a good mountain climber even to walk there."

"Can we get the *Loki* in there?" asked Henry.

"How much water does she draw?" asked Ingvild.

"About four feet," said Nate. "She was built for these waters, ya know. If we can get her in, we don't have to sleep in no tents."

"Should be no problem," said Ingvild.

"Good," said Nate. "You can have my cabin, Ingvild. I'll bunk in the main cabin. Hot showers and everything. Plenty of room for gear. Plus the bow winch on the *Loki* can lift two tons."

"It does sound ideal, but I was planning on staying there for four weeks, maybe longer."

"No problem for us. We've got nothing but time," said Henry.

"No problem here, either," Nate added.

"Alright then! We can go as soon as you are ready. I will bring my little *snekke* as well. There are some very shallow parts in the fjord, and we can use it go for supplies. You won't want to be moving your big boat around once anchored."

"We can go tomorrow, if you like," said Serene.

"Okay with me. I will telephone Sven about the diving gear. He's at his summer house on the fjord. It's on the way. But first I must install my muffler. Tell you what, I'll drop you back at your boat, and Nate and I will do the muffler," said Ingvild with a voice of urgency and a twinkle in her eye.

— Chapter 19 —

"Mr. Mayor. Thank you for seeing me without an appointment," said Boxer as he took a chair in Helge Austad's office.

"How can I be of assistance, Mr. Ryan?" asked Helge as he examined Boxer's business card.

"As you see, I'm a private investigator. I'm trying to locate two people. Have you seen them?" asked Boxer as he handed Helge the photos. From his days in the resistance and as a Nazi prisoner, Helge was conditioned to think carefully before responding to any question. Even when he did answer, it was usually with a question of his own.

"Who are these people, and why are you looking for them?" he asked in a casual, relaxed manner.

"His name is Kevin McCall, but he also uses an alias, Henry Langston. He's an American and so is she, although as you can see she's half Polynesian. I need to talk to them about an insurance matter."

"Are they dangerous?"

"Hard to say. Certainly dangerous to my client. It cost him ten million dollars. But I doubt if they're violent criminals, if that's what you mean."

"That is good. I find this very exciting. We have no crime to speak of in Flekkefjord. What makes you think they are in our little town?"

"I know they were headed to Norway to a town that has no tides, and Flekkefjord seems to fit that description."

Helge chuckled and dismissively said, "There must be many, many places like that … where are you staying?"

"I'm at the Maritime Hotel, Room 213. Nice place. The desk clerk suggested I speak to you when I showed him the photos."

"Yes, a good hotel. Mr. Ryan, if I hear anything about these people, I'll call you at the hotel. How long will you be staying with us?"

"Not sure. There are a few towns in the area I'll be visiting. I have a car."

"I hope you enjoy your visit. Good day, sir."

After Boxer left his office, Helge leaned back in his chair, closed his eyes and thought, "I wonder where this will lead? Ingvild left with those people this morning for Berrefjord. I just can't believe those nice people are criminals. All this interest in our tides is also most disturbing. I'd better call a meeting and brief the organization. Yes, that's what to do for now."

Boxer wandered through down through the town consumed in thought about the mayor. Soon he found himself at the town park, which overlooked the entrance to the river. He sat down on a bench. It was a sunny afternoon, and he was tired after the long flight and the drive from Stavanger. He still wondered about his meeting with the mayor. "He's a cagey one for sure. Never said yes or no if he had seen them. He could be lying, or perhaps Norwegian politicians are as adept as American politicians at avoiding direct answers. Couldn't tell from Helge's eyes if there was any recognition when he looked at the photos. My intuition, however, tells me that something isn't kosher."

Boxer's reverie was broken by a sharp gust of wind, which loudly whipped the Norwegian flag on the pole over his head. "This is a gorgeous place!" he said out loud as if just awaking and comprehending new surroundings for the first time. The smell of salt air, the brilliant blues of sky and water, and the endless view of the soft green mountains along the fjord were exhilarating. Suddenly he felt wide-awake, reinvigorated. The aching weariness he had felt just minutes ago had been miraculously replaced by alertness and a new calmness of being he had never before experienced. Reluctant to break this unusually fine feeling, he sat on the bench for hours until the setting sun sent a cold shiver through his body.

Earlier that day dawn sounded with the 'dunk … dunk … dunk' of Ingvild's engine as she brought her boat alongside the bulkhead astern of the *Loki*. The sound roused Henry, Serene and Nate to the deck where they watched Ingvild skillfully secure her bow and stern lines.

"*Hai! Hai!* Good morning!" she shouted as she flashed an eager smile and leapt to the dock. "From the forecast, we have excellent weather before us. Are you ready to cast off?"

"Good morning!" said Henry, Nate and Serene almost in concert.

Ingvild, who rarely hesitated and always felt she was in command, said, "Nate, you ride with me, and you follow. When we stop by Sven's for the diving equipment, he will have breakfast for us. Have you eaten?"

"Yes, we just finished," Nate said.

"To be polite, you must have coffee and cake at Sven's. It's a tradition here. Just follow my wake, and you won't have to worry about the rocks. Nate, let's go!" she barked.

Sven was on the dock emptying a crab trap when the boats reached his red summer house set on a narrow shelf of green lawn beside the water. He wore only tattered shorts. He was a large, well-muscled man in his late twenties with square, happy face, long blond hair and a drooping blonde mustache. "*Godt dag! Godt dag!*" he called to his visitors as they docked.

"*Hai! Hai!*" said Ingvild. Sven engaged her in a bear hug, lifted her off the ground and swung her in a circle. Ingvild made the introductions, and Sven invited everyone to a picnic table overlooking the fjord. He served coffee, bread, butter, jams, cheese and salmon that he had caught and smoked himself.

"Sven works on the North Sea drilling platforms as a diver. He was also the Norwegian junior kayak champion, an expert skier and mountain climber," said Ingvild as Sven shrunk in embarrassment. "His English is not so good so please speak slowly and clearly, and he will understand you. Otherwise, he's a wonderful person, the most eligible bachelor in Flekkefjord, and one of my favorite cousins," she added.

They spent a delightful hour chatting at the table on the green lawn. When his guests were ready to depart, Sven brought the diving gear and a portable compressor to the *Loki* and passed the equipment to Henry and Serene who lashed it to the safety rails.

A few minutes after bidding farewell to Sven, Serene said, "Henry, when Sven handed me a tank I noticed a small tattoo hidden on the inside of his bicep. It was the same insignia we saw on that wolf flag at Helge's barn."

"Maybe his father, or grandfather was in the resistance," Henry answered.

"Could be," said Serene.

"Look at Nate and Ingvild jabbering away like a couple o' monkeys!" said Henry. Ingvild stood at the tiller, and Nate sat on the motor hatch facing her, and they were involved in a highly animated conversation. "Now, there's an odd couple, indeed!" he added with a smirk.

"I think they like each other. I don't think Ingvild would let just anyone fix her muffler," Serene said with a wink.

The boats left the Flekkefjord, made a starboard turn north into Hidra Sound and traveled a few miles up the coast. Ingvild motioned to the *Loki* to slow down as she steered her boat towards a narrow straight between two rocky islands. It looked as if the channel headed directly into the coastal mountains. Henry pulled back on the throttle and followed closely in Ingvild's wake through a series of sharp turns through narrow channels between a maze of sharp rocks and tree-covered islands. As they got closer to the mountains, the channel widened and the mountains came down almost vertically to the water to form a long canyon. Ingvild turned and shouted back to the *Loki*, "Listen to the echo!" Her voice reverberated through the canyon.

"What echo?" Henry yelled loudly which was followed by more echoes of laughter from both vessels. The canyon opened to show the full majesty of the Berrrefjord. Ingvild had previously described it as the most beautiful small fjord in all of Norway. Henry, Serene and Nate could see no reason to disagree, especially on a perfect June day.

It was an oval body of water, about two miles long and about a mile wide and sprinkled with small islands around the shoreline. The dark, blue-green of the water was motionless with the exception of a few circular ripples caused by fish rising to the surface. Spectacular mountains with jagged, rocky summits surrounded the entire fjord. Most striking of all was the quietness of the place. Later, Henry could only describe it as profound stillness.

Ingvild pointed to their destination, a valley at the far end, which sloped down from a towering rock wall of cliffs behind it. It was easily apparent why there were no roads to Berrefjord.

As they neared the shore, outlines of stone walls emerged from the brush on the slope. At the water's edge were vestiges of an old stone pier. Fifty yards from the shore, Ingvild shut down her engine, and Henry followed by cutting the *Loki's* motor. Suddenly, Henry and Serene, Nate and Ingvild were momentarily arrested by the even greater, striking quietude of the environment.

"You can see why I adore this place," Ingvild whispered to Nate. Yet her voice carried across perfectly to Henry and Serene who were thirty yards away. Ingvild stood, stretched her arms over her head, waved to Henry and Serene and called, "This is good place for you to anchor. You dig in, and we will pick you up. There's a spot where I can run my boat up on shore."

That night at the Maritime Hotel, Boxer had the sleep of a lifetime. When he opened his eyes, he saw sunlight dancing on his balcony through the open doorway. For once in his life, he did not spring from his bed as if it were on fire, but lay there savoring a wonderful feeling which was reminiscent of his childhood. Moreover, he was clear-headed, thoroughly relaxed and felt more optimistic than usual about the day ahead. Unfortunately, rather than enjoy more precious moments in this pleasant state, Boxer succumbed to an all too human activity; he attempted to understand the reasons why he felt that way.

Oddly, he did not have any dreams during the night. Normally, after the vicissitudes of travel, especially on a long trip such as this, his dreams would have been turbulent and unsettling. Yet, after hours of sitting idly at the waterfront, strolling leisurely back to the hotel, and skipping dinner, he crawled into the crisp white linen, curled himself in the soft down comforter, and laid his head on the feather pillow. The last thing he recalled before falling to sleep was the sweetness of the night breeze. All else had been bliss.

It was, he concluded, an extraordinary night's sleep, a wholly unexpected blessing. If he could sleep that well every night, he calculated, more than a third of his life would be measurably enhanced. Most reluctantly, Boxer rose from his bed, stretched, and walked in his pajamas to the balcony. Directly across the river, he saw the Pizza Inn. The streets beyond were quieter than he remembered, only a few cars and people casually going about their morning business. It was a lovely, warm day. Small pleasure boats passed beneath him. Some held families with fishing poles and inflatable toys, apparently going to a picnic. Then he remembered it was Saturday. This gave him the perfect excuse to avoid calling Philly. Although he knew Philly would be eagerly awaiting his call, he decided to wait until Monday to resume his investigation.

Boxer sat in a deck chair and became increasingly fascinated with the townscape. It looked prosperous. Most of the buildings were older, but exceptionally well maintained, freshly painted mostly in white. The newer buildings looked plain but solidly built and blended smoothly with the older architecture.

The streets and sidewalks were clean and free of litter. Everywhere he looked there were window boxes planted with bright, colored flowers. Here and there he saw small, neatly kept patches of green lawn. There was the small park he had passed on the way to the waterfront the day before. Sunbeams twinkled off the water of a fountain made of what looked like three dancing goats. He chuckled in delight.

He watched cars crossing the bridge. They tended to be the more expensive models, such as Volvos, Mercedes, BMW's and Saabs. The autos were spotless, too. When a pedestrian put a toe on the street, traffic immediately stopped to let the person cross and then there was a wave or smile from the pedestrian and the driver, an acknowledgment that something civilized had transpired.

From his arrival at the airport he had noticed that Norwegians dressed simply and neatly, decidedly more formally than Americans. Now he observed their weekend attire. While it was more casual, it still had a freshly pressed look. Boxer had the same impression of the people, "freshly pressed" came to mind. The men looked healthy with richer skin color than he had been accustomed to in New Jersey. No one was overweight. The women were particularly good looking with trim, athletic figures, and they walked in an aggressive, no-nonsense manner. He remembered he had read somewhere that Scandinavians tended to be more matriarchal than other European societies. He made a mental note to research that further.

With his awareness sharp and sure, his mind in perfect harmony with his body and with this place, Boxer decided to start his morning meditation. He rested his head, smiled and closed his eyes.

"We must gather firewood and build a large bonfire tonight!" Ingvild said as she stood on the highest point in the valley she could climb without using a rope. Henry, Serene and Nate stood just below her and marveled at the magnificent vista of the Berrefjord, their reward for the long climb. The huge slabs of rock on which they stood had cracked off and tumbled down from the vertical cliff that barred their ascent any higher.

"Why a bonfire?" asked Serene passively, transfixed by the beauty of the fjord.

"We must celebrate the beginning of our undertaking by honoring the old Norse gods so they do not interfere with our work. It's solid pagan tradition. Besides, it will scare away the wolves, keep us warm, and I like the fires."

"Can't argue with that logic," agreed Henry.

"Now that you mention it, Ingvild, I feel a little pagan myself," quipped Nate. "It won't be much work. Tons of dead wood down by the shore. I have a question, Ingvild. This is such a gorgeous place. Why doesn't anyone live here anymore?"

"It was a good hideout for raiders in the old days. For hundreds of years after the Viking period, it was primarily a fishing village. Now, fishing has gone mostly to the north. They use big boats that can't make it through Berrefjord's shallow entrance. Even the old lumber ships avoided Berrefjord for that reason. That's why we have these old, fat trees in here. Also, as you see, there's no place to farm. They only kept small vegetable gardens in the old days. Some of my family was here until the mid 1940's. They left because of the war. It's been abandoned ever since. Once in a while, someone will build a small summer house. There are a few on the other side. You can't see them through the trees. I don't mind a few. I don't even charge rent. But I have told them to tell anyone else who comes that it's private property."

"Do you own that land over there?" asked Henry pointing to the far ridge.

"I own the entire fjord from the tops of the mountains down. Any water draining into the fjord is Berrefjord land. We have a deed from the king describing it so. The town of Flekkefjord has been after me for years to sell my property. They even threatened to pass a special law to make me sell. I finally got them to give me a permit to build a house. Someday, when I retire, I will build a nice home down there where the old village stood and live out my days here."

"That sounds beautiful, but quite lonely," said Serene.

"Oh, no. I will take a husband one day. I have to. I need someone to build the house," Ingvild said followed by laugher which echoed over the fjord. "It will be getting dark soon. We had better climb down and build that fire."

There was no wind. The reflection from the fire cast a long, narrow triangle of reddish-yellow reflections across the still waters of the fjord. The blazing bonfire, stoked with dry pine logs, cracked, popped and shot sparks high into the night sky. The light ring from the fire filtered out the view of the stars directly above the fire, but on the soft edges of the glow, large, bright stars began to be visible and then spread out more radiant against the blackness.

"This is so … so … exciting. I've never sat by a bonfire," said Serene.

"They never last long enough for me," Ingvild replied.

"I think it's romantic," said Henry as he put his arm around Serene.

"I find it soothing, myself," added Nate.

"Nate, I've been meaning to ask, what kind of readings have you been getting on your 'measuring instrument' lately?" asked Serene.

"Measuring instrument?" Ingvild interjected in a confused voice.

Nate laughed and said, "I am my own measuring instrument ... and it's never been better, Serene. Let me explain, Ingvild. This may sound silly to you, but as you know, the reason I wanted to come to Flekkefjord was because there are no tides here..."

" ... you mentioned it on the phone when we first spoke."

"I remember very well. Ya said not to ask around town and that you'd explain why."

"Oh, it's nothing really ... just provincial town folk ... let me hear about this 'measuring instrument' thing."

At length, Nate explained his sensitivity to tidal movements, learning about Flekkefjord from Alf, his subsequent studies on tides, his theory on the effect of tides on the human nervous system and how he was monitoring himself, and attempting to measure affects on himself due to the absence of tides.

"How do you do these 'measurements?' Do you keep a journal or something?"

"To tell ya the truth, I had considered keeping a journal. That was before I arrived in Flekkefjord. But the idea fairly much flew out of my head after we docked. Fact is, I've only thought about how I felt a few times."

"Have you lost interest in your project, Nate?" asked Henry.

"In a way, yes! I don't really care about the tides anymore. I know it can't be explained. What I've learned, more importantly, is I seem to have found my natural habitat; the place most harmonious to the living conditions of this strange old bird named Nate Nevins. It's a truth, and it can't be measured. But I also suspect Ingvild knows more about the non-tide effect than she's letting on," Nate said followed by a hard look at Ingvild.

It was, they all agreed later, a rare occasion when Ingvild was at a loss for words. She gazed into the fire while the others waited in silence. After her awkward pause, she said, "I suppose I won't be telling you anything that Nate hasn't already discovered, but as I told Nate people here do not feel comfortable talking about it. I wouldn't say it's a secret, but over the course of hundreds of years, many people here have come to realize that this small area of the coast has unusual, some even say, magical properties. Others say it's rubbish, of course, and perhaps that's because they are not sensitive enough to feel it. For many generations our leaders have recognized the uniqueness of this place. They have gone to extraordinary lengths to protect the quality that is possible here ... for certain people."

"Is that why there's no property for sale!" declared Serene.

"Part of it, Serene. Long, long ago the town fathers began discouraging outsiders from settling here. One way was by incorporating all the undeveloped land around Flekkefjord as town property and prohibiting private building on it. That's why they want mine so badly. You could say we have the earliest wildlife sanctuary in the world, and the only wildlife being protected is our people. That's why the town hasn't grown in a couple of hundred years and why no property is sold except to relatives. Since there's no economic growth here because of the building limitation, most young people go elsewhere to seek employment, like me to Oslo. Many go to the States. The weird thing is that people who move away are somehow compelled to come back on a regular basis. I come back on holidays and for my summer vacations. I can't stay away. In spring and summer, hundreds of people descend upon their relatives and spend months in Flekkefjord. I think we are like the salmon who must return to the spawning ground."

"When we met with the mayor, he seemed evasive about real estate. He said he'd let me know if anything came on the market," said Serene.

"Oh! So you've met my Uncle Helge!" said Ingvild.

"More than that. He had us out to his farm for lunch. We had a great day," said Henry.

"My Uncle is a man of his word. If anything does come on the market, Serene, he will let you know but nothing ever will, and he knows it."

"I take it Helge is in charge of keeping the secret," said Nate.

"Yes, he is the leader of our local militia. They meet in his barn."

"He showed us the barn. Seemed proud of it. Especially of the Black Wolves, his old war buddies group," said Henry.

"That's the militia, the Black Wolves. There still have a few old resistance fighters, but they have many more young men. Cousin Sven is a member, in fact," said Ingvild.

"Are they a part of the national government?" asked Nate.

"God, no! I doubt the government knows much about them. Did you see many policemen in town?"

"Yes!" said Serene. "I saw one writing a parking ticket by the Pizza Inn."

"We have two uniformed police officers. One works days, and the other works nights. There are no police from 1:00 a.m. to 6:00 a.m. or on Sundays and many holidays. Mostly they write tickets and direct traffic. If the rare crime occurs, or if someone makes trouble, the Wolves take care of it. We don't have a criminal court. Need I say more," said Ingvild.

"Vigilantes, eh," Nate said in a disparaging tone.

"I don't think they consider themselves as such. It's been that way for hundreds of years. They think of themselves as the men of the town doing what needs to be done for the community."

"What do they do with a serious criminal?" asked Nate.

"To begin with, we have practically no crime in Flekkefjord. When the rare crime does occur, the Wolves find out who did it and vote on the punishment. For minor crimes such as theft, they drive the person from the town with stern warnings not to return. For more serious matters, which has only happened a few times that I know of, the criminal disappears into what we now call *Nacht und Nebel*, a term we learned from the Nazis during the war. It means that the criminal is taken out at night and he disappears into the fog."

"*Nacht und Nebel*, a polite term for murder ... or perhaps as good a criminal justice system as any other, now that I think about it," said Nate.

"Maybe better," said Ingvild. "Everyone knows that punishment for a crime is certain and swift. And the men making the judgment, we know and trust. They are good men, good-natured and fair. It's like the old Norse justice system when small villages were no more than family clans, before the advent of large, complicated societies, which by necessity evolved into more technically complicated legal systems. Perhaps we need to return to small, manageable communities where everyone knows his or her neighbors and everyone is willing to take tough decisions for themselves and for the general good of the community at large."

"I don't know if I agree with you, Ingvild," said Henry, "but you make some good points. In the United States, we claim our criminal justice system to be the best in the world, yet it is fraught with corruption, deal making, and injustice. By and large, the rich and powerful get away with murder while the poor and desperate get raw deals and worse. It's not only highly inefficient, but enormously expensive to boot. We spend more on our criminals than we spend on the poor, it seems. So, I suppose we shouldn't criticize something that apparently works for you."

"Ingvild, you said earlier that this place is special ... magical. Can you tell us more about how the people are affected by no tidal movement?" asked Nate.

"For reasons which I don't fully understand, we have grown up with the idea that Flekkefjord is somehow the spiritual center of the world. Archeologists say that this area was the earliest part of Norway to be settled, which is odd when you think about it. There are so many other parts of the country that are much flatter and with better soil suited to agriculture, land that today is a hundred times more valuable than this rocky land.

"Pictographs carved in stone from ancient times have been found in Lista, just a few miles from here. They show ships with rowers and sails. Similar pictographs from the megalithic period have been found all over the Mediterranean and as far away as the Azores. So we know these people were highly mobile, and they could have settled most anywhere. These were sea people who traveled widely, and for some unexplained reason, they chose this spot of all the choices that they had in Norway. They knew first hand about oceans, currents and tides, and maybe for the same reasons you had, Nate, they were also drawn to this place.

"The other pictograph that is found in abundance in this area, and also found universally at megalithic sites is the circle, often carved in concentric circles suggestive of the pattern you see when you drop a pebble in the water and see ripples go out in a circular pattern. Many experts say it represents the sun, or moon, or even a round shield, or life itself.

"I tend to believe it represents a place, an elusive spot, that ideal home that people are always searching for where they can find peace and harmony; not just a place where they can seek out a living and find physical safety for themselves and their families, but a special place where they can find personal tranquility. To me, that's what everyone wants whether they are aware of it or not.

"Many of us believe the ancient people found it here. Maybe it's why they called it Flekkefjord, which in English means the 'spot' fjord. This spot is the spiritual center of the world for those of us who live here. Maybe others feel the same way about where they live. I don't know how much of the effect of this place has to do with Nate's biological tides, but I do know I have a feeling here I've found nowhere else. I've already said too much about Flekkefjord and our strange ways. Then again, I've always been considered by the town's people as a little on the strange side myself," Ingvild chuckled. "Please don't tell anyone what I've said."

"We find you delightful Ingvild. I believe I speak for Henry and Serene, too," said Nate. "We won't be repeating what you've told us. Consider the whole matter confidential. What you said about the 'spot' and those carvings of circles in rocks reminds me of the 'mandala' theory of Carl Jung. Are you familiar with it?"

"Vaguely ... something about the collective unconsciousness. We covered it in school," Ingvild replied.

"That's it! Jung believed that beyond individual consciousness and its deeper unconsciousness that we humans share an unconsciousness on a higher level, a common, universal, timeless, collective unconsciousness. I think he was kind of wacky myself, but anyway that was his hypothesis. He tried to prove it by showing that the same archetypal symbols reoccurred in dreams, mythologies and works of art throughout history.

"The circle, of course, which he called the 'mandala' was the most frequently recurring symbol. He seemed to think that many symbols, like the mandala, were autonomous agents and the collective unconsciousness was the realm in which they resided," Nate said.

"Nate! You are a much deeper fjord than I thought. But maybe Jung should have taken his nose out of his books and looked up at the sun or moon to find his circles," said Ingvild.

"I agree, Ingvild. Can you imagine primitive man looking into the sky and seeing perfect circles, a sight rarely found in nature in such precision? Perhaps that explains the circles carved in your local rocks," replied Nate.

"Obviously it was the impetus of sun and moon worship by pagans. However, I wonder what Mr. Jung would have thought about concentric circles and the fact we have no tide."

"How do you say *touché* in Norwegian?" asked Henry.

— CHAPTER 20 —

Even the thought of resuming the investigation was repulsive. If anyone had asked Boxer how he spent his weekend, he would have been embarrassed to say. Most of Saturday he spent on his balcony and much of that time was in meditation. He ordered a late breakfast and an early dinner from room service. By early evening he welcomed his bed as never before and enjoyed an even more blissful sleep than the previous night.

On Sunday he plucked a tourist folder from rack in the lobby as he left the hotel. Another wonderful day of sunny, warm weather greeted him and the town seemed deserted. He glanced at the map and noted a scenic overlook marked on a hill across the fjord. He wandered in that direction. First he strolled along the waterfront, and then he walked up a hill on a narrow, winding road that led through a residential section. Soon the houses gave way to a heavily wooded pine forest with thick beds of dark green moss covering the ground between light gray stones. The road ended at a well-worn footpath, which continued upward.

As he walked quietly on a carpet of soft pine needles, he caught glimpses of blue water and orange tiled roofs through the trees. *What a thoroughly delightful pathway this is! What makes it so? Every few seconds it turns and presents yet another scene. It's good not to know exactly where you are going and what you will see next. A long, straight stretch may offer easier walking but you can see far ahead and always know what to expect.*

The path jogged around several giant slabs of granite that had tumbled down from the mountain. The heavy scent of pine mixed with a fresh breeze blowing in from the sea. As he came around a boulder, he found a small, rustic park bathed in full sun with a breathtaking view of the town. There were a few picnic tables and benches set on a series of small, grassy plateaus. Boxer sat on a bench in the shade of a broken, weathered old pine tree. He stretched out his legs, spread his arms out on the back of the bench, closed his eyes and laid his head back to let the sun dry the perspiration on his forehead. It was at that moment Boxer achieved what he later described as 'clarity'.

The grimness of Monday morning and the work ahead now confronted him. The dark gray skies and misty drizzle complemented his mood. His misery was compounded by guilt when he thought of Philly anxiously awaiting his call while he had whiled away the weekend. Boxer's entire outlook had refocused yesterday at the scenic park. Now, as much as he detested the job ahead, he knew he had to finish it. Philly now became the only obstacle to be overcome before he could begin the new life he had glimpsed in yesterday's moment of enlightenment.

Boxer put on his raincoat, opened his umbrella, walked across the bridge and began canvassing the shops. After an hour of showing the photos of Henry and Serene to people and no one recognizing them, he went into a restaurant, sat at a booth and ordered coffee. The waitress served him, and he took out the photos and placed them on the table. Boxer starred blankly at their images and seriously questioned whether they were even in Norway much less this town. He had proceeded on the thinnest evidence, perhaps even faith, but that was all he had. Now, he really regretted taking the case, except that it had brought him to Flekkefjord.

"You are a friend of Henry and Serene!" said a heavily accented voice. Boxer turned to see a large, red bearded man in a white apron.

"Yes!" Boxer lied. "They told me they would be here, but I have not been able to find them."

"Ah. You missed them," said the large man apologetically as he slid in the booth opposite Boxer. "They were here until a few days ago. I think it was Friday morning they left. Yes! Friday, I'm sure," he added.

Boxer offered his hand and said, "I'm Frank Ryan, but my friends call me Boxer."

Rom introduced himself and guilelessly related the friendship he had formed with Henry, Serene and Nate. Rom also told Boxer how his cousin Ingvild had befriended the crew of the *Loki*, and that they had gone on an excursion together to Berrefjord. Boxer lied again saying he had met Henry, Serene and Nate in Cape Cod, and then asked how he could get to Berrefjord to catch up with them before he had to return to the States. Rom told Boxer where to rent a motorboat and drew a map to Berrefjord on a napkin. Rom advised Boxer to wait until the weather cleared and to get a guide at the boat rental place. Rom insisted the coffee was on the house. Boxer thanked him profusely and left a hundred crown tip for the waitress.

On his walk back to the hotel, Boxer faced a dilemma. Should he go to Berrefjord first or just call Philly and tell him where they were? He decided to do both. First, he was intrigued by the crew of the Loki and wanted to meet them. Secondly, he was overdue calling Philly, and he was the wrong guy to keep waiting.

Back in his room, he placed a call to Philly's cell phone.

"Yeah?" Philly answered.

"Philly. It's Boxer."

"Tell me some good news," Philly said impatiently.

"I have good news. I've found them. They were docked here in Flekkefjord until last Friday. Now they've gone to a nearby fjord with a local woman named Ingvild Berrefjord."

"How far is that from where you are standing?" demanded Philly.

"About ten miles. This guy who's Ingvild's cousin told me they'd be there for a few weeks."

"I'll get the Moran brothers over there as soon as I can. What's the name of the place you're staying?"

"The Maritime Hotel in Flekkefjord."

"Okay. You stay put until they get there. I'll let you know the Moran's ETA. You show the Morans where they are, and you're out, like we said."

"Don't you think I should scout them out first?" asked Boxer.

"Whatdaya mean?"

"The only way to get to this fjord is by small boat. I was going to go there tomorrow just to verify that they are actually there."

"Not a good idea. The last time I talked to Scardino he was taking a boat to find them. He came back dead," said Philly.

"That was an accident ... lightning never strikes twice in the same case," chuckled Boxer. "They don't know me from Adam. Besides, I may be able to wangle some information on that big pearl. You know what a charmer I am."

"You know best about these things, Boxer. It'll take a couple 'o few days to get the Morans together anyway. You be back at the hotel by next Friday to brief them on the situation."

"All right, Philly. I'll call you on Friday after I brief them."

— CHAPTER 21 —

The abandoned village of Berrefjord sat at the base of the steep valley. It had been literally carved out of the slope in a series of interconnected terraces that descended to the old stone pier at the water's edge. The valley was flanked on both sides by cliffs that looked as if it they had been gouged out of the mountain. Where the cliffs met the water, there were piles of granite chunks that had crashed down from above. The crash that dislodged the rune stone that Ingvild had discovered looked to have happened recently from the unweathered color of the rock.

Nate had carefully anchored the *Loki* so the bow winch was directly over the spot where Ingvild found the first stone. Since this positioned the bow only 20 feet from the jagged shore he had set all three anchors. Although the *Loki* seemed secure, Nate was ready to reposition the boat farther offshore if the weather showed any sign of turning foul.

The water was amazingly clear. Nate and Serene could watch every move made by Henry and Ingvild at the depth of fifteen feet. Only their air bubbles breaking the surface blurred their view from time to time. It was easy to see what they were doing, simply examining each rock carefully from every angle. Though it was mid-June, the water was still ice cold, and Henry's teeth chattered even though he was protected by a heavy duty wetsuit that was specially designed for North Sea diving. Ingvild, on the other hand, did not seem to mind the cold water and jokingly claimed that Norwegians, like Eskimos, have extra layers of fat under their skin to keep them warm.

After several dives, Henry and Ingvild surfaced with great excitement and called for the winch cable. After repeated warnings from Nate and Serene to be careful, they submerged and were back on board within ten minutes.

On removing his mask, Henry said, "It doesn't look like it weighs too much! Wait until we get out of this gear, and we'll give you a hand." Ingvild and Henry went below to change into dry clothes.

Nate had cleverly rigged the winch cable to a crane he had fashioned using an extra spar. He attached one end of the spar to the bottom of the main mast and used block and tackle secured to the top of the mast to raise and lower the boom. This enabled him to pivot the crane out over the water and back over to the deck.

By the time Nate fired up the engine to power the electric winch, Ingvild and Henry were back on deck to assist. Nate engaged the winch. As the rock lifted off the bottom, the bow of the *Loki* dipped lower into the water. When the rock broke the surface, Nate stopped the winch to inspect the catch.

"Before I bring it aboard, spread out the life jackets on deck so we don't mar it," Nate said. Serene got the jackets from the wheelhouse and laid them on the deck while Henry unhitched and lowered the safety lines. Nate slowly raised the rock until it was a few feet above deck height and locked the winch gear in place. Nate pushed on the boom and slowly swung the rock around while Henry guided it with a boat hook. Once the rock was positioned directly over the life jackets, Nate unlashed the rope to the block and tackle and lowered the rock. "That was easy!" said Nate.

"Sure! It's always easy when you have a marine engineer on board," said Ingvild proudly as she knelt to examine the flat side of the stone that was coated with green algae.

"I'll get some detergent and a brush," said Serene.

Nate knelt down beside Ingvild who was busily wiping away the slime with her hand. "There are runes here. I could more feel them underwater than actually see them. Many runes!"

After scrubbing and rinsing, the surface of the stone revealed three long lines of runes that were cut off at both ends where the rock had broken. A foot below the bottom row was the black stripe of the tidal line.

Ingvild sat cross-legged in front of the stone looking at the inscriptions and referring to her books and research materials. Occasionally she would make a note on her pad. Nate, Henry and Serene went below so as not to disturb her. Two hours later, Ingvild entered the main cabin with her pad in hand, a puzzled look on her face.

"Any luck?" Nate asked.

Ingvild sat at the booth, Henry poured her a cup of coffee and she began reading from her notes. "It appears to translate as something like this. 'Ingvild. of Edred went to her family in the small knorr to the land of the Danes ... '"

"What's a knorr, again?" interrupted Serene.

"It looks like a Viking dragon ship, but much fatter ... more for carrying cargo."

"Sorry, I forgot," Serene apologized.

"That's okay. The next part says there was a big storm and the winds blew them across the great sea. After many days, they found a island where they drank sweet wine."

"That could be Madeira, or the Azores," said Nate. "I've been to both, and they are renowned for their sweet wines. If they were blown down south through the English Channel it would make sense," he added.

"Hum ... may be," replied Ingvild. "But here we call it the *Norway Channel*," she jested. "Then it says they suffered greatly until they found the blue islands of black people, or black islands of blue people ... probably the former!" she laughed and then continued. "But they did not go to the land for fear?" said Ingvild in a perplexed tone of voice.

"Could be the Caribbean," said Henry. "From the sea those islands look bluish and the black people could have been Caribs, which were very warlike tribes who practiced cannibalism. Maybe that's why they found fear! If they were farther south, there would have been Arawacks who had light brown skin and were more peaceful."

"Or they could have been off the African coast," said Nate.

"Anything else?" asked Serene.

"In the sea of weak winds, a home wind blew them to the dying sun. What does that mean?" asked Ingvild.

"I think Henry is right. Sounds to me they entered the Gulf of Mexico. It's a sea of light winds compared to the Atlantic. The home wind is obviously means blowing to the north, which is where they wanted to go. The dying sun is west. Where it sets. Bet ya they was sailing north by west. What else does it say?" said Nate.

"The last part is broken off. There's only one other rune, the symbol for the sun."

"Henry, don't get me wrong. I just love what we're doing here, but you and I have got to get away by ourselves for a while."

"That would be great, Serene, but I think it would break Ingvild's heart if we pulled up anchor now. Maybe Nate's, too," said Henry as he pulled on his pants.

"I'm only suggesting you and I take the day off, launch that dinghy, and poke around Berrefjord."

"You have the best ideas! I could use a break. I don't think they'll miss us at all," said Henry as he winked and left the stateroom.

Everyone had a few good laughs getting the little dinghy launched and rigging the tiny sail. With a packed lunch, a bottle of wine and a light breeze, Henry and Serene sailed off toward the north shore where Ingvild had earlier pointed out the location of the summer cottages. It was another brilliant summer day, and although they were squeezed tightly into the dinghy, they felt a new sense of freedom.

"Serene, have you seen my blue hat, the one you got me in Provincetown?"

"No. It's probably somewhere on the boat. Why?"

"I haven't been able to find it. My nose is sunburned, and it looks like another hot day."

"Poor Henry," she said as she leaned over and kissed him square on the nose. "Henry is there something odd about this place? Do you feel different since we've been here?"

"You mean ... how's my measuring device?" They both laughed, and Henry continued in a more serious tone of voice. "As a matter of fact, I've never felt better ... I mean in my entire life. My senses seem keener here, and I seem to be ... it's difficult to articulate."

"Do you feel more at peace with yourself?" asked Serene.

"Without doubt. But that's not what I was trying to get at. It's sort of a new state of mind. In the past there's always been this quiet, whispering voice inside my head weighing the pros and cons of every decision and action. It's perfectly normal I suppose, just everyday thoughts reviewing options. But here my thoughts are whole, more unified, less suspicious and questioning. That sound crazy, honey?"

"No. To a large extent that describes how I've been feeling lately. I've noticed a definite change in myself since we've been here. That's why I asked."

"How do you see it?"

"Something is going on. That's for sure. Yesterday, while Nate and I were watching you diving, this weird thought popped in my head. It suddenly occurred to me that I felt more like my real self. I've never thought anything like that before!"

"It could be that we've both never been this relaxed. After all, we've been on vacation for nearly two months. It's been pleasant to say the least," said Henry.

"I suppose you're right. But whenever I'd been vacationing before, I was always anxious to keep moving on to the next new thing, never quite satisfied. You know what I mean?"

"Yup. There's something different here. Nate's noticed it, too. I've seen some definite changes in him as well. He mentioned the other day that he feels a 'constancy' in himself. I almost understand what he means."

"Hmm, constancy. Yes! Persisting. Kind of like a sustained, underlying sound that that you can't quite hear. Only this is a feeling. Anyway, I'm glad we're here, and I don't want to leave. All I need is a little dinghy ride once in a while," said Serene with a giggle.

In southern Norway in June, you can still read a newspaper outdoors at midnight by the soft light of sun just over the horizon and reflected back by the sky. It was nearly midnight by the time Henry tacked the dinghy back and forth to cross the fjord and reach the *Loki*.

"Look, Serene!" said Henry. "There's a yellow launch tied along side."

"Looks like one of those rental boats I saw in town. Some people on an outing, I suppose."

As they drew closer, they saw Sven on deck waving and putting his finger over his lips for them to be quiet.

Henry lowered the sail and deftly brought the dinghy alongside. As soon as the dinghy's bumpers touched the *Loki's* hull, Serene took the bowline and stepped quietly aboard. Henry followed.

Sven motioned to follow him. He led them to the bow, stopped at the winch and whispered, "Helge telephoned last night for me to work for the boat rental company today and guide this man Ryan here. He below. Helge say he ask questions in Flekkefjord about you. A detective, Helge say. Ryan showed your photos to cousin Rom and told him he was your friend."

Henry and Serene looked at each other. They both saw fear. Serene sat on the winch and sighed deeply. Henry was stunned in disbelief. His head slumped in thought. After a few seconds, Henry whispered to Sven, "Did he say anything to you about us?"

"No. I say I do not understand English good. He not talk much. Ryan saw boat anchored. He talked to Ingvild and Nate. Ingvild was surprised I was the guide. I tell her I help a sick friend for the day. They have been talking and drinking coffee for hours."

"This guy Ryan. Does he look dangerous?" asked Henry.

"No! Very nice man. I like him," Sven answered with a grin.

"Okay. We'll play dumb. Let's see what this guy is up to," said Henry.

"Think he's connected to the 'Red Cross' affair?" asked Serene with a tremor in her voice.

"What else."

"I have this," said Sven as he pulled out his shirt to reveal a pistol tucked in his belt.

"Thanks, Sven," said Serene. "Please try to avoid any violence."

"Yes, Sven, let's avoid trouble at all costs. If you don't mind, would you stand guard on deck while we go below?"

"Good," agreed Sven. "I will come if I hear trouble. That's why Helge sent me."

"Thanks," said Serene.

— Chapter 22 —

"I thought I heard footsteps on deck," said Nate as Serene and Henry entered the main salon. Boxer stood as they reached the table and introduced himself with a handshake, first to Serene and then to Henry.

After the introductions, Boxer said, "I want to thank you for the hospitality of the boat. I understand you are the owners."

"Our pleasure, Mr. Ryan," said Serene politely. "Please sit down."

"Call me Boxer. Everyone does."

"Did you have a nice sail?" asked Ingvild.

"We had a wonderful day. Henry and I agreed that as much as we love you and Nate, we have to get off by ourselves once in a while. We just love that little boat, Nate. You made her beautiful. Henry and I have decided to name her the *Princess Ingvild.*"

"Yup, we're going to paint the name on her stern," said Henry.

"And a good name it is," said Nate as he put his arm around Ingvild's shoulder and gave her a friendly hug.

"So, Boxer, what brings you to Berrefjord … to Norway?" Henry asked.

Before Boxer could speak Nate interrupted excitedly. "Ya not going to believe this! Boxer here came for the same reason we did, the tides!"

"You're kidding!" said Henry.

"Remarkable," added Serene.

"Yes. This is the only place that doesn't have tides. That's what sparked my curiosity. I had some time so I thought I'd see for myself," said Boxer.

"And, what line of work are you in?" asked Henry.

"I'm an electrical engineer by profession, but for the past several years, I've been mostly engaged in research," Boxer said modestly.

"That field has always fascinated me. How does one become an electrical engineer?" asked Henry.

"I suppose you have to have an interest in the subject. Me, I tinkered with electricity in high school for a science project and was offered a scholarship."

"To which school?" asked Henry.

"Stevens Institute in Hoboken. I grew up in Jersey City."

"Great school. I'm originally from Nutley myself. Another coincidence!"

"The sun never sets on the Jersey empire. Here's to the Garden State," said Boxer as he lifted his coffee mug.

"Boxer's been telling us about a new theory he's been working on. It's quite amazing. Boxer, would you mind explaining it to Henry and Serene," asked Ingvild.

"Of course I wouldn't mind, but I'm sure Henry and Serene are tired from their outing and aren't interested in my babble. Besides, it's getting late, and I'm sure Sven will be wanting to get back to town. I've already imposed enough on your kindness."

"Boxer, I'm sure Sven would prefer to stay overnight here and go back in the morning. Going through those skerries at night is dangerous. You're welcome to sleep over as well. You can have my cabin, and I can sack out with Nate and Sven on the couches. There's plenty of room as you can see," said Ingvild as she pointed to the couches in the salon. Before Boxer could answer, Ingvild sprang from the table and said, "I'll check with Sven." A few seconds later Ingvild returned with Sven who had a wide toothy smile on his face.

"*Jah. Jah.* Morning better. Many rocks," said Sven.

Ingvild pulled out a sleeping bag from a locker, threw it to Sven and in Norwegian told him he could sleep on the couch in the wheelhouse. Sven left with the same smile he arrived with.

"Ingvild, you make it impossible for a man to say no," Boxer jested.

"You have revealed my true genius," she quipped. Everyone laughed.

"Great!" said Serene. "Now tell us about your theory. Henry and I are wide awake. We had a very relaxing day." As she said this she caressed Henry's cheek with her hand and gave him a provocative look.

"Well, I guess I'm on the spot," Boxer began to say when Ingvild interrupted.

"In more ways than you know. Sorry, I'll explain later. Just remember 'spot.' Please go on," said Ingvild.

"Ingvild, you remind me of an intricate jigsaw puzzle I once bought," said Boxer in an avuncular tone.

"How so?"

"It came in a sealed box, I opened it carefully and put every piece on the table. I worked on it for days, but could not finish it no matter how hard I tried.

You know why? There was one missing piece. It drove me crazy. Be assured, I will not leave here until you tell me everything about that spot."

Ingvild blushed while everyone laughed. "So obviously I am not on the spot, at least not yet," she said.

Boxer continued, "My theory, I have recently named 'Surfacing' for lack of a better description. From my brief visit here with Nate and Ingvild, I have gathered they are extremely well read and highly intelligent. I assume this is also true of you two, as most companions seek similar company. I must preface my theory this way because I know that less intelligent, closed-minded people would find my ideas absolutely absurd. And, who knows? They may be right. You will have to judge for yourselves.

"To put it simply, I believe that we have not even scratched the surface of the potential of the human mind. Not a potential that may evolve over future time, or that we have the capacity to develop within our own lifetimes, rather an untapped wealth of intelligence that currently exists in each of us, but which is unavailable for reasons I will explain.

"I base my theory on the fact that nature, by necessity, has developed man over millions of years as a creature primarily designed to reproduce though our ability to survive. Obviously, I think we can all agree on that for without our ancestors ability to mature and reproduce none of us would be sitting here tonight. Survival itself, I believe and many have thought, is only possible because our sensory perception to those innumerable factors in the environment that threaten our survival trigger human reactions which are necessary to sustain that survival. Over time, those reactions become instinctual and permanent only to the extent they remain useful.

"My theory, I must tell you, is also based on singularity of mind and body. In other words, I'm a non-dualist. I believe the mind and body are one in the same. I have come to believe that *all* reactive memories have been stored, not just in the brain, but also widely dispersed throughout the body's cellular structure. When I say *all*, I mean all the reactive memories of the living individual plus all the reactive memories that have been accumulated over the full span of his or her genetic history. If I am boring you, or if this is too bizarre for table talk, please stop me now," said Boxer.

"On the contrary, it's very thought provoking," said Serene. "I do have a question, however. Are you saying that we remember everything that happens to us as well as everything that has ever happened to all of our ancestors?"

"Yes! But not in a way that you would consider specific memories, such as remembering a house you lived in as a small child, or your first bicycle, or lines from a favorite poem. I mean those ingrained memories of intelligent decisions and actions that have been validated by the fact they have positively contributed to the survival of a family line and the resulting living individual.

"My theory rests on the foundation that man is not an animal designed for remembering, but rather designed for *forgetting*. We must forget everything that is *not* immediately useful for our preservation and *only* retain only those memories that are necessary to survival.

Now, the key point in my theory is this. Do those lost memories that were forged through perception into useful intelligence, which are not critical to today's immediate survival, exist somehow, somewhere in our present biological form? I became convinced they do exist.

"Based on that premise, I devised an experiment that is attempting to prove that this storehouse of deeply buried intelligence can be retrieved and be useful."

"That is a far out idea!" declared Henry. "I must admit, however, I follow the logic of what you're saying. But, tell me about your experiment."

Boxer told about the Surfacing Technique he had developed for himself, how he had his own IQ benchmarked by tests, and how he had been practicing the meditation and self-hypnosis technique several times a day for nearly a month.

"Wow!" said Serene. "You and Nate have a lot in common. Has he told you about his own experiment with the tides?"

"Yes, in fact, he did just before you and Henry arrived. An amazing coincidence I confess. Then again, coincidences are amazing."

"Henry and I *are* one of those amazing coincidences," said Serene as she squeezed Henry's arm.

"What's with all this self-experimentation is what I want to know?" said Ingvild who had been quietly listening for a change.

"Ingvild, to my way of thinking, ya have to look at it this way," explained Nate, "we are all self-experiments when ya hit rock bottom. We begin life as a biological experiment of our parents. They start us off by mixing up genetic fluids, and the experiment is launched into this old world to see what happens. How it turns out depends to a large measure on the genes ya start with, but is nevertheless at the whim of nature and the environment in which it finds itself. It could fail at any time, ya know. If it proceeds, and as it grows the experiment gains the ability of limited self-determination and in rare cases develops the intelligence and willpower to affect great things or horrible things, as the case may be.

"In essence we are our own self-experiment and in the end the only experiment that counts. If the experiment turns out good, it's good for everybody on Planet Dirt. If it turns out bad, good people suffer. I also agree with Boxer that most people are unaware of their own potential. Remember, the ancient Chinese believed that life is limited but knowledge is limitless. No matter how educated or enlightened we think we are, we are all stupid when it comes to realizing what we really are, never mind what we could be. And finally, the results of anyone else's experiment are always questionable when it comes to you. We have to be our own arbiters of the truth as we see it."

"Nate, you are a man after my own heart! You've hit the nail square on the head. One of the biggest problems I see in this world is people who are living by the truths of others rather than discovering their own. The intractable mechanisms of the bureaucratic educational systems are responsible to a large degree. A true human tragedy."

"So, Boxer what has your experiment revealed thus far?" asked Ingvild.

"All I can give you is a very preliminary, a subjective evaluation," said Boxer as he laughed at himself. "There's no question that I have experienced a marked increase in my intellectual power. I noticed an improvement after only of week of practicing the surfacing technique. Since then there has been a gradual improvement each day, that is, until I arrived in Flekkefjord. You may not believe this, but here my improvement has soared beyond anything I expected. My progress here has also been accompanied by a phenomenal sense of calmness, a sense well being, and a new clearness to my thinking ... hard to describe. I'm sure you all think I'm a lunatic."

"Far from it," said Henry. "Most thinking people are searching for something or other. All of us here have that in common."

"I try to not dismiss any new idea I encounter," said Ingvild. "At least not right away," she added with a laugh.

"What do you think, Serene?" Boxer asked. Serene did not answer immediately and ran her slender finger around the rim of her coffee mug for several seconds in thought.

"Honestly, I don't know what to think. The theory you have put forward is quite interesting. I'm in no position to question it, nor do I want to. The only question I have is this. Why have you come here under false pretenses after having shown our photos to Rom and saying that you were our friend?"

A dead silence fell. Every eye fixed on Boxer. The silence was broken by footsteps. Sven entered the cabin without his smile and his hand flat against his belt. He had been listening from the wheelhouse door. Without a word, he sat down on the couch opposite the table.

"You've found me out," said Boxer as he slumped back in his chair. "I should have never come here," he added with a sigh and mumbling to himself.

"We know why you came!" shouted Henry in a rare outburst of anger. "Now you present us with a problem."

"Will someone *please* tell me what's going on here?" demanded Ingvild.

"It's a long story, Ingvild. Before I met Henry, he was working on a container ship and was blown overboard in a storm. He found a floating container that saved his life. He broke into the container and found it filled with Red Cross relief supplies and ten million dollars in cash that was being smuggled by the mob.

"Henry built a raft from the materials in the container and took the money just as the container sunk. I found him weeks later on a deserted island near our hotel in Fiji. Henry's real name is Kevin McCall. He changed it because he feared, correctly as it turns out, that the mob would be looking for him thinking he stole the money.

"One day this nasty goon, Dom Scardino, showed up at our hotel, kidnapped me and forced me to take him to the deserted island where Henry was in hiding. By this time, Henry and I had become lovers. While Scardino was pushing me around the island, Henry was spying on us waiting for an opportunity to rescue me. It came when we went to the top of the hill during a thunderstorm. Henry charged this guy with a steel spear he had made on the container. Scardino knocked Henry down with his pistol and picked up the spear. Then a huge bolt of lightning hit the spear, and Scardino was instantly killed.

"We took his body back to the hotel and made it look as if he had been playing golf when he was struck. The island authorities bought the story, and we thought the mob bought it too. Anonymously, Henry sent the money to the Red Cross in New Guinea where the supplies had been originally destined. We thought we were free and clear of the whole mess, that is, until Mr. Ryan showed up here today."

"That's quite a different version than I was told," said Boxer. "Quite different. When I accepted this case, Henry, I was told that you planned and hijacked the money. It was only after I got into the case that I learned you gave the money to the Red Cross."

"How on Earth did you find that out?" asked Serene.

"Let me explain. I was a high school friend of Philly "Gumdrops"

Costello. He was smuggling the cash. That's what he does for a living, among other things. We grew up in the same neighborhood, and we stayed in touch over the years, mostly him calling me. After I retired from engineering, I began doing private investigations, part-time, in order to pursue my personal interests. Philly always tried to steer business my way. I always politely declined because I knew he was connected. A few months ago, Philly called me. This time he begged me to help him with a personal matter. I was extremely reluctant to do so, but I was desperate for money. I have some income from my patents, but I'd been ignoring the detective work for my private studies and dug myself and my family into a financial hole. Philly offered me a lot of money to take this case. He said he'd been ripped off and he was near financial ruin. I weakened and took the case, but only to do the investigation.

"We had a clear understanding that after I found you I would call him and then get out of the way. No way did I want to become involved with violence. I knew I was fooling myself. Trying to justify something that I knew was wrong, but I desperately needed the money. I'm truly sorry.

"To answer your question, Serene, Philly read in the paper that the missing Henry Langston had returned home. That's what prompted him to call me. I'm very good at finding things. But during my investigation, I learned a lot about you two that didn't add up. When I found out the Red Cross got the money anonymously, it proved that you didn't steal it. From talking with various people in New Jersey, Fiji, Mandavu, Cape Cod and with Rom the other day, I learned that you are both nice, honest people. I found that to be true of Nate as well. That's probably my real reason for coming here myself. I already knew from Rom that you were here in Berrefjord. I didn't have to come here myself. Honestly, I was more curious to see the people I'd been tracking. My conscience has been nagging me all through this case. I think I secretly wanted to warn you. I don't want any blood on my hands," said Boxer.

Light was beginning to stream through the portholes. Even though several pots of coffee had been consumed the company was bleary eyed. Henry stretched, and yawned saying, "I think we all need some rest. Boxer, we can discuss this later. Come, I will show you to Ingvild's cabin. Good night all."

Sven, who looked as though he was sleeping, rose from the couch and returned to the wheelhouse. Serene cleaned off the table. Nate and Ingvild pulled out sleeping bags from the locker and sprawled on the couches. Before Serene was through with her chores, Nate and Ingvild were fast asleep with their hands touching.

When Serene entered their cabin she found Henry loading the small shotgun. "I hope this doesn't frighten you," Henry whispered.

"No, I'm a practical girl."

— CHAPTER 23 —

Cars for Stars was located in a warehouse in a slum-infested neighborhood one block off McCarter Highway in Newark. Philly had no problem finding it as it occupied a large city block. A big, flashy art deco style sign looked out of place on the nineteenth century brick factory. Roll after roll of razor wire topped the ten-foot chain link fence, which surrounded it. As he pulled his Cadillac up to the chained gate he was greeted by a pack of vicious looking dogs with saliva running from their mouths as they jumped against the gate. "No need for an intercom. People five blocks away know I'm here," Philly laughed to himself.

Within minutes a fat, greasy man in blue coveralls with a tipped up welding mask came out of a small green door, looked at Philly's car and pushed a button on the wall. A huge metal garage door opened. The man unlocked the gate, kicked and yelled at the dogs who ran off looking disappointed, opened the gate, and motioned Philly to drive inside.

Old mercury vapor lamps cast a surrealistic yellowish light over rows of the oddest assortment of vehicles he had ever seen. Overhead signs directed him through the lanes to the office where he saw neatly painted visitor parking slots each with a big white star. Philly was surprised to see that the office was quite modern, black metal and tinted glass. It was literally a new structure built inside the cavernous old one.

He walked through the entrance and was greeted by clean, fresh air, a sharp contrast to the stale, toxic smell in the warehouse. The décor was tastefully corporate. The Moran brothers looked prosperous. Philly knew them when their father ran numbers out of a gas station in Jersey City.

A slim Hispanic receptionist, a would-be model or movie star Philly guessed, took his name and asked him to take a seat. Philly stood at the desk, and within ten seconds Joey Moran, the youngest brother, burst through the padded swinging doors with a nervous, phony smile on his twenty-ish face.

"Welcome to *Cars for Stars*, Mr. Costello," blabbered Joey. "I'm Joey. Don't know if you remember me?" he said as he pumped Philly's hand.

"Sure, Joey. You're the retarded brother, right?" said Philly.

"Good one! Good one!" stammered Joey. "Let me show you to Mike's office. Jimmy and Pete have come in for the meet." Joey led him though a large room of gray and mauve cubicles with dozens of people working on headsets and computers, many of whom were attractive young women. Joey stopped at a black, glass revolving door. "This is Mike's office," said Joey as he motioned Philly to push through. The office was one room, almost the size of a basketball court with twenty-foot high ceilings. The far wall was steam-cleaned brick with a series of floor to ceiling glass block windows. Another wall displayed an enormous antique gas station sign of a red flying horse.

"Mr. Gumdrops!" bellowed a large, gray bearded man dressed casually in black. He stood in front of an antique roll top desk set against the brick wall.

"Mike! You're looking fat and happy these days," said Philly as the two large men embraced. This was followed by embraces with Jimmy and Pete and a few minutes of small talk with the four brothers. A tiny waiter in a white smock brought a tray of Portuguese pastries, placed them on a large round conference table, and took orders for coffee.

Jimmy Moran was the eldest and by far the toughest of the brothers, the de facto enforcer. A tall, lanky Irishman of about fifty, it was said he could charm the birds out of the trees when it suited his purposes. Over the years, he affected a brogue developed through his long-standing association with the Irish Republican Army. He was well known for his cashmere turtleneck sweaters and leather patched shooting jackets he imported from the old sod.

Over the years, Jimmy had called on Philly several times for one of his 'short' containers, one specially built for smuggling. A false wall hid a two-foot deep hidden compartment, which could be loaded with arms, drugs, explosives, or whatever. Philly did not care as long as he was paid cash. He would drop off an empty container, pick it up after it was loaded, and ship it to Ireland. Ownership of the actual container was blind, the customs declarations were false, and if caught, Philly could always say, "I don't know nothing. I'm just the freight forwarder." He was totally insulated. Jimmy would fill the rest of the container with a tangle of used auto parts. No sane customs inspector would think to unload a box of junk.

Mike was the smart one, a born entrepreneur and a business graduate from Seton Hall University in South Orange. He ran the family businesses, which consisted of a modeling agency/escort service, a real estate company that specialized in urban renewal scams and a used auto parts company which was supplied by their chop shops. The wellspring of their success came from the longtime family business of car theft. They had risen to be the best in Newark, quite an accomplishment in the car stealing capital of the world. Port Newark/ Elizabeth is the largest east coast importer of automobiles and trucks. A never-ending stream of car ships dock there. They are attacked by gangs of longshoremen who are driven by vans into the ships, which are more akin to floating, multilevel parking garages. The drivers speed the vehicles to vast, fenced in parking lots, and as instructed, leave the doors unlocked and the keys inside the vehicles. The Morans take over from there as they had been doing for decades. Based on insider information, they select the cars they want and pay off the right people to look the wrong way at the right time. They had been known to steal up to thirty cars in one shot.

The Morans got their drivers through deals with neighborhood gang leaders. Just like their unionized counterparts, they drove their thieves to the port in vans. Then they cut away a section of chain link fence, the drivers would be directed to the selected inventory and the merchandise driven to a nearby Moran warehouse. The Morans had been known to employ portable ramps to bridge the drainage ditches next to the fences. The primary driver qualification was that he be under sixteen years of age. If a teen were caught, they would hardly ever spend a night in jail. The precious few juvenile cells in Essex County were reserved for rapists, armed robbers and murderers. In Newark, car theft was treated more like a parking ticket. Some juveniles had rap sheets with hundreds of possession of stolen vehicle arrests, yet until they came of age, they never received more than endless probation.

Pete was the quiet brother, the third eldest. Because he said little, people never knew what to make of him. Philly saw Pete more frequently than the others. They did business shipping stolen luxury cars in containers, mostly to the Caribbean, Central and South America.

Joey was the baby. Now in his mid twenties, Philly remembered him as a drooling toddler from the old neighborhood. Today he dressed sharply and seemed like a nice kid.

"So Mike, what's with this Cars for Stars business?" asked Philly.

"It's a gold mine, Philly. Almost legit. We'd been doing it sub rosa for years through the New York families with connections in the film business. Used to be mostly for police cruisers that they could crash up. We'd buy 'em up for peanuts at city auctions and store them in the warehouse. We'd paint 'em up however they wanted and rent at outrageous rates. Then we'd charge to haul away the wrecks, back here, naturally, where we'd patched 'em up and rent 'em again.

"Around five years ago we had a boom in film and TV on the east coast. That's when Joey came into the business. He started handling the calls. Whatever anybody wanted, Joey told 'em we had it. He'd either boost it or buy it, but he always delivered. Now we got everything, old moving trucks, double-decker buses, old cars, new cars, hot rods. We even got a Sherman tank. Whatever they want, Joey delivers it," boasted Mike as he leaned over and patted Joey on the shoulder.

"You Moran boys was always good," said Philly. "Is this place clean?" asked Philly as he looked around the room.

"Clean as a nun's bib. Just had it swept. This place is like a fortress," answered Jimmy.

"I saw when I came in," laughed Philly.

"Even our neighborly thieves got the word," Mike added.

"Okay. Like I said on the phone, I got this nagging problem I'd like you boys to clean up." Philly explained the McCall situation.

"Norway? That's a problem these days. You can't get a gun on a plane anymore. Well, at least it's harder," said Mike.

"Not a problem for me," said Jimmy. "I can get the men and materials in from Ireland, and go to Norway by small boat."

"I was hoping for something like that, Jimmy. Far as I know, these people are on their boat anchored in a remote fjord. It should be easy," said Philly.

"Nothing's easy these days. It'll cost primo, Philly," said Jimmy.

"That I expected, Jimmy. I want the best for those two, actually three, another guy named Nate, I mentioned."

— Chapter 24 —

By mid morning they had gathered at the winch with cups of hot coffee in their hands. Boxer was still sleeping soundly in Ingvild's cabin. Serene and Henry had slept uneasily. Sven had stayed awake, yet he looked to be the most rested. Nate and Ingvild awoke early and confessed to only a few hours sleep.

"Now what do ya think we should do?" asked Nate with a yawn.

"I haven't a clue. I'm hardly awake yet," replied Henry.

"The best thing, I think, is for Sven and I to go back to town with Boxer and for you guys to sail away," said Ingvild.

"That sucks!" declared Serene in no uncertain terms. "I love it here, and we've got to look for more stones."

"I'd hate to pull up anchor and leave Ingvild in the lurch," Nate gulped as a blush came over his face. "What do ya think, Sven?" he added.

"I would have to speak to Helge. I heard all the talk last night. Helge always knows."

"I'm sorry for this trouble," said Henry with a sigh. "I'm not afraid of Boxer. In fact, I like him, and I believe him when he said he regretted getting involved. It's his employer Costello that worries me. I've got to put an end to this somehow. Getting out of here was my first reaction, but there's a lot to what Serene said. I really don't want to go. If we did run now, I'd always be looking over my shoulder. There must be someway out of this."

Just then Boxer stumbled out of the wheelhouse door spilling black coffee from his mug and muttering something to himself. When he saw the others standing on the foredeck, he walked forward with a serious look on his face and said, "Have you decided what to do with me?"

"Yes!" said Ingvild. And then added in a singsong Scandinavian accent: "We are going to tie a heavy stone to your neck and put the stone in the fjord. What do you think of that?"

Boxer laughed spilling more coffee. "I have a better idea. Today is Wednesday, and I am supposed to call Philly on Friday to confirm I found you. I'll call him today and tell him you vanished and that I have no clue where you went. I'll tell him your case is a waste of his time and mine. When I get back to the States, I'm going to return the fees and expenses he's fronted. Then my conscience will be clear, and I can get on with better things."

Henry looked Boxer directly in the eyes and said, "That sounds good, Boxer. We trust you to do that, but to be absolutely sure, we want to listen in on the conversation, just to make sure that Costello has given up looking for us. Serene and I have decided that we must put an end to this. We can't live like this any longer. Besides, now we've got Nate, Ingvild and Sven involved in our mess. Maybe even Helge and Rom. This Costello is determined and relentless. We've got to be certain."

"I have no problem with that. I understand. There's one little twist, however, I failed to mention, but I don't think it's going to be a problem. When I last spoke to Philly, he said something about sending the Moran brothers over here to follow up on my detective work. I think you know what he meant by that, but I don't think he'll make that move until he hears from me on Friday."

"Who are the Moran brothers?" asked Serene.

"I don't know them," said Boxer. "But I assume they're goons. Philly knows a lot of people like that."

"I'm sure," said Serene.

"Well, now that that's settled. How about looking for rune stones!" piped up Ingvild.

"I was thinking of going back to bed, Ingvild, but a few dives are definitely more appealing," said Henry sarcastically.

"May as well, ya know. It's a fair day for it, all considered," said Nate.

"Sven, I think we'll be fine here if you want to take Boxer back to the hotel," suggested Ingvild.

"I'd rest easier if Boxer stayed aboard. We can take him back on Friday morning in your boat, Ingvild. Sven, you can take off if you like," said Henry.

"I can stay and help with the diving. I am on vacation," said Sven in a perfect American accent.

Boxer laughed. "You sure had me fooled, Sven. Henry, I don't mind staying here. In fact, I'd very much like it. I'd just be hanging around the hotel anyway."

With everything settled for the moment, the crew of the *Loki* enjoyed a large, late breakfast during which Ingvild told Boxer and Sven about her runes. After breakfast, Henry, Ingvild and Sven dove to search for more stones. Within fifteen minutes of the first dive, they surfaced and asked for the winch. Five minutes later, Ingvild surfaced and climbed aboard.

"Nate, I am going to tug on the line three times to let Henry and Sven know that we're ready. Then lift at the slowest possible speed, and they are going to guide a very large slab, about three meters long, out of an awkward position," said Ingvild.

Ingvild tugged on the line, and Nate engaged the drive, which began to move the steel cable at a snail's pace. "If it's that big, I'll stay at this speed," said Nate.

Minutes later, Henry and Sven broke the surface, climbed aboard, removed their gear, and went to the winch. A blurry image of the stone soon resolved into focus as it neared the surface and broke water. Nate locked the winch in place. Meanwhile, Ingvild and Serene had spread out the life jackets and removed the safety lines.

"It looks heavy. I hope this little crane I rigged will hold. I'll man the winch. Henry, Sven and Boxer, you boys grab fast to that tackle line and heave to gain a bit 'o slack so Serene can unlash the rope. Ingvild, after we lift the stone high enough, ya pull that line and swing it aboard, slow. Everybody ready!" commanded Nate.

Nate used the winch to raise the stone out of the water and engaged the locking gear. Then the men heaved on the block and tackle to raise the crane higher and the sounds of strain on the ropes became unsettling. By that time, Nate had his head down on the deck eyeballing the stone to see if there was enough clearance to swing it aboard. He motioned to Ingvild to start pivoting and then went to assist her by braking the great slab as it swung over the deck. They lowered it slowly onto the deck, which groaned as the weight settled. A collective sigh of relief from the crew was audible.

"That's some whopper you caught, Ingvild!" exclaimed Nate.

"Yes, with many, many runes!" she replied as she jumped up and down with joy.

After washing and scrubbing the stone, Ingvild was once again left alone with her papers to begin the translation. The rest of the crew went below for an afternoon snooze.

A few hours later, they assembled in the main salon, everyone except Ingvild, who was still working on deck in the dimming light. Henry was in the middle of explaining the runes to Boxer. "Our best guess was that Princess

Ingvild had entered the Gulf of Mexico, and they were headed north by west when the runes ended on the last stone. Oh yes, then there was another symbol for the sun. The big slab looks like a continuation of the story. The broken edges match up perfectly."

"Henry, on the first stone, did you say she brought back the moon back from the land of the sun?" asked Boxer.

"Yup, that's the mystery, and why we're here. Nate thinks it has to do with the tides because the runes are carved just above the water line and dead parallel to them. We learned from Ingvild that this is an unusual place to find runes, so close down to the water, that is. The only other carvings ever found close to the water are what they call mooring holes. Those old Vikings didn't take any chances with their ships. When they stopped along the shore to spend the night they would send men ashore with hammers and hand drills to bore holes in the rock, two or three feet deep. Then they inserted a mooring pin, a long iron rod with an eyehole at the top. That's how they anchored the ship, not trusting to tie up to a tree or rock. Ingvild pointed out several holes to us."

"Clever," said Boxer. "People today don't give enough credit to the ingenuity and hard work of the ancients, or their raw intelligence. In terms of pure perception of life, we don't know much more than they did."

"Maybe a might less," chuckled Nate.

"I know exactly what you mean, Nate, or at least I think I do. Today, much of the information that fogs up our thinking is of a conceptual nature, or a jumble of trivial facts totally unrelated to our lives. I fear it's diminished our perception of the reality we face at everyday. That's why most people are alienated, oblivious to nature and the people around them. They watch weather reports on TV rather than open a window. They act like vegetables in many ways, extremely passive, afraid to express themselves much less discuss issues that force them to venture an opinion. Many people have no concept of how other people feel, or perhaps not even how they feel themselves," said Boxer.

"I agree with ya. Our heads are stuffed with facts and figures and theories, dogmas, laws, systems, formulas and histories. So much claptrap in there it's a wonder there's any room for genuine personal thought anymore," said Nate.

"Exactly! Too much time is spent trying to figure out what the so-called experts are saying about a subject and not enough time thinking a subject through for yourself. I always get a good laugh when I hear some educator saying that the first job of education is to develop 'critical thinking' in their students. Next day he goes back to the classroom and spoon-feeds their heads with preapproved, prepackaged thought that they have to learn like trained elephants so they can perform on homework and tests. Talk about brainwashing," said Boxer.

"You two are a pair of odd socks," gasped Serene. "Haven't the great thinkers of the world already gone though the metal gymnastics and distilled their findings into knowledge and wisdom that can benefit others?"

"Ya got a point there, Serene. Education is and can be a wonderful thing. But what I think what our friend Boxer here and I are talking about, and I suspect that some of those great thinkers would agree on is this, a person has to do the hard work of thinking through a subject on his own for it to have meaning as an internalized truth. Otherwise, formal learning can be mere trivia, an ersatz measurement of intellectual progress, or used to exercise power over the less educated, for example, but never valid to the student in the sense of being 'known.' That's what we are talking about.

"Take some of the enormous philosophical systems that have been constructed by geniuses, like Spinoza, Hegel, or Kant for instance. I believe they went about their work, the thinking out of things, not to inform or educate others, but as their attempt to learn about themselves and how they might fit into an un-understandable universe. There's too much studying and diploma dispensing and not enough thinking. Too much learning about nature and not enough conscious engagement in observing and existing as a part of it. That was our point," said Nate.

"So, you propose some sort of Rousseau-istic idealism where we just sit around thinking and appreciating nature," said Serene with a wink at Henry.

"Actually, it sounds very pleasant to me, however impractical as it is and has been proved by history," said Boxer who paused a moment then continued. "No, perhaps a better 'balance' is more realistic, or as the ancient Greeks believed, the truth is somewhere in the middle. As far as 'nature' is concerned, many people understand the word differently than I do. They envision some kind of Sierra Club paradise, the ideal pristine environment, much like this fjord, for example.

"I see nature as including all the matter of the universe and everything on Earth, including man and all the extensions of his industry including the pollution he creates. Not that I am pro-pollution, mind ya. Pollution does, however, serve many useful purposes, among which is the obvious job of trying to solve it. It keeps a lot of good people busy. The true horror of pollution, I believe, is the sense of guilt it promulgates. Do we hold our planet responsible for a volcano and the pollution it spews? Or how about these giant forest fires! Yet, mankind is condemned daily by science and environmental groups for driving cars, poking holes in the ozone layer, and melting icecaps.

"I believe all acts of man are in perfect accord with nature for our actions are in perfect accord with our imperfect human natures. Poets praise the songbird, the sound of thunder, the laughter of children, but who pays tribute to the sound of a garbage truck picking up trash, the whoosh of a passing bus, or a siren of an ambulance or fire truck? Are these not also manifestations of our humanity, which should be revered as much as the sound of wind rustling through a pine tree? No, there's no way of going back to nature. It has been with us all the way along our road of progress, banging out its tune with stone axes, tractors, factories, trains, planes, and jackhammers. And, yes, even garbage trucks. These are the sounds we make. The sounds of life! They are as valid to nature as is the call of the mockingbird.

"I think the intellectuals, writers and politicians who have a deep seated and innate sense of guilt for producing no more than commentary have taken up the criticism of the noisemakers, the real workers of the world, as a way of justifying their vacuous existences. I hope I live long enough to see people begin to fully occupy their rightful place in nature, as a part of it and not apart from it. Life can be wonderful, if people could only develop the capacity to enjoy it."

"Boxer, you and Nate have more in common than you realize. I could listen to you nuts all night, but I'm getting worried about poor Ingvild. I don't think she's eaten since she started. I'm going up to check on her," said Serene as she hurried up the steps.

It was almost midnight, yet with the soft light of the sun still reflected from the sky, the flashlight Serene carried was unnecessary. Ingvild sat hunched over her stone, bathed in a pool of brightness from a spotlight on the wheelhouse.

"Hi, Ingvild. Wondered if I could get you some coffee or a sandwich?" Ingvild stood up and stretched out with a yawn. "Oh thank you, Serene, but I'm finished for now. I made a translation and took a rubbing from the stone, but I worked too long. I'm exhausted and my leg fell asleep. It tingles," she said with a small laugh as she shook her foot.

"Come on, put your arm around my shoulder, and I'll help you below. You need sleep. Boxer can bunk in the main salon. You're going right to bed," declared Serene.

— CHAPTER 25 —

Jimmy would use any excuse to go to Ireland. One day he planned to retire to his cottage in County Armagh. Now he rested his arms on the ornate marble balustrade in front of The Four Courts, a graceful 18th century building fronting the river Liffey. While he was waiting for his contact, he stared down at the blackish river, which runs through the center of Dublin. "Ironic," he mused. "This city was conquered by Vikings from Norway by bloody raids on good Irishmen. Now Norway is going to get a taste of their own medicine. It's payback time."

"Aye, it's a right old ugly stream," said a slender man who leaned on the railing beside Jimmy. "The river never stops running."

"And neither do the damned English," said Jimmy with the pre-arranged response.

"Aye, so you're the man, you are. You can call me John, or Johnny, whatever you like. O' course, 'tis not my name," he said with laugh. "You're Jimmy, they tell me," said John, a pale man dressed in a faded black raincoat.

"Yeah. So did they also tell you what I wanted, John?"

"Aye. We can go next week."

"Next week! I thought you guys could move fast."

"Nay, 'tis Ireland. Everything's right careful here. Eyes and ears everywhere."

"You have a good boat?" Jimmy asked.

"Aye. We have one. A good captain and his mate as well. So how many boys you be wanting?"

"I told Sean I wanted four," Jimmy answered angrily.

"Not his name you know. Don't know what 'tis," laughed the little Irishman. "Six 'tis better than four, you know."

"Why is that? Aren't they good men?"

"Aye. The best fighters we have. We need the work, ya see. It's the

156

troubles."

"You're beginning to sound like a union delegate from New York," said Jimmy in a voice of growing frustration.

"No need to get the teapot boiling. We're all in the cause together."

"You're right, John. I could use a few days at my cottage."

"Americans are always in a thither. We'll all be dead soon enough. So bless each of the good Lord's days whilst ya can. Meet ya here next Friday evening at six. Bring what you will. We'll have all the necessaries and drive you to the docks," said John as he tipped his wool cap and walked away.

The crew of the *Loki* gathered at breakfast, all bursting with curiosity about the translation. Ingvild sat down, keenly aware of the nervous expectancy of her companions. No one wanted to rush her so they sat silently. Deliberately, Ingvild loudly slurped her coffee and began to laugh. She opened her notebook and said, "My skill in translation is improving. Unfortunately, I don't believe I'll be using it much anymore. I'm fairly sure that these runes complete the inscription. Look at this sketch I made."

She put the notebook on the table and her crude drawing illustrated how the three pieces of stone fit together like a jigsaw puzzle with the black watermark line running like an underscore across the bottom. She had also indicated the lines of runes, which showed a complete inscription with a beginning and an end. She pointed to the drawing.

"Here is where our last stone left off with the sun symbol, and here's where it continues on the large slab. And here is where the first stone fits, the part about Ingvild bringing the moon from the land of the sun and it being a curse. It fits in near the end of the inscription. The bulk of the story is on the large piece, which, I'm fairly certain reads as follows, '*They found the land of sun people and went to the king of the sun and worked to speak.*' I assume this means they learned to communicate with these people, probably through gestures or by drawing pictures. '*The people worship the sun. At night their spirit men worship the moon in secret from the people. Ingvild told the spirit men that the moon does not move the great waters by her homeland. They believe Ingvild's land is the womb of world where moon rests from her husband the sun. Ingvild sailed home, and spirit men give her the time of the moon to take to the moon's place of rest. Ingvild found her father dead. Ingvild's people forsook the old gods and began to worship the silver moon.*'

"Now here is the part from the first stone," Ingvild said. "'*The moon from*" *the land of the sun was a curse upon her people.'* Then the story continues on the large slab. *'When the gods of the north were dishonored, Ingvild hid silver moon from people at the spot where the moon sleeps.'* That's the complete inscription as far as I can tell."

"Whew! I'm guessing they landed in Mexico or thereabouts, Central America even," said Nate.

"Yup. Makes sense ... land of the sun ... sun worship ... spirit men must have been their priests," added Henry.

"Ingvild?" asked Serene. "That last part about the spot where the moon sleeps, could that be Flekkefjord?"

Ingvild looked up at the overhead for a few seconds in thought and jumped up from her seat, "Yes! I bet you're right, Serene. All the word Flekkefjord means in Norwegian is 'spot fjord.' And, it's the only fjord named in such an odd way. Most fjords are named after a family who first settled there, or after a saint, or a geographic feature. The big Oslo Fjord, for instance, literally means 'mouth of grain' because there was so much good farmland around it. I always felt 'spot fjord' was an undistinguished, blah name which could be any place or spot on any fjord. Not a distinctive at all. It also makes sense that she would take the silver moon out of Berrefjord to get it away from her people and hide it."

"I read about it meaning 'spot' in a guide book Nate gave me," said Serene.

"I still have no idea what the silver moon could be," Ingvild answered.

"My guess is that it's a moon calendar," uttered Boxer sheepishly. "If it is, I'd say they landed on the Yucatan Peninsula and had contact with a Mayan civilization."

"Why do you say that, Boxer?" asked Ingvild.

"In one of my past reading binges, I became interested in Mesoamerican civilizations. The Aztecs who populated present day Mexico worshiped the sun, among a whole host of others gods like jaguars and snakes. They developed very sophisticated calendars that tracked the movement of the sun throughout the year, exceedingly precise and practical to their agricultural needs, the planting time for maize seeds and so forth. Nowhere in my Aztec studies did I ever come across even a mention of the moon.

"The Mayans, however, had both the sun and the moon as their primary deities. They believed the sun and moon were the first inhabitants of the earth. The sun was considered the male hunter. At sunset, he passed into the darkness of the underworld and became one of the lords of the night and emerged at dawn with the insignia of death. Maybe because of the orange-red color of the rising sun, which they likened to blood. The moon was female and the goddess of maize and earth. Even today, there's still a widespread belief among people there that eclipses are due marital fights between the sun and the moon.

"The Mayans had amazingly accurate sun calendars. If they plotted out the movements of the sun so carefully, and if their priests secretly worshiped the moon, it would make sense they would have had moon calendars, too. Secret ones, I suspect. These ancients were great astronomers ...

"Sorry, folks, I almost lost my point. What made me think of this, Ingvild, was your translation, the part about the sun people giving Princess Ingvild, 'the time of the moon to take to the place of rest.' I believe that the 'time of the moon' could only be a calendar. They had no other way of measuring time other than by celestial observation. No clocks. No hourglasses. Not even any evidence of sundials. They just divided their daylight into nine approximate periods of time. And, I think, 'where she rests,' is not referring to the Princess's homeland, but to the place where the moon goddess takes her rest during the Mayan day when the sun god reigns. Where the moon is resting, there are no tides!"

"You're astounding, Boxer!" said Nate. "Now that I think about it, you're probably right about the Yucatan. Most likely they sailed south with the Canaries Current until they hit the North Equatorial Current, which starts to turn east. Then the wind and current get kind of tricky around the Lesser Antilles, 'round about Saint Martin. If they passed through the blue islands in that vicinity, they would have picked up the Caribbean Current, which flows north by east and would have driven them directly into the Yucatan Peninsula. They must have sailed through the Caribbean Sea, which is calmer than the Atlantic, but not as calm as the Gulf, as we first thought."

"One thing doesn't make sense, Nate. Archeologists have found large stone calendars, even small gold calendar discs made by the Aztecs and Mayans, but when I think of a silver moon, I think of a disc made of silver. The problem is the Mayans had very scant supplies of precious metals, only tiny bits of gold and copper have been found in the Yucatan and no silver that I know of. For decoration, the Mayans used primarily stone, jade, obsidian and shells," said Boxer.

"Maybe it's not literally made of silver," Nate suggested.

"We've got some brain trust at this table!" Henry exclaimed. "You've solved your mystery, Ingvild. Congratulations."

"Thank you Henry and all of you for all your hard work helping me. You too, Boxer, for your important contribution. I've got the runes, and I have the story, but it's only an interesting story. I have no proof it actually occurred."

"Wait!" yelped Serene. "Henry, remember when we first entered Flekkefjord?"

"Sure. What of it?" he answered.

"Remember, I was reading the guide book the day before, and we joked about Flekkefjord meaning the spot of the fjord. Remember, I took it literally and the morning we entered the fjord I saw a round shape on the mountain which you thought was a shadow?"

"Yup. I recall," said Henry. "I was humoring you."

"Well, if I were Princess Ingvild, I would have put it there. That is, if I wanted to honor the moon, a place of honor at the entrance," she said.

"*Jah.* I think I know of what she is saying," said Sven who had been listening silently. "I have noticed it also. It is to the right just as you come in, very high on the flat side of the cliff."

"Yes, that's the place," said Serene.

"It could be most difficult to get up there," Sven responded.

— CHAPTER 26 —

At first light on Friday morning, the *Loki* hauled anchor and the little flotilla set out for Flekkefjord. Ingvild's *snekke* led the procession, Sven and Boxer followed in the yellow rental boat, and *Loki* brought up the rear.

It was a damp, misty morning when they entered the Flekkefjord. All eyes were on the mountain, however, the curtains of dense mist that obscured the view only served to increase their curiosity.

As prearranged, they docked in line next to the Pizza Inn. Sven dropped off Boxer and with a wave and a smile, motored away to return the rental and to report to Helge. The others were enthusiastic about breakfast at the Gestapo Headquarters, as they now called it. While walking though the parking lot next to the Pizza Inn, Henry froze in his tracks and said in a baffled voice. "My blue hat!"

"What Henry?" asked Serene.

"Now I remember ... I was taking a photo of you and Nate ... I took it off and put it there. That was over a week ago." Henry walked over, picked up his hat, put it on, and the group continued walking.

"Nice hat," said Boxer. "I'm surprised nobody clipped it."

"I doubt it's been touched," Henry replied.

"Our people do not steal. They are honest, good people," said Ingvild.

"Lord, help them...," Serene stopped in mid sentence remembering their promise to Ingvild. Recovering, she continued, "Boxer, perhaps one day when you have a lot of time, Ingvild will brief you on the efficiency of the local criminal justice system."

An hour later, they were in Boxer's suite at the Maritime Hotel. Henry, Serene and Nate listened in on the sitting room phone while Boxer placed the call from the bedroom.

"Philly, Boxer here."

"Good. I'm glad you called. You found them?"

"Bad news, Philly, they're gone … disappeared again. I looked all around this fjord where they were supposed to be, and it's deserted." Boxer heard no response from Philly. "Philly, you still there?"

In a voice of despair, Philly answered, "Yeah."

"What's the matter, Philly?"

There was another long pause before he answered in a sad, cracked voice, "Boxer, this McCall thing is a curse. It's killing me, I tell you. I have to pay the money back and the interest … it's gutting me … Scardino's dead, his expenses, now your fees and expenses, and I had to pay the Morans everything up front to finish the job. Now there's nothing to finish," sighed Philly.

"Philly, forget my fees and expenses. Consider what I've done as a personal favor for an old friend. I just learned I came into a windfall from one of my old patents. They told me the check is in the mail," lied Boxer.

"No. Boxer, but it's nice of you to offer."

"No. I insist. Remember I had my reservations about this case from the beginning."

"Yeah, I remember."

"Besides, you can call off the Morans and cut your losses."

"Too late. Jimmy's already in Ireland getting his crew together. He may be on the way already. I don't know."

"Can't you call him in Ireland?"

"Nah. All this IRA secret crap of his. He was bragging about all these phony passports and secret passwords. He's gone. I doubt if his brother Mike could find him. Jimmy gets off on all that cloak and dagger stuff."

"Sorry, Philly. I'll book the next flight out of here. I'll call you when I get back."

"No! You stay at the hotel. Jimmy has your name and room number. When he shows up, tell him to call it off. We made a deal for an in-and-out job in one day. If you're not there to stop him, he'll keep looking around there and charge me an outrageous day rate. You don't know this Jimmy. He's relentless and mean. He won't stop. It will cost me a fortune, which I don't have at the moment."

"Okay. Okay. I'll wait. When will he arrive?"

"I'd say in about five or six days. He said it would take a couple of days to get the boat and crew together in Ireland and another day or two to get to

Berrefjord. When he finds nothing there, he'll head over to your hotel."

"Okay. I'll wait for him. And, then I'm out of here," said Boxer.

"Thanks, Boxer," said Philly in the most sincere voice Boxer had ever heard from him.

Boxer hung up the phone and went to his guests in the sitting room. "You heard?"

"Yup. We covered the mouthpiece and crowded around the receiver. Serene, are you all right?" Henry had just noticed that Serene's face was flushed and tiny tears were on her cheek. "Don't be afraid, honey. We'll work this out," he said sympathetically.

"I'm not afraid, you fool. I just feel bad for Philly. He sounded so pathetic," she said as she reached for a tissue and blotted her eyes.

"Ah ... Serene. Remember, this is the guy who's trying to kill us," said Henry.

"I know dear, but still..."

"He's not really a bad guy, kind of likable when you get to know him. Probably his upbringing. The paradox is he does horrible things," said Boxer.

"As long as he doesn't do horrible things to us, I have no problem with him," added Nate.

"'Now what?' is the question," said Henry.

"You guys stay out of sight. When Moran arrives, I tell him you're nowhere to be found, which will be absolutely true by then. You people just continue on your travels. Simple," Boxer suggested.

"That's fine. Except the fact he now knows where I live," said Nate. "My home and my friends are there. I wouldn't be comfortable going back there now."

"Same here," said Serene. "My father and Lani are at the hotel. I fear he'd try to get to Henry and me through them. I'd be continually worried about them, and now I'm even afraid to call my father. Philly may have his phone tapped. Henry and I can't return to Mandavu either, which means I may never see my father again," said Serene now sobbing. Through her tears, she added, "And now we've got Ingvild and Sven involved, too."

"But, Serene. You heard Philly. He's giving up the search for you," said Boxer.

"Don't worry, honey. We're going to end this mess for once and for all. Philly might feel like giving up today, but he could be angrier tomorrow and change his mind. Then where would we be? There's got to be a way out," said Henry.

"We have to talk to Helge," said Ingvild.

"Why?" answered Henry.

"Because by now Sven has already told him what is going on. We should call him right now before he confronts us. It will be better ... ," Ingvild was interrupted by a loud knock at the door.

"I'll get it," said Boxer. "Probably my laundry." A minute later Boxer entered the sitting room followed by Helge and Sven, both holding pistols.

The next morning found the *Loki* anchored in calm water between a skerrie and a ledge at the bottom of a high cliff. The day had emerged as clear as Helge had predicted, and although there was a chill in the shadow of the great mountain, they expected the afternoon would grow hot. Sven warned that they would bake in the full sun during the assent.

Nate and Boxer agreed to stay with the boat and keep in touch with the climbers with a cell phone Helge had provided. Sven would carry his own phone and lead Henry, Serene and Ingvild up the mountain.

As Sven inspected the ropes, the group watched. "*Jah*, I have never climbed this one. I have often thought of it while coming in and out of the fjord, and I have seen a route that should not be too difficult. I have climbed this type of rock many times. The big danger, of course, is falling, but you must also watch out for loose rocks. Be careful with your foot placement so you do not dislodge them and if someone is climbing above you watch out in case one falls down.

"I will free climb with the rope and secure it and then you can come up one at a time. Wait until the climber before you gets to the top before you start. And again, watch for rocks falling down. Even a small one can hurt badly. We will climb up along the tree line until we think we are even with the spot. There appear to be several narrow ledges running horizontally across the face. I hope we choose the right ledge to cross over, because we will not be able to see the spot from where we start.

"Nate and Boxer, that's when we will need your help. After we leave take the boat out on the fjord. When you see us coming close to the right height, call me. We can coordinate from there. It should take us a few hours to get up to the approximate elevation. Is everyone ready?"

Nate and Boxer watched the climbers disappear into the pines. They raised anchor and brought the *Loki* into the middle of the fjord. Beneath them it was 300 meters to the bottom. Since it was impossible to anchor at that depth, Nate killed the engine and they drifted. Since there were no tides, an almost imperceptible current flowed out to sea cause by the fjord being fed with fresh water from a chain streams and lakes that reached many miles into the coastal mountains. Occasionally, Nate would have to restart the engine to correct for the drift. Earlier, Sven had estimated the top of the cliff at 300 meters and the spot to be about 50 meters below the summit.

Nate and Boxer stretched out in the aft cockpit to wait. After scanning the mountain with his binoculars, Nate saw a flash of bright yellow. "There they are, just above the tree tops."

"I see them. That's going to be a long climb," replied Boxer as he lowered his own glass. "You know, Nate, I suspected something wasn't kosher with Helge after I first met him. I always rely on my intuition."

"Know what ya mean, Boxer. He's quite a remarkable fellow. Wise of him to suggest we continue today, otherwise we would have sat around rehashing the subject."

"I still can't get over the shock of having guns pointed at me. That was a novel experience that I hope never happens again."

"He's a cautious man. Probably why he's still alive. Oh! That's right. You never heard his story," said Nate.

"Tell me," said Boxer.

"Have you seen the statue of him by the church?" asked Nate.

"No! You're kidding. He has a statue?"

"Oh yeah. We saw it before we met him. He was in the resistance and a war hero. Later we met Lilly who volunteers at the town museum. That's where we saw Ingvild's first rune stone and learned about her. Well, this Lilly, a very sweet woman, told me all about Helge, and she showed me some books about the war. Even though it was written in Norwegian, I bought it. There is a whole chapter on Helge. I know some Yiddish, German and Latin, and from what Lilly told me and the little Helge told us at his farm, I was pretty much able to understand the story.

"He was fifteen years old when the Germans invaded. His older brother Kora and a friend escaped to England. They actually rowed there! Kora was trained as a radio operator and parachuted back into Norway. He got a job that allowed him to travel all over the country by train, and he became a key spy for the allies. Helge, who wasn't old enough to be officially in the resistance, began to help his brother by running errands, hiding resistance fighters, and passing messages.

"One day the Germans arrested another spy in the train station here and found Helge's name written down on a piece of paper he was carrying. Helge was arrested, imprisoned and tortured by the local Gestapo, but he wouldn't talk. They sent him to Grini, an infamous concentration camp near Oslo where he was condemned to death under a special program that they had for Norwegian spies called *Nacht und Nebel*, which meant the prisoner would disappear into the night and fog. In this way, his family would hold out hope he was still alive and he wouldn't become a martyr and further stir up resistance.

"In the middle of the night, Helge was taken out of the prison camp. He thought he was going to be executed. Instead he was put on a ship and sent to Germany, then to a prison in Poland, then to a horrible camp called Natzweiler, 8000 feet up in the French Alps in the dead of winter where he contracted pneumonia in one lung and pleurisy in the other. They put him in an unheated barracks that they called a hospital, but was just a place to go and die.

"Fortunately for Helge, he was young. He didn't die, and when the Allied forces started getting close to his camp, he was evacuated and sent by train to another camp in Poland. Along the way, his train was bombed, and he was re-routed to Dachau, near Munich in southern Germany. There, because of efficient Nazi record keeping, he had been tagged as a hospital patient, and luckily he was sent to the hospital barracks. He was still very sick, barely alive, but that's what saved him from the ovens. It was getting near the end of the war, and the Nazis were killing Jews and other prisoners with wild abandon, trying to get rid of the evidence so to speak.

"Helge was lucky. Right at that time, the Swedish Red Cross made a deal with the Germans to get the Scandinavian prisoners out. One day he was put on a bus, driven north and put on a ship to Sweden. He had been tortured, beaten savagely, starved, frozen, worked like a slave, and hovered near death with illness in the worst concentration camps imaginable for nearly three years. Yet he survived. It took him years to recover. That's the kind of man we're dealing with. Tough."

"You'd never know. He's so pleasant. Maybe he's just one of those people who is in a constant state of being happy to be alive. What do you think he's got up his sleeve?" asked Boxer.

"Have no idea. You heard him. Said he'd think about it and for us to go about our business and not to worry."

"How are our friends doing?" asked Boxer.

Nate lifted his binoculars and scanned the mountain. "Thanks. I'd better call Sven. Looks like they're getting close." Nate placed the call and advised Sven as to their position. Sven decided to go a bit higher and then work their way down if needed. "By the way, Boxer, what makes you think it's a calendar?"

"The Mayans were obsessed with time as no other people have ever been before or since. They literally worshiped it. Some archeologists believe they calculated, quite accurately, back in time as much as 400 million years ago. You see, the Maya thought that if they tracked time long enough, the history of time that is, that they would be able to predict what would happen in future time. When Ingvild said they gave Princess Ingvild the 'time of the moon,' I didn't think it could be anything else but a calendar. I've visited their ruins. Everywhere you look they erected these stone monuments, stele, with carvings of their gods and hieroglyphics, this picture writing they developed. Most all the monuments were references to time and dates."

"What do ya think the reference to 'silver moon' means?"

"That's really got me stumped. The Mayas had no metals in their lands. That whole area is limestone with only a thin layer of poor soil. They would slash and burn a section of jungle, plant it for a few years until the soil was exhausted and then move on to another piece of jungle. They were, however, master architects and engineers. With an endless supply of limestone, they built magnificent structures. They also developed an excellent concrete from a mixture of calcium carbonate and lime. Very advanced for the time.

"As I mentioned the other night, only tiny pieces of gold and copper have ever been found there and these were imported from far away. The nearest silver mines that I know of were on the west coast of Panama. So I doubt it could be made from silver. Their prized possessions were jade, feathered coats and jaguar skins. If that's where Princess Ingvild landed in the early 900's AD, it was about at the end of the Mayan classic period which was the peak of their civilization. After that, they began to come under the rule of the Mexican civilizations, which the Mayans considered as barbaric and decadent..."

"Boxer! They've made it over to the spot. Sven's way over six feet tall ... I'd say the spot is maybe twenty feet in diameter. First I've been able to make out its size."

"What are they doing?" asked Boxer.

"They seem to be standing on a ledge in front of it, although you can't really tell that it's a ledge from here. Sven seems to be poking around with something. Wait! It looks like they are crawling in underneath the spot. Now they've disappeared!"

"I'm getting no answer … just some message in Norwegian. He must be out of range or have a low battery," said Nate.

"They've been in there for some time now," said Boxer looking at his watch.

"There they are!" said Nate looking through his binoculars as his cell phone rang. "Sven, everything alright? Okay. Okay. We'll talk when you get down."

"What's up?" asked Boxer.

"Sven said he didn't want to talk on the phone. He'll fill us in when they get down. We can head into shore now. Probably take less time for them to descend."

For nearly an hour Nate and Boxer watched the woods until Ingvild with a big smile on her face popped out from behind a boulder followed by the others. She looked as fresh as when she left and shouted *"Hai! Hai!"* as she approached the boat. After greetings and small talk on deck, they adjourned to the main cabin where Nate had already brewed a pot of coffee in anticipation of their arrival.

"What's the big mystery with the phone, Sven?" asked Nate.

"I did not want to talk on the phone. There are many radios and phones on the fjord, and people can sometimes pick up signals. I did not want to say what we found."

"Nate! It's amazing!' said Ingvild. "Just under the spot is a crevice. In it we found a cave. The entrance had been cleverly walled up with rocks. It looked so natural. We could have easily missed it, but Sven was poking around with his walking stick and must have knocked a rock loose. We heard it roll down inside the cave. We removed enough of the wall to crawl inside. Luckily, Henry had a flashlight in his daypack. Guess what we found?" she gleefully teased.

"The time of the moon," Nate replied.

"Yes! But we also found Princess Ingvild!" She reached in her pocket, removed several Polaroid photos and laid them on the table. "This is a shot of the moon stone. It's propped up against the cave wall. The cave is very dry, and it is thickly covered in dust. It's about a meter in diameter and looks like stone with some kind of decorations. You really can't see much with the cobwebs and dust. I didn't dare touch it until we get a professional archeologist." She uncovered the next photo. "This was carved on the cave wall."

"More runes?" asked Nate.

"And they are exactly like the ones we've found at Berrefjord. I translated enough to learn that the princess was buried with the silver moon. I wished I had my stuff to make a rubbing. Anyway, we searched around and in the back of the cave we saw this." The last photo showed a grouping of tightly fitted stones. "This, we think, is her tomb."

"Mother of Mary!" exclaimed Boxer as he jumped to his feet. "This is the discovery of the century. Incontrovertible proof of Viking contact with Mesoamerica before Columbus, maybe before Leif Erickson. And, if it's Mayan, we may have an actually have a date to prove it beyond a doubt!"

"That's why we didn't want to say anything on the phone," said Sven.

"That's something," said Nate. "What about the spot itself?"

"It's hard to see it's a spot up close because of the gradual change in color. May have been some kind of black dye that's faded," Henry replied.

"So guys, what's the next step?" asked Serene.

"We must keep this to ourselves for now. Tell no one until we organize a proper archeological team and do this right," said Ingvild.

"We must tell Helge," said Sven.

"Sven, I agree. We've already taken him into our confidence, and he wants to help us," said Henry as he looked at Ingvild.

"I would trust my uncle with my life."

"You already have, my dear," said Nate.

They were all glad to get out of Ingvild's crowded car but apprehensive about the meeting with Helge.

The big doors had been left open, and although a floodlight lit the ramp leading up to the entrance, it appeared to be dimly lit inside. As they entered they saw Helge and two other men sitting at the long table facing them. The only light came from candles set on the table. Several wooden folding chairs had been arranged in a semicircle facing the table.

Helge stood and ceremoniously said, "Welcome, please be seated." Behind them they heard the barn doors close, and they turned see Sven closing a wooden latch. Sven walked towards them and motioned them to be seated. When everyone was seated, Helge cleared his throat and spoke, "Thank you for coming on such short notice. I would like to introduce Mr.

Edvard Olsen, a member of our tribunal." Edvard, an elderly, well dressed man with white hair and a kind face stood and bowed. "And, this is Jan Eivind, our other member." Jan looked to be about fifty, was very tall with a round face, and thinning hair. He stooped when he stood as if fearing to hit his head on something. "And, of course, you all know me. I have asked Sven to be here as well. I hope you will forgive the candlelight, but it has been our custom since before we had electricity. We also think it keeps us in touch with the lessons of the past and reminds us of those who are no longer here, that is, members of the Night Wolves.

"I have already told Edvard and Jan Eivind of what I know about your predicament and also about your discovery today on the mountain. Sven is your friend but his first loyalty is to the protection of the good citizens of Flekkefjord, which is the domain of the Night Wolves as it has been for many generations. Remember, it was I who sent Sven with you, Boxer. Not only for the protection of my niece Ingvild but for Henry, Serene and Nate. It was also for your protection, Boxer. We do not tolerate situations that are potentially violent."

Boxer spoke up, "I don't want any violence, either. As you know, I accepted this job reluctantly only because I needed the money. Now I'm doing all I can to neutralize this conflict between Philly Costello and Henry."

"We are aware of that, Boxer. Before we came up to your room last night, Sven and I also listened in from the lobby on your conversation with Mr. Costello. I was most impressed, especially the kind way in which you offered to return his money. We also think that Henry and Serene are innocent victims in all of this, an unfortunate chain of circumstances stemming from Henry's finding the smuggled money. Now Nate and Ingvild are involved, even Sven and by inclusion myself, our organization, our entire community. On top of all that, we now have to deal with your discovery on the mountain today…"

"Uncle Helge, what's the discovery have to do with any of this?"

"Ingvild, your discovery is potentially more dangerous than a hundred Philly Costello's. If the world learns of this find, our peaceful town will be overrun by outsiders … tourists … the curious, and what our forefathers worked so long and hard to create and protect will be jeopardized. The last thing we want to do is attract attention to Flekkefjord. We have here something that is very precious, perhaps the last bastion of tranquility in a world that has seemingly gone mad. My dear niece, I want you to think about what I am going to say. I think this discovery of yours is wonderful. You are extremely smart. Everyone knows that. And you are loved by everyone, mostly by me. We even love to talk about your different ways and the good fun you bring to everyone.

"You didn't embarked on your search for Princess Ingvild for money or fame. It was only out of your natural curiosity to learn about your ancestor. Now you have done that. You don't need more money. You have plenty. You own the whole Berrefjord besides the all the farms, houses and the apartments you inherited. What would fame bring you that you don't already have? The price of the notoriety of your discovery would be high. It would disturb all our lives in Flekkefjord, including yours and all your relatives. Your gratification should be the discovery itself, the knowledge it brings to you, and to your new friends who helped you and shared in the experience."

As Helge finished speaking, Ingvild put her hand on Nate's and squeezed it firmly. "Uncle. I understand what you are saying, but this find proves conclusively that Princess Ingvild discovered the Americas more than 500 years before Columbus, maybe even before Leif Erickson!"

Helge looked tenderly for a moment at his distraught niece and said, "Our ancestors accomplished great things. They discovered Iceland, Greenland, Labrador and Newfoundland. Some experts claim they sailed further south to Cape Cod and into New York Bay. Some believe they sailed up the St. Lawrence River, went through the Great Lakes and went as far as Minnesota. They colonized Ireland, explored and traded throughout the vastness of Russia and became their first kings. They sailed the Mediterranean and down the coast of Africa. One more unknown accomplishment would be among a hundred of such. Think, would Princess Ingvild want the tranquility of her people endangered?"

"I will think about it, Uncle."

"Whatever you decide, Ingvild, you can count on all of us to support your decision," said Serene. Everyone voiced his or her agreement as Nate placed a kiss on Ingvild's cheek.

"But Uncle, I need to get a professional archeologist to record and excavate the sight."

"That would be unwise. I know you are excited to return to the cave. But isn't this something you could do yourself?"

While Ingvild was pondering the question, Henry said, "Ingvild, before I did films and videos, I was a professional still photographer and worked a few times documenting archeological digs. I know how to set up grids and use rulers in shots to show the size of objects. As long as we're careful, shoot everything in sequence with time-date slates and tag anything we find as to its measured depth, our work would be as legitimate as any professional team of archeologists."

"Besides, Nate and I are both engineers. We can measure and plot the site and draw accurate maps," said Boxer.

"I can dig!" volunteered Sven.

"And so can I," added Serene.

"Do-it-yourself archeology. I love it! Why not, we've all watched public television," said Henry.

Helge looked to Edvard and then to Jan Eivind who both nodded in agreement. "It is decided then. Ingvild, you will say nothing about your discovery until this matter with Jimmy Moran and his friends is resolved. Then we will talk again. You have a few days before Moran is expected to arrive, so continue with your work at the cave. Meanwhile, we will take other measures for your protection. Immediately, you must hide the *Loki*. Cover over the name on the boat and Sven will show you a remote cove where you can safely moor her. We used to smuggle men and arms from there during the occupation. Use Ingvild's *snekke* for your work at the cave, and I will alert the organization to be on the lookout for this Jimmy Moran. The meeting is adjourned."

The following day was a busy one of preparation. Early that morning Ingvild and Sven arrived at the Pizza Inn in her boat. By that time, Nate had finished obliterating *Loki's* name with black paint. Then the *Loki* followed in the wake of Ingvild and Sven across the fjord to a secluded cove on the northern bank. The entrance was hidden from the view of harbor traffic by a hilly island. After double anchoring the *Loki*, they returned to town to gather supplies. Besides his climbing gear, Sven also brought a small, folding shovel, three battery powered spotlights, a one-meter ruler, and a ten-meter tape measure.

Henry, who had so readily volunteered to take photos the night before, now needed the equipment needed to do so. Ingvild led the group to the town's only photo shop, which was owned by yet another cousin named Vigdis. Henry was surprised to find a large selection of new and used equipment. Vigdis explained that the Norwegians are as nearly compulsive as the Japanese in taking vacation photos, and since they have long vacations and the wherewithal to travel, they gravitated toward buying better cameras.

She had a stock of new and used Cannons, Minoltas, and Nikons. Henry was interested in a quality 35mm with interchangeable lenses, particularly one that had fast macro and wide-angle lenses. Henry found his solution in the form of a vintage black bodied Nikon F2 and a 28mm wide angle, a 43 to 86mm zoom, and 50mm Macro Nikkor lens. Henry also bought a cable release, a dozen rolls of high-speed color film, a portable strobe unit with an extra battery, a tripod, and a cheap, nylon backpack style camera bag. Vigdis gave Henry the special 'cousins' discount'.

A few doors away from the photo shop, Nate and Boxer found a hardware store. They bought a rock hammer, a bundle of metal garden stakes, a variety of soft bristle paint brushes, paint scrapers, a hand trowel, a small chalkboard and chalk, several balls of string, a few line-levels, bottled water, and a pad of chart paper.

Next, they stopped at the Gestapo headquarters for a large breakfast, as they did not want to haul food up the mountain. At the table Henry asked, "Boxer, think you'll make it up the mountain?"

"Sure. I'm in good shape, but I don't know about my old friend Nate here," he jested.

"From what I've seen of Nate, I believe he could carry you up," parried Ingvild.

"It shouldn't be too bad if we split up the loads," said Henry.

"The good thing about my boat is that we can beach it and all climb up together," said Ingvild as she nudged closer to Nate. "Tonight, I think I should continue to stay on the *Loki* with you guys. It will be much more convenient," she added.

"That's good idea. Boxer can stay with us, too," Serene suggested.

"Shouldn't I return to the hotel in case Philly calls?"

"Nah. You can use Sven's cell phone and check the hotel for messages and even return calls if you like," said Henry.

"And that way you can keep an eye on me," Boxer replied.

"No, Boxer. We like you. It'll just be cozier that way … and perhaps safer," said Serene.

— Chapter 27 —

Jimmy stood outside the Four Corners in the drizzle and dense fog. He'd selected what he considered a proper Irish wardrobe for the upcoming caper – a lightweight, black wool watch cap that could be rolled down into a ski mask, a black cashmere turtleneck sweater, and a black leather bomber jacket for which he paid a fortune only to find out later it was made in India, not Ireland as he supposed. His costume was completed by dark blue jeans and a pair of black, US paratrooper jump boots. Slung over his shoulder was a dark blue Gore-Tex daypack with a change of underwear and his shaving kit.

Feigning a true Irishman's pose, he leaned on his prized blackthorn shillelagh. A British soldier would immediately know he was a tourist. A Hollywood casting director would describe him as perfect for 'one of the IRA boys'.

A battered airport shuttle van stopped at the curb, the sliding door opened and out shot John's head. "Och! Jimmy. Ya come to the scratch?"

Without understanding John's meaning, Jimmy nevertheless jumped in the van and closed the door behind him. "What was that you said?" asked Jimmy.

"Och. In the ole faction fightin' days, ya scratched a line in the dirt. The boys put their toes to the line before they'd begin t' flailing. It means ya come to fight, Jimmy. That's a handsome stick ya have. Has it got the lead in it?"

"Lead?"

"Tis the head of your stick been drilled and filled with molten lead. To give weight to the blows, man. Och, you must be recent to carrying the stick," said John.

Jimmy was shocked. He had expected a dirty old fishing boat. Rather, shining in the yellow floodlights alongside the pier was an ultramodern, sleek white luxury cruiser of about 70 feet in length.

"Tis a beauty. Fast it is. The big fella owns it," said John. "The boys are

174

already on board."

"You're coming?" asked Jimmy.

"Och. Surely I am. Think we'd send you out with a bunch o' strangers?"

As they neared the boat, Jimmy saw the name *The Shooting Shamrock* lettered on the stern with a graphic of shamrock with speed lines coming off it like a shooting star. "An appropriate name!" commented Jimmy.

"The big fella does have a sense of humor. If you only knew," said John with a laugh. John led the way up the aluminum gangway, though a hatch, and into what appeared to be a plush drawing room. Mulling around the room were three of the largest Irishmen Jimmy had every seen and a small man with a white goatee and a captain's hat.

"Boys. This is our friend Jimmy from the States. Jimmy, this is the captain of the boat." The captain tipped his hat. "These big fellas ... well you can call 'em whatever you want and whenever you want," he chuckled.

"Suits me," Jimmy replied with his signature smile. "You boys bring the hardware?"

One of the men picked up a heavy duffel bag, walked up to Jimmy, and opened the drawstring. Inside, Jimmy saw an assortment of automatic rifles, handguns, and ammunition. "You can call me John," said the large black haired man with bushy eyebrows.

"Och! I'm already John," said John. "You can be Johnny, if ya please," he laughed. "Enough of this nonsense. Captain, how long to get us there, ya calculate?"

"Just checked the weather. We're clear all the way for the next 48 hours. It'll be most of that time to get there. I'll have the mate cast off then. There's plenty o' fine Catholic whisky behind the bar."

"How would you like a nice fishing trip?" Ernst was awakened from his afternoon nap and was utterly confused by the telephone call. "Is this Helge?" he responded in confusion thinking it was a practical joke.

"*Jah.* So ... how about doing some fishing for me?"

"What kind of fish you liking, Helge?"

"There is a new species I'm told to be swimming in the Berrefjord over the next few days."

"What kind of fish?"

"Irish fish and a big New York whale named Jimmy. They want to bite some friends of ours, including my niece Ingvild."

"They sound like nasty fish, but we have caught those kind before. Ha! *Jah*, I could go tomorrow morning. I like the Berrefjord, you know. Very quiet and peaceful. A good place to read a book. What if I find these fish?"

"Telephone and tell me what they look like and if they say anything. When they find no one there but an old fisherman who cannot even catch a fish, they will swim to town."

"*Jah!* I could use some fishing."

Droves of people were returning to Flekkefjord for the holiday of St. Hans as if compelled by some unexplained phenomenon of nature like a rare species of birds returning to their nesting grounds. There was not a hotel room nor campsite to be had for miles around the town. All the extra beds in private homes had been spoken for by visiting relatives.

One of the great mysteries of life is not the celebration of feast days, rather the reasons for them. Granted, most people enjoy a good time and could care less about the reasons why, but the celebration of St. Hans defies explanation by even most Norwegians. Ask one about it and he will tell you it is midsummer night, the summer solstice, the longest day of the year when it is light for almost all of the day. It has always been celebrated they will say, a tradition going far back into their dark, pagan past. But it was only after the land was Christianized and after King Hans the 1st, who ruled Denmark, Norway and Sweden in the 15th century and was later canonized, did it come to be known as St. Hans Day. It happens every year on the 21st of June, the summer solstice.

From all outward appearances it consists of eating, excessive drinking and the burning of large bonfires most of the night. Up and down the coast, old wooden boats if available, or rafts, stacked with piles of wood are taken out into the fjords and set ablaze. This ignition is preceded by a parade around the fjord by ships, fishing boats, ferries, kayaks, and pleasure craft of every description. The parade is led by one of the larger boats, which has the honor of carrying the town's brass band. As the band plays patriotic and popular songs, they lead the procession around the fjord. These large flotillas of closely packed boats, overstuffed with people of all ages eating, drinking, talking, laughing, and listening to music rarely, if ever, collide, a miracle in itself deserved of sainthood.

As midnight approaches, the boats, many of which are decorated with evergreen trees and pine boughs, circle around to watch the bonfire being lit.

As the flames blaze up high into the sky and create eerie reflections across the waters, it makes one think of an ancient Viking funeral. The event definitely celebrates of the apex of the summer, but it also marks the crossing of the threshold of the journey into the dreaded northern winter with all its deeply rooted, primitive fears of survival and death. The latter may account for the excessive consumption of alcohol.

— CHAPTER 28 —

By 11:00 a.m. they had all climbed the mountain and reached the spot. As they sat resting on the ledge, Henry organized his camera gear and addressed the party. "Ingvild is our project leader, and we will follow her instructions in every respect, however I do have one suggestion. Before we all go in, I think just Ingvild and I should go in and do a complete photographic documentation of the site. We already have some footprints from our last visit. Ingvild can place the ruler and tape measure to establish size relationships, and I'll shoot with the strobe. It shouldn't take long."

"I agree, Henry. Then you can all join us. After that, I want to brush off the moon, and see what's under all that dust. As I do this, Henry, you can document the various stages. Then I want to pack up the stone and haul it down with us. People may see us up here, and I don't want to take any chances. I also want to make a good rubbing from the runes. If we have time, I'd like to open up the tomb, although the thought of doing so gives me the shivers."

"Don't worry about that, Ingvild. We can take care of that if you prefer. While you're dusting the stone and before you move it, Boxer and I will measure the cave, do the elevations and plot the objects," said Nate.

Henry stood. "If you're ready, let's go Ingvild!"

"It's small cave, Ingvild. We've shot everything to death." Henry looked at his watch, "And, it took less than half an hour. Call the others. Now, I want to get a group shot of all of us gathered around the moon stone."

While Ingvild went out to call the others, Henry set the camera on the tripod, positioned it opposite the stone and framed up the shot. As the others entered, he posed them around the moonstone, set the automatic timer, and joined the group just as the flash went off. He retrieved the camera, popped in fresh roll of film, and moved the tripod closer to the stone. "Okay, Ingvild, you may commence the brushing of the stone." Illuminated by spotlights, Ingvild sat cross-legged before the stone and picked up a brush. Henry's strobe unit went off and continued to flash intermittently as she worked. Nate and Boxer began taking measurements. Sven and Serene watched Ingvild.

Henry monitored the scene though the viewfinder. The strobe revealed tiny sparkles of green in the area where Ingvild was brushing.

"What is this?" Ingvild said to herself.

Boxer, who was working nearby came over to look. "That's jade, most likely. A square piece of jade, highly polished and carved."

"These little bumps surrounding it? I've dusted them off but the dirt still sticks."

"Here, try a little water," said Nate as he opened a bottle of water and sprinkled a few drops onto his handkerchief.

Ingvild carefully wiped off one of the small bumps. Serene leaned over her shoulder and whispered, almost in disbelief, "That's a pearl."

"Well, if the Mayans didn't have silver, they certainly had a lot of pearls. My God, there must be a couple of thousand of them!" Nate added.

"I have to admit that the color is about as close to the silver luminescence of the moon as you can get," Boxer commented.

Meanwhile, Ingvild had aggressively brushed off the remaining layers of dust from the jade and the object began to reveal its splendor. "It's magnificent!" she said in awe.

Around the edge of the disk were thirteen oblong pieces of pure green jade, each equally spaced along the circumference. Each piece was carved in bas-relief with a different glyph. In the center was a stylized depiction of a coiled snake magnificently crafted in a mosaic of smaller, square jade tiles. The snake's head looked somewhat like a dragon with fangs and the one eye that stared back was a darkly empty, concave socket. The snake's head rose between the oblong jades almost to the edge of the disk. The entire field of the disk was composed of closely set bumps, one of which they knew to be a pearl.

"Ingvild, may I take a closer look?" asked Boxer as he kneeled down beside her. Ingvild nodded. Boxer brushed the edge of the stone, picked up a searchlight and looked closely at the stone with a magnifying glass. "This is not stone. It's a very fine aggregate, like a hard plaster or poured concrete. The jade and pearls look like they were inset while the aggregate was wet. My guess is they worked in small sections. After each section dried, it bonded the jewels, and they moved on to another small section."

"Concrete?" Ingvild sounded puzzled.

"Yes. In fact, I was telling Nate about Mayan building techniques in the boat yesterday. They were expert architects. They used their own type of concrete to cast enormous corbelled vaults, their version of the arch." Boxer continued to examine the material. "This looks like an interesting mixture, probably finely ground limestone and ash mixed with water. There are also these flecks of green, perhaps ground up jade from the carving scraps. I wouldn't be surprised if there was rubber mixed in there as well. The Mayans were among the first people to use rubber. They played their games with rubber balls in large stadiums. Even made raincoats with it. They were also proficient with tempera paints, made from egg whites and mixed with pigments. Tempera is in effect a colored glue, very adherent. Most of their great murals have been lost due to time and moisture, but a few examples have been preserved. An extremely talented and clever people."

"And talented artists. Look at that workmanship," said Serene.

"Boxer, have any idea what those thirteen jade pieces are?" asked Henry as he clicked off another shot.

"Yes I do. I believe it's a thirteen-month Mayan moon calendar. Give me some time to let me try to recall what I know, and I'll tell you later. Some say I have a photographic memory, but with all the crap I've put in my head over the years, it often takes time to get it together. Why don't we open the tomb? I'm dying to see what's in there."

"Me too," Ingvild agreed. "But I want to finished up here. Why don't you guys open up the tomb while I make a rubbing of the runes? I will try to get up some courage to look."

"Okay. But first let me set up to shoot the opening," said Henry.

"Good idea. We'll help Sven open the wall while you shoot," said Nate.

It was still light enough to read a book at 12:00 a.m. By that time however, everyone was too tired to read or do anything else. The long day had been exhausting enough, but Ingvild had also insisted they close up the tomb, erase all signs of their presence, and finally wall up the cave entrance before they left. But it was the climb down the mountain that did them in. Nate estimated that the calendar weighed about 70 pounds. They carefully wrapped it and lashed it to Sven's backpack frame. The gear Sven had carried up was distributed among the others. It was slow going and dangerous traversing the face of the cliff. Soon after they started, it became obvious that Sven needed assistance. Henry passed off his pack to Nate and helped stabilize Sven by helping hold his weight in towards the cliff. Their greatest fear was that an abrupt shift in the load would pull Sven off the mountain. By the time they reached the tree line, a long rest was required. Then they lowered the calendar with ropes using the pack frame as a skid. They tied one end of the rope to the pack and ran the rope around a tree. As Henry let out on the rope, the others took turns guiding the load downward. When the rope ran out, they would brace the load and Henry would climb down, select another tree and repeat the process. It took nearly three hours for them to descend, load Ingvild's *snekke*, and return to the *Loki*.

After a quick snack, they all turned in and slept until late the next morning. Around 11:00 a.m. Nate awoke and quietly made coffee so as not to disturb Boxer who was snoring away on the couch. Sitting down with his coffee, Nate could not help but think about Princess Ingvild lying peacefully in her tomb. She was much taller than he expected and big boned. From the top of her skull to her heel bone, she measured five feet, ten inches. Her body had been laid out in the open on a low platform of flat stones, her hands neatly folded over her midsection.

Her jewelry, however, immediately arrested everyone's attention. Around her neck was a silver chain and pendant that rested on her breastbone. In the center of the pendant a large pearl was mounted. Each wrist had a thick silver bracelet. Four silver rings graced her fingers. There was no doubt the design of her jewelry was of Norse origin. Only the huge pearl looked out of place. It set Nate to thinking, "It stands to reason that when she went off to Denmark, she would have worn her silver jewelry and perhaps taken silver as currency. An assay could easily tell where the silver was mined, and it probably originated in Norway or northern Europe. I'd wager when the Mayans saw her silver for the first time, they would have equated it with the moon. They'd never seen silver before. And when they learned there were no tides in Ingvild's homeland, that would cinch why they believed it was the place where the moon resided during their daylight hours."

"What are you mumbling about, Nate?" growled Boxer as he sat up on the couch and yawned.

"Just rambling, my friend. Have some coffee. Wake up, and I'll tell you."

Shortly thereafter, the rest of the crew was up and at the coffee pot. Nate explained his theory about the origin of the silver. Boxer agreed that a spectrographic analysis of its chemical composition would tell them exactly where it was mined. Meanwhile, Ingvild had recruited Sven to help unwrap the stone and prop it up on the couch opposite the table.

"Now, Boxer, tell me what you recall about their calendars," Ingvild asked.

"Okay. Before I went to sleep last night, I hypnotized myself and did my surfacing technique, specifically on whatever information I know about Mayan time. Here goes.

"As I already mentioned, the Mayans were obsessed with the study of time, not just measuring and recording its passage, but in a deeper spiritual way. I remember when reading about what archeologists said about the Mayan concept of time, it reminded me of Einstein's attempt to come up with a Unified Theory to reconcile the relationship of time, space, energy and matter. The reason the Mayans tracked time so carefully was that they thought everything in time repeated itself in the future, that time itself was a living, breathing, real thing with its own unique dimension, kind of like a fourth dimension as Einstein expressed it. For the Mayan, time was not something that just neutrally passed by them, but a vital energy that passed through them much the same as blood flowed through their veins.

"That's why their measurement of time was based on the female biological time, the menstruation cycle of 28 days. Each of those 13 jade symbols represents one of their lunar months. What we have here is their secret lunar calendar. It takes the Earth one year to make one complete orbit around the sun. During that time there are 13 cycles of the moon, each of 28 days for a total of 364 days in the Mayan lunar year."

"But there are 365 days in a year, aren't there?" asked Serene.

"Approximately 365 days, actually 365.2422. That's the true, what they call a 'sidereal year', which is the exact time it takes the earth to revolve once around the sun as measured by modern, precision instruments. The Mayans, in fact, calculated the solar year at 365.2420. Just an incredibly accurate accomplishment considering they had no telescopes, water clocks, or even hourglasses. The Mayans knew precisely how long a solar year was. But with the lunar year of 13 cycles of the moon, each of 28 days, they were roughly one day short. They solved this fractional difference, by rounding off, by adding one extra day to each year, which they didn't count. A kind of 'time-out' from time itself. See where the snake's head breaks the circle of the 13 jades. That's the mysterious, missing day."

"That sounds whacky. What kind of mushrooms were those Mayans eating?" Henry said.

"It's not as crazy as it sounds. It also made perfect sense to the Druids who devised a lunar tree calendar of 13 moons of 28 days each, plus one day. The ancient Egyptians, the Incans, the Polynesians, even the Lakota Sioux had 13 moon, 28 day lunar calendars. It's really the most practical and natural way to measure time. The moon circles the earth almost precisely 13 times a year."

"Yes, that is true. The old ones in Fiji counted time that way," commented Serene.

"I agree," Nate said. "In studying tides, scientists often mentioned the 13 month lunar cycle because it relates exactly to tidal movement. When ya think about it, time can be spliced up almost anyway ya please. Take the 12-month Gregorian calendar we got today. It was ordered up by Pope Gregory in the late 1500's, based on the older Roman Julian calendar. The year begins on January 1st, just because Julius Caesar picked that date out of thin air. We got 12 months of different lengths, some 30 days some 31 and one of 28 ... and every four years a leap year month with 29 days. Crazy! September, which means seven in Latin, is actually the 9th month, and we got them leap years which I still can't get my little brain around."

Boxer nodded in agreement and said, "The 13 month calendar is a natural cycle, not just an arbitrary division of time. The Mayan year begins on July 26, which corresponds to the rising of the great star Sirius. When you think why the Mayans went this route, it makes even more sense. It gave them a uniform way of calculating exactly where each day they lived would fall in the future. With this uniform, harmonious system they could actually calculate where a specific day of the week, like a birthday, would fall 400 million years into the future! They believed that long periods of time repeated; by observing what occurred on days during consecutive life spans, they felt they could accurately predict what would occur on those same days in the future. In a way they were trying to 'tune into' the frequencies of the universe by calculating how frequently things occurred and how they fell on their calendar over long periods time."

"This is most interesting, Boxer. I must study Mayan time further. Also, you must tell me more about your surfacing technique. It has served you well today. I must also learn more from Nate about tides. There are a number of interrelationships here that should be rigorously pursued. But tell me, what do you think is the significance of that snake on the moon?" asked Ingvild.

"That's a representation of the primary Mayan god, *Quetzalcoatl*, which they visualized as a feathered serpent. I think it represents the highest form of animal life, the flying bird, and the lowest form, the serpent that slithers across the earth. My guess is the snake rears its head at the rising of Sirius, breaks the circle, and represents that one day time out and the beginning of their year on July 26th. If that's the case, the first jade to the right is their first month of the year.

"Let me ask you something, Ingvild. Do you think Princess Ingvild's ship had one of those Viking dragon heads carved on the bow?"

"Yes, at that time it certainly would have ... the dragon head was quite necessary to frighten off the sea monsters, you know," Ingvild said with a wink.

"That must have shocked the Mayans. Imagine them seeing a ship with the head of what looked like their own god on it, led by a woman ornamented with silver, the same color of the moon, who came from the other side of the world where there is no tide."

"It must have blown their minds!" exclaimed Henry.

"The whole thing is certainly blowing mine," Serene added with a laugh.

Ingvild looked somewhat distressed, "And now we're faced with the problem of what to do with our moon calendar. I promised Helge not to say anything about the cave. I dare not take it into town, and ... as seaworthy as the *Loki* is, all boats can sink."

"We could take it back to Berrefjord and stash it in the old village," suggested Henry. "We still have a couple of days before Moran is expected."

"Not a bad idea. I know exactly the place. We can go in my *snekke* to be extra safe. I think Henry, Serene and Boxer should stay here. Sven and Nate can come with me. We would look like locals out for the day and would be back by early evening."

"And we have our cell phones to stay in touch," said Sven.

Everyone nodded in agreement and then Serene spoke up, "Ingvild, I've been meaning to say you did the right thing by not taking her jewelry." She looked pointedly at Henry. "As tempted as some of us were, I admire your decision."

"I was tempted as well but couldn't be a grave-robber, especially the grave of her, a relative. Besides, a girl is lost without her jewelry," she laughed.

"Not this girl," said Serene as she put a small leather pouch on the table. "When I saw that pearl on Princess Ingvild's pendant, I knew this was the missing eye of the serpent on the calendar." Serene opened the pouch and rolled out the Daughter of the Moon into the palm of her hand.

"My God! That's even more beautiful than the one on her pendant!" exclaimed Ingvild.

"Yes, I believe it is," Serene rose from her chair, walked over to the disk, and placed the pearl in the eye socket. "It fits perfectly."

Because the moon calendar was set on the couch at an angle, the pearl remained in place and Serene returned to the table to join the others who looked at the disk in astonishment.

"Will someone please explain what's going on here?" said Boxer in a puzzled voice.

"Yes, I don't understand either," said Ingvild.

"That pearl is called the Daughter of the Moon. It belonged to my great great grandfather, by the name of Manowee. You might say that I inherited it, and in a way you might say it has cursed my family. For many years Manowee waged a spiritual war with himself over that pearl because it represented the last symbol of his wealth and greed, a destructive greed that was a barrier to his spiritual harmony. He finally won a battle in his war by throwing it away, but not a complete victory because he threw it in a place where he knew he could retrieve it. To his credit he never went back for it, and he lived and long and harmonious life. Then it came to me by pure happenstance, an accident of fortune, and it's been weighing heavily on my mind, and spirit ever since.

"Ingvild, yesterday you taught me something new. Your respect for family, for Princess Ingvild, was much greater than greed. I can think of no better resting place for the Daughter of the Moon than in the time of the moon to finally bring Manowee's spirit to rest."

"That is beautiful, Serene. Thank you. I think it brings a sense of completion to both the Princess Ingvild and Manowee," said Ingvild as she embraced Serene.

With a tear running down his cheek, Nate said, "If you like, Boxer and I can whip up a little tempera glue and set that eye in right and proper."

— CHAPTER 29 —

The Irish Sea and the North Sea are turbulent waters even in fair weather; however, an unusual midsummer calm had quieted the sea like a placid mountain lake and the *Shooting Shamrock* shot across the water at full throttle. While the mate steered, the captain left the bridge to inform his passengers of their remarkable progress. As he entered the salon, he announced proudly, "Gentlemen! Neptune has been kind to us. We have been at full speed most of the night, and if it stays this calm, we should be off of Berrefjord by this afternoon. I have a general chart of that area, and while the entrance to the fjord looks tricky, we shouldn't have any problem if we take it slow and easy."

"Och, yer a good man, captain, and 'tis a fine boat too. I slept like an infant, I did," said John. "Yer fine whisky may have helped," he added.

"I always like to be ahead of schedule. You get the money faster," said Jimmy as he wiped off his automatic pistol with an oily rag.

Ernst was having a fine day. He welcomed the solitude and his ice coolers were nearly filled with small, tasty mackerel, his personal favorites. He fished with a hand line with hooks spaced every few feet on the line. He didn't bother baiting any longer. The flashing hooks were lure enough.

He heard the echo of Ingvild's boat before it entered the fjord, and he knew it was hers the minute he saw it glisten in the sun. No one but Ingvild would waste that much varnish. Ingvild immediately recognized Ernst's boat and made a beeline towards him, standing at the tiller, waving and shouting, *"Hai! Hai!* Cousin Ernst. Did you take all the fish from the Berrefjord already?!" she laughed.

"Jah! Jah! They know me well here and live in dread of a good fisherman," he answered with a rolling laugh.

Ingvild pulled alongside, jumped to Ernst and gave him a big hug and kisses. "It is so great to see you. It has been too long. Since last summer."

"It is good to see your bright, smiling face again. You always make me feel so fine and special."

"You are one of my favorite cousins. But why are you taking all my fishes?" she kidded as she opened a cooler.

"I have always loved this place. It is so pleasant in summer. So very quiet. A good place for an old man to think."

"Well, you know our cousin Sven, and this is my good friend Nate from the States." They exchanged greetings. "We will leave you in peace and quiet and wish you more fun with the fishes. We have some little jobs to do at the old village." And with that Ingvild jumped back to her boat and pulled away throwing kisses to Ernst.

Ten minutes later Ingvild beached her boat next to the old stone pier. Sven and Nate wrestled the stone out of the boat and carried it following Ingvild a short distance to an old stone foundation.

"Put it down here and come help me open up this old root cellar," said Ingvild. She led them to the back wall to a pile of rusty sheeting that had once been the roof of the old house. "I covered this over years ago to keep the rain out. I thought it would be a good place to go in a bad storm but never used it. Too stinky and dark down there."

Nate and Sven slid back two sheets and removed the old beams Ingvild had lain across the stairwell to support the metal sheets. Ingvild pulled a flashlight from her daypack and handed it to Sven. "Sven, you go down, and Nate and I will slide it down with the rope. Put it up against the back wall."

In a few minutes, the task was complete. They replaced the sheeting and Ingvild covered it with brush.

"Excuse me. I must go and make a tree happy," said Sven as he jogged off towards the pine forest. Nate looked confused.

"He has to go to the bathroom, silly. You make a tree happy by watering and fertilizing it. Come, let us sit by the front of my house."

"This where ya planning to build, Ingvild?"

"Yes. Sit on my front steps, and enjoy my view."

They sat down together on the old stones, once the entrance to the little house. "I will make my house larger, of course, but I think this is the best spot on the fjord. I will leave the other foundations as they are and plant flowers, shrubs and trees among them and have lovely gardens around my house. I will use the old stones and bricks for pathways and run pipes down from the stream to water my garden and flood some of the foundations and make water gardens. Perhaps a small waterfall or two."

"Ya have it well planned out, Ingvild. And you're right. It is a beautiful view from here. What's it look like in winter?"

"In winter I won't be looking here. Too dark and cold. You'll find me in Spain or Portugal. Someplace warm."

"Same with Cape Cod. I love the spring, summer and fall, but wintering there is horrible. Ya know ... if you ever need a hand to build your house ... well ... I'm pretty handy."

"Mr. Nevins, whatever are you saying? Are you looking for a construction job?" she teased.

Nate blushed and looked down at his feet. "No. What I'm trying to say is I would like to spend some time with you. To be honest, I've fallen in love with you ... and you seem to take to me. I'd like the pleasure of your company under whatever circumstances you think best."

Now Ingvild's face flushed pink, and she stuttered, "Is ... this ... a proposal ... of marriage?"

Nate looked her in the eyes. "Yes, if you'll have me."

Ingvild gulped. "Of course, Nate. I would be proud to be your wife."

They embraced. Tears ran down both their faces. Nate gave her a light kiss on her lips. "Thank you for making an old sea dog the happiest man in the world."

"No, thank you for giving me such joy. We are a good pair us two ... a good match as they say. And you are not so old. You climb mountains like a young goat," she laughed.

Nate reached into his pocket, removed a gray velvet pouch, and took out a diamond ring. "I bought this in Flekkefjord after we installed your muffler in hope that one day you might accept it. I had no idea it would actually happen to be today."

Ingvild extended the fingers of her left hand, and Nate slipped on the ring, which fit perfectly. "I eyeballed your finger size right," laughed Nate.

As they kissed once again, Sven came running out of the woods with a look of panic on his face. "They are here! They are here! Ernst just called me on my cell phone. The *Shooting Shamrock* out of Dublin just stopped and spoke to him. Let's get out of here."

They ran to the boat, shoved off and Ingvild started the engine. "We'll head down the south shore. Maybe they won't even see us."

"I see them," said Nate as he looked through his binoculars. "They are

188

moving very fast. Headed right our way."

She pointed down the shoreline, "See those skerries over there. We can duck behind them and hide." She set her single cylinder engine to full speed and the normal 'dunk dunk dunk' sounds nearly blended together, yet her top speed was a small fraction of her pursuer.

Jimmy Moran stood on the bridge and held the captain's powerful telescope to his eye. "Over there captain!" he pointed. "There's a boat with two men and a woman. That's probably them. Go get 'em," he commanded. "I'll rouse the boys."

They were almost at the chain of small rocky islands that stood about a hundred yards off shore. Sven pulled out his handgun, cocked it, put in on his lap and covered it with his jacket. Nate pulled the steel tipped boat hook closer to him.

Moran returned to the bridge with his boys, all heavily armed, looked through the telescope, and shouted, "They're on the run. Must be them. After 'em, Captain."

"I see them," the captain replied. "They're heading into that channel behind those islands." The captain quickly consulted his chart. "I've got no depths marked for that channel. We'd better not chance it."

Moran cocked his pistol and pointed it at the captain. "I said follow 'em," he said in a vicious subdued voice.

"You're the boss," the captain replied.

The *snekke* went behind the first island and for a few minutes their pursuer was out of sight. When the *snekke* reached the last island, the *Shooting Shamrock* entered the channel at full speed and bore down furiously upon them. Sven could now see armed men on deck.

Nate looked back and thought they might stop and try to bluff their way out, when he heard a gun shot and saw a bullet strike the water close to their stern. A loud boom, almost like an echo, instantaneously followed the shot and then he saw the *Shooting Shamrock* rocket into the air and land sideways in the water with a loud thud and screams. The men on deck were thrown overboard, and the boat slid to a stop, engines silent and dead in the water. They heard violent cursing, which was soon drowned out by the 'dunk dunk dunk' of their own engine as they moved further away from the scene. Ingvild yanked the shift lever into neutral. They stood up, looked back, and watched men swimming ashore as the *Shooting Shamrock* went down by the bow and slowly slipped beneath the surface. Only diminishing belches of bubbles marked its fjord grave.

"It's 200 meters deep there. They will never see that boat again," Ingvild announced proudly.

"You knew it was shallow there?" Nate asked in disbelief.

Ingvild put her arms around Nate. "Of course. There's a big ledge that sticks up in that one spot. That's why I came this way. Sven! Did you know that Nate and I are to be married?"

— Chapter 30 —

Henry's cell phone rang, but it was a few moments before Henry could get to it since he was on deck rushing to up-anchor and get underway. Minutes earlier, Helge had called him with information from Ernst that Moran was in the Berrefjord.

"Henry?" the unmistakable voice of Sven asked.

"Yes, Sven. You guys all right?"

"*Jah*. It's okay. Ingvild sunk the big boat that was chasing us."

"What?!"

"*Jah*. She some smart cookie, that Ingvild. She make big boat follow her over shallow rocks. Her little *snekke* go over like a cork, but Moran crash and boat sinks."

"So, where's Moran?"

"Some men swim ashore. I will call Helge. He will know what to do. We are coming back to you. And big news. Cousin Ingvild and Nate are to marry! What you think of that now?"

"Er … I'd say; you've had quite an afternoon!"

"Och. I'm drenched to the bone," said John as he wrung out his sweater. "Tis a lot of explaining and paying you'll be doing to the big fella."

"I'm sure he has insurance," replied Jimmy as he sat soaked and dumbfounded on a slippery green rock.

"Maybe so. But there's the poor families of the captain, the mate and Big John to be settled for."

"Don't meddle in my business. I'll work it out with my contact in New York. You keep your mouth shut. Understand? I got to think."

Jimmy had much to think about. He, John, and two others had survived the crash. They were all on the rocks trying to dry out in the last rays of sunlight.

Jimmy looked around the fjord and saw no sign of human life. They were stranded. He recalled from the maps that Flekkefjord was about 15 miles away to the southeast, but he had no idea how to get there. It was too late in the day to do anything, and no one had a light to start a fire. He still had a gun in his shoulder holster, and he desperately wanted to use it.

That same lovely summer evening found Boxer and Serene lounging in the cockpit listening intently to Henry as he related Sven's phone call.

"Nate and Ingvild! I'm so happy for them. So suddenly. I knew there was something there, but my God, already," said Serene.

"That's wonderful," Boxer commented, "and Moran's boat sunk as well. A good day for all of us. I'd say…"

"Wait, I hear a boat. There … it's coming in the cove. It's Helge and Baby. And there's another boat behind them … Ingvild's!"

Boxer began singing 'Here comes the bride,' and Henry and Serene joined in. Helge and Baby began to sing but in Norwegian. Then everyone in Ingvild's boat started singing. As the singing petered out, the boats came alongside, and everyone was laughing and in good cheer.

"You picked a beautiful night for an engagement party. Congratulations!" said Henry as he helped Ingvild aboard and gave her a hug.

"We have brought some champagne. Give me a hand, Boxer," said Helge as he lifted a wooden case.

As soon as everyone was on deck, the impromptu celebration began. Henry found a local radio station and piped music throughout the boat. Serene busied herself in the galley preparing trays of hors d'oeuvres. The sound of corks popping brought periodic bursts of applause. With everyone gathered on the afterdeck, Helge called for attention and proposed a toast, "I have often thought what kind of man my Ingvild would get and now I have finally met him. I knew he would have to be special for Ingvild herself is special. Welcome to our family, Nate, and may you both have many joyous years together."

As the evening progressed, the ladies retired to the main salon for tea and the men gathered in the cockpit. "So, Helge what will be done about the men at Berrefjord?" asked Sven.

"It is a national matter now for the Royal Norwegian Navy in support of the local civil government. A gun was fired at innocent Norwegian citizens and a foreign boating accident happened in Norwegian waters. I hope they have their passports in order and the proper visas to land on Norwegian soil," he said with a wink and smile at Henry. "I would not be surprised if a Coast Guard patrol boat was in the Berrefjord in the morning. We will have no more problems with these people. I am personally happy this is over as I have many official duties for St. Hans. It comes so soon every year, the day after tomorrow, you know."

The little cabin that had been Nate's and then became Ingvild's was now Nate and Ingvild's. Whatever chemical reaction had transpired between them at Berrefjord resulted in their early rising and found them both electrified with energy. While the others slept, Nate hummed as he made breakfast, and Ingvild spread out her cave rubbing on the table and began to translate.

"Nate, I get better at this."

"It must be the practice, my dear."

"Yes, once you learn the rune symbols, it becomes easier. This one is not difficult at all. Come sit. I will read it to you."

Nate served her bacon, eggs, and toast, and poured her a cup of black coffee.

"Why thank you, Nate. You have the makings of a fine husband."

"It says, '*Ingvild of Edred sleeps in peace with the time of the silver moon. Rejoice for the blessings of the gods are upon our homeland sea and the wealth of life is the treasure learning.*'"

"What a wonderful epitaph. She must have been an extraordinary woman. Just like you, Ingvild," said Nate as he kissed her. "Well, you've solved the mystery, and I can only hope for many days of happiness and love for us."

"Yes. I believe it will be so. Remember, however, that when one search is over another always begins."

"That seems to be the pattern of life. Always searching for something and most times not even knowing what it is. It's the vital energy that powers all of life."

"Together, I believe, we will do more than just sit around and be happy, although I like that idea, too. I think there are reasons why certain people find one another."

"There is always a reason why."

Everyone at the prison was allowed to make as many telephone calls as they needed. Jimmy was used to just having one phone call, which was to his brother Mike who would arrange for a lawyer. The Norwegian Navy personnel were extremely courteous and accommodating. They led Jimmy to a small room with a chair, a table and a telephone. It looked like it was soundproof, but Jimmy, always suspicious, suspected it was bugged. He punched in the numbers.

"Mike, I'm busted. You need to get lawyers on this right away."

"Where the hell are you?"

"The Stavanger naval prison, in Norway."

"What happened?"

"I haven't been charged yet. Don't want to get into it too much on the phone. Let's say we had an unfortunate accident with the boat. Remember Mikee D?"

"Yeah."

"Call him and tell him the *Shooting Shamrock* sank and the captain, mate and Big John are gone. Dublin John and the other boys are with me."

"You do the job for our friend?"

"Nope. We were on the way when this accident happened. Somebody's gonna have to make good on the boat and for the guys who went down."

"Who?"

"I don't know. You're the business brain. Work it out."

"Okay. Okay. Guess we got to get some square head lawyer. I'll make some calls. How they treating you?"

"Handcuffs and leg shackles. The place is immaculate, and the jumpsuits are a quaint shade of blue. Aside from that … . it SUCKS!"

Mike Moran's phone call was short and to the point, "Philly, we got to talk in private. Meet me at Spain's parking lot at noon."

It sounded so urgent that Philly arrived at the restaurant on time. So was Mike who jumped into Philly's Cadillac. Mike told about Jimmy's phone call and the call he had earlier that day from the lawyer who met with Jimmy.

"It's a royal screw up from hell, Philly. The lawyer said they got 'em on a dozen charges. Attempted murder of Norwegian citizens. Terrorism. Illegal discharge and possession of firearms. Landing without visas or passports. Reckless operation of a boat in Norwegian waters. Resisting arrest. The lawyer said it could take several years. All kinds of red tape because it happened in a foreign country."

"Bad break for Jimmy. But that's not on me. He didn't do the job. I get my cash back, right?"

"Right. If we don't deliver, you don't pay. I'll eat the miscellaneous expenses, the legal bills and have to pay large for the subcontractors who died on the job. But remember, you said you'd be responsible for any transportation costs?"

"Yeah. That was our agreement."

"Well, the boat that sank belonged to a top IRA guy, and he wants the money for it."

"How much?"

"Three million and change, he says. He's got a recent ship's surveyor report for the amount. He'll send it if you want."

Philly's face turned ashen. "Ain't he got insurance?"

"What idiot would sell insurance to a well known IRA leader?"

It was mid afternoon when Boxer returned to his room at the Maritime Hotel. He drank too much champagne the night before. He downed some aspirin, took a long overdue shower, closed the curtains, turned up the air conditioner and got in bed. He lay there thinking, "I'll call Philly later and play dumb about Moran. I'm glad it worked out this way. They're such a stimulating group of people. I'm going to miss them and this place. I'd better call the airline and book a flight for the day after tomorrow, late in the day. I can't miss this St. Hans thing tomorrow. Too tired to surface..."

A few hours later, he was wide awake and the headache was gone. He dialed Philly's number, and his Spanish housekeeper answered.

"Where is ambulance?" she screamed hysterically. "I call two times!"

"This is not the ambulance. This is Boxer, a friend of Philly's. What's going on?"

"Mr. Costello ... I think he dead."

"What? What happened?"

"Maybe he have heart attack. I call 911 two times!" She began to sob.

"You sure he's dead?"

"He no breathe. No move. Chocolate drip from mouth. Candy all on floor. Doorbell! Must go!" and she hung up.

Everyone in Flekkefjord always planned for perfect weather on St. Hans. This year they were not disappointed. The unusually fine weather they had been having all summer was holding, as contrasted to many other Norwegian summers when it rained continuously.

The *Loki* was once again docked by the Pizza Inn on a clear, crisp Norwegian afternoon. Boxer had returned to his hotel just across the river, and Ingvild had gone back to her house to attend to some business matters. The boat was long overdue for a cleaning. Serene was busily vacuuming below, and Henry and Nate were scrubbing and polishing on foredeck. They wanted the *Loki* to look her best for the parade.

"Nate, I suppose you'll be staying here with Ingvild for a while."

"Yes, Henry. We're going to be married here in the big wooden church, the one by Helge's statue, as soon as we can make the arrangements."

"Will you be living here or at the Cape?"

"Definitely here. I called my pal Shep this morning and asked him to check around for anyone interested in buying my place. It'll sell fast, and I'll get a good price. The real estate market on the Cape is booming. I'll have to fly back for the closing, of course, and pack up my books and things. We're going to build a place at Berrefjord and then go south to Spain or Portugal for the winters. Ingvild wants to wind down her job in Oslo, or get early retirement, so we'll be in Oslo over this winter. I hope you and Serene can stick around for a week or so. I'd like you to be my best man."

"Nate, I'd be honored. Beside, we're in no rush to leave. In fact, Serene and I have come to love this place. We were talking about staying the rest of the summer and exploring the fjords. And if you need help building your new house, I'm fairly handy and so is Serene."

"Fantastic, Henry. Ingvild will be as delighted as I am to hear that."

The time set for the *Loki's* departure was 8:00 p.m. Henry and Serene had already laid out the food and beverages which included a large supply of beer, a case of local shrimp, smoked salmon and dozens of pastries. Nate had strung lines of paper Norwegian and American flags from the main mast.

Ingvild arrived at little after seven, the sound of her car trumpeting her arrival. They might not have recognized her had they not heard the car. Not only was it the first time they had seen her in a dress, but the outfit was a marvel of folk art. Over a starched white blouse with balloon sleeves and trimmed with fine needlepoint eyelets, she wore a long black shift, trimmed in bright red and intricately embroidered down the front with multi-colored floral designs. Over the shift she wore a vest embroidered in silver threads and trimmed in red with silver buttons.

One of the business matters she had to attend to was obviously a trip to the hair salon. Her blonde hair had been beautifully trimmed and was swept up and topped by a large red bow that matched the trim on her dress and vest. Her lipstick also matched the bow, and she was wearing makeup which none of them had seen before. She could pass for Ingrid Bergman.

Most striking of all was her walk. Her dress somewhat restricted her otherwise animated movements and toned down her demeanor. She hiked up her shift a few inches and walked daintily towards the boat in black, patent leather pumps. Spontaneous applause came from the crew punctuated by a wolf whistle from Henry. It made Ingvild smile, and her entire countenance was one of sublime happiness. Nate, the gentleman he was, extended his hand to help her aboard, kissed her hand, and bowed from the waist.

Next to arrive was Boxer who wore a dark double-breasted blazer with gray slacks and a white shirt with an open collar. He had an expensive bottle of cognac in each hand.

Sven and his girlfriend Laila then arrived. She was lively and fun and seemed to be a good balance to Sven's serious nature.

Just before eight, Helge and Baby came aboard. Baby was also dressed in an exquisite folkloric costume, and Helge wore a formal black suit with his medallion chain of office around his neck.

With Henry at the aft cockpit helm, they shoved off and moved at idle speed down the river and out into the harbor. There, boats of every description were converging from all directions and circling around a large fishing boat. Aboard it the town's brass band was crowded into the bow and tuning their instruments. Music of every other style was heard coming from the other boats, which was mixed the lively chatter of happy, expectant people. The sky was a rich combination of blue and white clouds to the east, which melded overhead with soft streaks of oranges and reds coming from the midsummer sun that hung just above the mountain.

"Henry," commanded Helge. "Move out in front of the band boat. The mayor must lead the procession."

"Aye aye, sir," he replied with a stiff salute and a smile. Henry slowly wound his way through the sea of boats, took position and shifted into neutral.

"When I give the signal, Henry, go at your slowest speed and head to the left of that big raft. You can go close by the raft. Then just continue all the way down the fjord on the right, circle around the big island and come back to the raft. You can't do wrong. Wherever you go all the boats will follow," he said with a roaring laugh.

"It is a big honor to lead the boats," said Ingvild.

"Yes, I imagine," said Henry. "But I didn't plan on having so much responsibility this evening."

Helge signaled to the bandleader to begin. They started playing the Norwegian National Anthem and then he motioned to Henry. Henry moved out slowly and headed towards the raft. When the anthem finished, a loud cheer came from the boaters, and the band played on with a lively waltz. Several minutes later they passed the raft, a huge steel platform floated on oil drums and piled 20 feet high with wood. At the bottom of the pile the bow of an old wooden *snekke* protruded. Many of the boats began to lash themselves together so that people could climb back and forth and party. The mobile feast accompanied by the brass band proceeded down the fjord in high merriment on a perfect midsummer evening.

"Uncle Helge, can we speak to you privately for a moment?" asked Ingvild as she stood arm and arm with Nate.

"Certainly. Shall we go below?"

Seated in the main salon, Ingvild began, "We have a proposal for you about our discovery. You want us to keep it secret to avoid calling attention to our town. We agree. We also want to maintain our tranquility, however we want something in exchange for our discretion."

Helge clasped his hands on the table and assumed an official demeanor. "And what would that be?"

"Two things. First, we want a variance from the town to build an institute at Berrefjord that we will name the Institute of Harmonic Convergence. It will be a study center, dedicated to the memory of Princess Ingvild, which will promote the exchange of learning in pursuit of attaining spiritual tranquility for people. We will invite small groups of students, maybe a dozen at a time for a few weeks to be instructed by people like Boxer and Nate, and other people we choose. Secondly, we may want some people to stay at the institute for extended periods of time, Henry and Serene, for example. You will facilitate this with the immigration authorities. That's all we want."

"Ingvild, you know the years of debate we've had with the council just to get you that permit to build a single family dwelling. Everyone wants to exercise eminent domain over the rest of your lands and make Berrefjord common land. We have offered you a very generous price."

"I know, Uncle. But you could explain to the council that there is a new, special situation that has arisen, that demands this concession."

"You are a sly one, Ingvild," Helge chuckled. "Yes, perhaps some new action is demanded. As far as immigration is concerned, they rely on the local authorities in these matters. So that's not a problem."

"Can you say we are agreed, then?" asked Ingvild.

"Yes, I believe decisions are easy when there is only one option." Helge glanced out the porthole. "Come, we are nearing the raft!"

Henry shut off the engine and stood 50 yards off the raft. His wake of boats began to circle the impending sacrifice, and the excitement was growing among the people, especially heard in hoots and shouts of the children.

Boxer, holding Sven's cell phone in his hand, stopped Ingvild, Nate and Helge as they came on deck and led them to Serene and Henry who were standing in the cockpit. Nate began, "I have something to tell you all. Philly 'Gumdrops' Costello will not be bothering you anymore. He's dead. He died of a massive heart attack about ten minutes ago. I just spoke to the hospital."

"Poor man," said Serene. "He sounded so unhappy on the phone."

"He was my boyhood friend, you know. Believe it or not, he had many good qualities. He was morbidly obese. That's what got him in the end, I believe. Just one too many gumdrops."

A roaring cheer went up from the crowd. They all looked to see two men in a rowboat reach the raft, ignite two torches, throw them on the raft and then row away. The kindling flames from the torches spread quickly over the dry wood, and in minutes the sounds of the crackling fire and exploding pine knots silenced the crowd. Sharp tongues of orange and red flame shot higher and yet higher into the midsummer night.

Serene put her arm around Henry and whispered in his ear, "It's ironic that the man who brought us together is dead. He was a pagan in his ways. So let's consider this his funeral pyre and leave that part of our past in the ashes."

"I agree. Now that the past is behind us, I want to ask you to marry me."

Serene kissed him and looked him in the eyes lovingly, "Henry, if we got married, I fear the adventure might disappear from our lives. But I'll tell you what, I'll think about it."

THE END

Printed in the United States
54943LVS00002B/265-297

9 781413 729832